The Theta Timeline

Chris Dietzel

This is a work of fiction. Names, characters, places, and incidents are the products of the author's imagination or are used fictitiously. Any resemblance to actual events, locales, or persons, living or dead, is coincidence.

Published in the United States by Watch The World End Publications.

ISBN-13: 978-0692303955

ISBN-10: 0692303952

Cover Design: Levente Szabo

Editor: D.L. MacKenzie

Author Photo: Jodie McFadden

By Chris Dietzel

The Theta Timeline

"And so tyranny naturally arises out of democracy, and the most aggravated form of tyranny and slavery out of the most extreme form of liberty?"

"As we might expect."

Plato - The Republic

"All moments, past, present, and future, always have existed, always will exist."

Kurt Vonnegut Jr. - Slaughter-House Five

PART ONE – THE PRESENT

"The present is theirs; the future, for which I really worked, is mine."

Nikola Tesla

1 – THE BAG MEN

The men shifted their weight back and forth from one foot to the other. Each had been told not to move from where he stood. Trying to run was pointless anyway; all of their ankles were tied with a continuous length of tubing so that every man was anchored to the other nine in the row. While the men all obeyed the directions they had been given, keeping their feet on their assigned spots, none of them could remain perfectly still. As if in a completely unorganized talent show dance line, the men leaned from one side to the other, bumping shoulders with the men next to them, some pushing, others pulling, as they all fretted.

A few of them wore baggy pants that hung down over their feet. Others had pants that were slightly too small, ending at their shins, making the coil around their ankles impossible to ignore. This was because the men were wearing identical burlap outfits that were only made in three sizes. No one, not the men wearing them, nor the scientists on the other side of the room, cared about perfectly tailored clothes. It would not have been possible to find a cheaper outfit. Even a curtain removed from a window and worn like a toga would be worth more.

The very last man in line, barely five feet tall, looked like a living potato sack because he had been stuck with the last set of clothes, which happened to be the largest size they made.

"Make a note," the oldest of the scientists said as his associate, holding a clipboard, withdrew a pen from the pocket of his lab coat. "Next time, make sure we have correct sizes for everyone. They don't have to fit perfectly, but for god's sake, look at that poor bastard."

The poor bastard in question couldn't think of anything to say in his defense, only sucked in air and looked down at where his feet would be if they weren't drowning in burlap.

The tubing around their ankles appeared from a metal cabinet positioned on the ground next to the first man in line. If the ten men wanted to make a run for it, not only would they all have to keep the same pace, they would have to drag the solid, cumbersome box with them.

The tubing wasn't meant to restrain them, however. The Security Services would never try to handcuff a suspect with something soft and flexible.

The man in the middle of the row, the only one with blond hair, was bumped by the men on either side of him. "I'd rather be strapped to a table than stand here like this," Blondie said. "At least then I wouldn't have all of you making me lose my mind."

He was immediately jostled once more by the man to his right, who muttered an apology as he picked at his fingernails.

The men stood exactly where they were told to stand even though none of the five scientists on the other side of the room had a weapon. Any of the men in burlap could try to undo their bindings and make a mad dash across the dimly lit room, toward the exit. They wouldn't be gunned down if they attempted such an act. And yet they remained in place, exactly as they had been told.

Each man in the row held a sack made of the same

material as his clothes. Some let it hang from one hand, nonchalant and casual, trying as hard as they could to give the impression they were the only ones in line who weren't scared shitless. A few hugged the bags to their chests as if it would offer protection. It had worked when they were kids and their favorite blanket protected them from the bogeyman. Maybe it would work now.

Only the men's ankles were bound, not their hands, yet none of the bag men bothered to untie the string keeping the sack shut so they could find out what was inside.

"Hell of a way for the valedictorian to go out," the first man said."

"You were valedictorian?" the third man said. "All I got was being voted *Class Clown.*"

The man in between them grimaced and said, "I was voted *Most Likely To Die An Unusual Death.*"

"Um," the class clown said, shutting his eyes.

The men only spoke to each other, allowing the scientists on the far side of the room, where a table was littered with four laptop computers and various charts and even a map of the world, to finish with the final preparations. No one else was around. Being in the heart of an otherwise abandoned factory, surrounded by double-thick cinder block walls, guaranteed that.

The ninth man in line, who seemed taller than he actually was simply because he was standing next to the poor bastard, who would no doubt be immortalized in clothes that were a hundred times too large for him, looked down at the sack he had been given, then at his feet, then at the other men beside him. He did all of this as though his next action would be to toss down his bag, untie the tubing wrapped around his leg, and try to make a run for it.

Instead, he took a deep breath and said, "No one knows what the future holds."

No one offered a response to this.

Almost everything the scientists said to each other was whispered so the bag men couldn't hear them, but every once in a while the men overheard things such as "If you don't get it right, we might as well just kill them now," and "*No one* knows if this is going to work but we have to give it a try," and "Damn, I need a drink. You wanna get a beer with me after we make these guys disappear?"

The oldest of the scientists withdrew a calculator from his lab coat pocket, then said something that made the other four shrug their shoulders and run back to their notebooks. One of the scientists rushed over to press another button on a computer, then scribbled more numbers. These rapid motions and hushed tones made the men lined against the wall squirm even more.

Other than to point and whisper, the scientists barely acknowledged the bag men. None of them kept a constant watch to make sure an escape wasn't attempted. None of them offered a reassurance that whatever happened next would be quick and painless.

"How much longer can this possibly take?" Blondie said. "I'm about to file a motion for cruel and unusual punishment."

When he looked to his right to see if the man beside him was entertained by his bravado he realized nothing he said had been heard. The man beside him was mumbling nonsense and gripping his burlap bag so tightly that his knuckles turned white.

Finally, Blondie called out, "How much longer?"

One scientist was scanning various pages filled with equations while the others scribbled numbers in their logs. None of them acknowledged the question.

"Can we get this show on the road?"

There was no response to this either.

At the end of the line, the poor bastard focused all of his energy on rolling up his pants and shirtsleeves so he didn't look quite so foolish. It didn't work. Now, instead of looking like a man who was only allowed to shop in the *Big & Tall* department, he resembled a character from one of those movies where a man wakes up to find himself trapped inside a child's body.

"We're almost ready," the oldest of the scientists said, not looking at the bag men when he said it, but finally offering something they were supposed to overhear.

One of the other scientists walked next to the first man in line, then reached down and flipped a switch on the black metal box where the length of tubing appeared. A humming began, soft at first, barely noticeable, but then it grew steadily louder, fuller. Even in the cinder block confines, the entire room, the entire factory, began vibrating.

"I didn't like this life anyway," *Most Likely To Die An Unusual Death* said.

All the *Class Clown* could say to that was, "Um."

One of them, forgetting the tubing around his ankle, attempted to take a step forward, but stumbled when Blondie didn't also move. The man was so nervous he simply forgot he was tied to everyone else, forgot the order to remain still.

"Do not move!" the oldest scientist yelled, the few strands of silver hair he had left bouncing when he did so.

As the humming increased, the room began to fill with white light. The cinder block confines changed from shadows and dark corners to having every single drip of water, scurrying bug, and cracked piece of concrete put on display. At least four of the men in line shut their eyes. There was no point to watching what was going to happen. It was all going to be over soon enough.

"I feel like I'm on the firing line," the valedictorian said.

"Um."

The men were not prisoners at all, though. And definitely were not going to be executed. On the contrary, the scientists prayed that at least some of the men would live through the day.

No matter if they lived or died, though, no one who knew them, not their friends and not their families, would ever see any of the bag men again.

Amidst the intense light, the line of men vanished.

Four of the scientists looked into the light while the fifth walked back over and flipped the switch on the metal box. The bright light began to evaporate. With it, the incredible humming eventually quieted down.

As the scientists packed up their gear, one of them said, "What now?"

It was the one with silver strands of flimsy hair that said, "Hope that at least one of them didn't die. And begin getting ready for the next batch."

2 - THE CHICKEN OR THE EGG, AND THE MUSHROOM CLOUD

Everyone remembered exactly where they were and what they were doing when they heard the first news reports. An atomic bomb had erased part of the country's southern coast. A million people died in the initial blast. Millions more would perish from radiation sickness. It was impossible not to know someone who had died. It had never been a perfect world but, for most, it had never been so devastatingly pain-filled.

For as long as people could remember, bombs had been falling on the other side of the world. Perhaps it was inevitable that they would finally destroy part of their own land. It was one thing to see cruelty and destruction on TV and know it was happening to someone else. It was quite another to know death and suffering were occurring where many viewers had friends and family.

In the long history of endless bombings and military campaigns, the leaders had noticed that nothing brought people together like a good war. They needed war because it rallied everyone behind a single cause and offered a distraction from how bad things were at home. When people aren't paying attention, rulers can get away with anything.

And, sadly, things hadn't been going well for a long time, so the leaders needed *a lot* of distractions.

Random countries were deemed immediate dangers. New security threats were identified and had to be dealt with. Sure, the motivation for going to war was always cloudy. Yes, the evidence to validate the war was never clear. But the bombs fell anyway. And each time, people forgot about their own problems in order to hope for a quick end to the fighting. Eventually, though, the drug-like high of bombs destroying far-off peoples faded away. Protests began to pop up over an ever-worsening economy, too much of the public without jobs, and people having no faith that things would improve. More distractions were needed. The leaders couldn't help themselves. They were, after all, used to being out of touch, unintelligent, inept, and crooked. They didn't know how to do anything else but serve their own interests.

The next war returned everyone's attention to the need to get rid of some evil dictator. People stopped complaining about not being able to afford food for their children and called for the dictator's head. The war could only keep people waving flags for so long, though. Then they once more marched in the streets. Some chanted catchy slogans calling for change. Others held signs with crudely drawn images of politicians with their heads up their own asses.

The leaders knew what they had to do. The previous wars hadn't been big enough. The enemies that were being fought didn't seem dastardly enough.

That was when a small bomb went off near a local bus station. People rallied like they hadn't rallied in a long time. Tanks and missiles were sent abroad to ensure some evil men would be killed for what they had done. For an entire year, no one complained about corrupt politicians or anything else.

However, when the fervor for blood eventually did die down, the protests were louder than ever. Cars were overturned and windows broken when a peaceful gathering turned into a riot. People demanded that the current leaders step down so new leaders, ones who weren't so blatantly rotten, could lead the country. The protests only quieted down when the police were brought in and curfews were imposed.

That was when the leaders realized two things: first, that a normal war would never suffice again; and two, that if an entire population could be controlled, it didn't really matter how mad the public got. The leaders would never need to fear for their livelihood again.

From that point forward, every time a new war started, it was in response to some attack in the homeland. And to prevent a similar attack from occurring again, batches of laws were passed to control what people could do and what they couldn't do.

When the next attack occurred, there was another war. Then, more restrictions. Or was it the other way around? Was the next war in response to the previous attack, or was the latest attack in retaliation to the most recent war? It was too confusing to figure out, and most people were too busy just trying to survive to expend much energy trying to solve the puzzle.

After a bus was strewn across two city blocks, laws were passed that allowed the authorities to search anyone they wanted, anytime they wanted. Almost as a side note, an otherwise inconsequential country on the other side of the world was obliterated. When reporters began to uncover witnesses who claimed the bombing was carried out by the government on its own people, these reports were largely dismissed as paranoid ravings.

Later, a train derailed, its track sabotaged. A video posted online clearly showed men with government badges working on the section of tracks where the train would eventually explode. But by then another country had already been invaded. And back home, laws had been passed to restrict where people could go.

While the majority of people forgot their own

problems each time their was a terror attack and a subsequent war, there were always a few people who not only questioned the bombings and destruction but who also pointed out that, war or no war, the leaders never accomplished anything to help the people. These were the few who refused to believe what the leaders said just because they were saying it.

Each time a new attack occurred, these voices were drowned out by the public outrage that some group of people on the other side of the world would try to hurt them. The leaders had learned that new enemies, either real or imagined, were easy to identify and that the majority of people could always be counted upon to rally against the common foe. And so, no matter how bad their own standard of living was, leaders focused entirely on "keeping people safe" and bringing radicals to justice. Each new sweeping set of laws was marketed as the solution to protect the population. Each new military campaign was billed as international justice.

After one attack, it was decided that checkpoints would be needed across the land to monitor everyone's movements. After another, it was decreed that no more protests would be allowed until the suspects were caught. The leaders offered reassurances: public demonstrations would only be illegal until everyone who could commit such violent acts were brought to justice. Of course, it could never say it had caught everyone, and so the law would last forever.

"We understand the importance of free speech," the Ruler said. "But safety is even more important."

Anyone caught marching would be arrested. And now, just to enter the city, people had to have their vehicles searched, explain where they intended to go, and sometimes receive full-body cavity searches.

It wasn't long after the bombing that a video was posted online which certainly made it appear as though the attack had been carried out by some of the government's own men. Or else the culprits had borrowed a government vehicle that had never been reported missing.

"Only a radical or a traitor would think their leaders

are capable of something like that," the Ruler said into the cameras.

But the footage looked awfully convincing. One by one, though, the videos disappeared from the internet. The people who had posted them vanished as well.

Life got worse. More people lost their jobs. The quality of schools kept declining. Another, even more urgent war was required. The leaders needed to up the ante if they expected to rally everyone together, though. It wasn't good enough to destroy a little country in the desert. The people were so desensitized to war or else were so cynical about what it accomplished that even wars on larger countries no longer elicited a sense of unity. Nor did two military campaigns at once.

During the next war, it was decided that future attacks could be prevented if the government had little robotic cameras flying all over the place recording everything below. After yet another war, it was noted that future cyber attacks could be prevented if the government assigned Internet IDs to everyone and then monitored everyone's online activity. Unhappy with this law, a kid wore a T-shirt that said I HAD MY INTERNET ANONYMINTY TAKEN AWAY AND ALL I GOT WAS THIS LOOSY T-SHIRT. The boy was arrested for being part of an illegal one-man protest.

The leaders never offered a reason for why the seemingly haphazard new laws were necessary other than saying they addressed identified threats and would keep people safe. What threats? Well, these had to be kept secret.

Each batch of laws promised safety, but after each war the people found themselves a little less free. And the attacks continued. No one knew if the attacks occurred because more laws were needed, or if more laws were needed because the attacks took place. What they did know was that somewhere along the way, something fundamental had changed.

The government had grown into an all-knowing and all-controlling beast. It had power it was never intended to have, and it was despotic in its exercise of that power. It was hypocritical, accountable to no one. It was oppressive and severe. And that meant it was no longer the government the people had been raised to believe in, but something evil. A monster.

A tyranny.

Without knowing exactly when or where it had occurred, people realized they were being ruled with fear— fear that more attacks would happen unless more laws were passed, fear that they might end up dead if they exposed the State's lies.

And still, the wars continued. They had to. There was no other way for the leaders to temporarily unify the public and also justify the additional security measures they would pass in order to control the increasingly restless population.

As far as people could remember, there had always been war and there had always been the leaders' excuses for why war was unavoidable. But no one could remember which came first: war rooted from need, or the need for war.

The wars kept escalating. It was inevitable that a mushroom cloud would eventually appear. No one could have guessed, though, that the first such cloud would form over the homeland.

The second largest city in the State was now gone. Only the steel skeletons of skyscrapers remained. Their windows and ornamentation had been turned to dust. When it rained, the water droplets were thick and chalky. Cars were turned into grey outlines. Some people were left as charred skeletons. A few were vaporized onto nearby walls, marking the place where they had changed from being living people to ghostly shadows. The few survivors wandered the streets aimlessly, their eyelids covered in radioactive ash, unable to keep food or even water in their stomachs.

The Ruler's address to the nation was immediate: "Intelligence indicates this was the effort of multiple nations working together, in conjunction with a group of our own citizens who are trying to tear this great country apart by disparaging its leaders."

When the countries were named, everyone gasped.

"But they're our allies," one reporter said.

"But they have no reason to attack us," another said.

But the State was adamant that classified intelligence reports proved what they were saying. The reports couldn't be made public, so everyone would have to trust what the State was saying.

"This is insanity," the President of one of the accused countries said. "We are a peaceful people."

The Prime Minister of another accused nation appealed to reason: "What do we stand to gain by carrying out such an attack?"

But nothing would prevent the State's Ruler from calling for war: "Obviously, our enemies aren't foolish enough to claim responsibility for the attack they carried out, but the intelligence we gathered is overwhelming."

The counterattack was swift. Two hours after the Ruler's portentous address, two countries were blanketed in mushroom clouds. Tens of millions were dead. Strong winds would ensure that a billion people would eventually die. It would be impossible for the defeated countries to grow consumable food for at least two decades. If they wanted to eat, they would need to buy the State's crops.

Just like that, two of the most powerful countries in the world were crushed, their people starving and dying in the streets. Within the State, people were once more unified, glad that the countries responsible for the initial attack had been held accountable.

To help keep everyone safe from future attacks, the leaders passed a whole new series of laws. No longer was anyone allowed to criticize the State. Even more checkpoints were set up. To enter a city, everyone had to put their right hand into a threat detector, a machine designed to determine if someone was likely to commit crimes.

The State, its sense of humor as strong as ever, called the new set of laws *The Freedom Act*.

A week after the State's southern coast was destroyed, the first incriminating videos surfaced online. One such video clearly showed a white van with official license plates pulling up to the spot where the bomb would eventually go off. A group of four men got out of the van, got into a black car, then disappeared. The closest the State came to acknowledging the video was to offer the statement that if anyone questioned the State's account of what happened they would be violating the Freedom Act.

The madness couldn't continue. Something had to be done.

3 - A MEETING OF THE MINDS

Watching the game at 10:00 a.m. at Dakota's on Browning St. Should be fun. Arrive right on time.

That was the message waiting for Isaac when he checked his computer. When the State read the email, they would think nothing of it.

He did not write a response. Looking at his watch, he figured he would have to start getting ready right away if he was going to pass through the checkpoints and make it to the meeting without being late.

His girlfriend had just left for work, so he had the apartment to himself. He changed and brushed his teeth in silence, preferring the quiet to the chatter from the television or whatever music Jessica had left in their stereo. With the quiet he could let his mind wander. He could think about the things he might hear at ten o'clock.

Outside his window, a squadron of little robot cameras flew in all directions, capturing the actions of the people below. He thought about what it must have been like to live in simpler times, imagined himself standing in the very same spot, only two hundred years earlier. How many stories had the tallest building been? What was it like to hear horses on the streets instead of cars and trucks? How many places were covered with flowers instead of concrete?

He felt silly thinking about living in different times unless he was with other people who wanted to discuss the same thing. It's one thing to read *The Time Machine* and be mesmerized by the story. That's normal. It's quite another thing to spend your days telling anyone who will listen that time travel wouldn't be as simple as H. G. Wells made it seem. That's not normal.

In truth, no one knew more than anyone else about what it might be like to go back in time. All anyone could do was speculate. Or, as Isaac was fond of saying, make educated guesses. That's why few meeting participants wasted much time on that type of speculation. Would they pass through a tunnel of stars? Would they be bathed in pure energy? It was a waste of time to argue over these things because no one could know for certain unless they experienced it for themself. And once they did, they would be unable to attend meetings and offer their firsthand accounts.

No one was even sure if time travel was possible. Like the early days of nuclear technology, there were facts and rumors and misinformation and only a handful of people knew which was which. Isaac was only told what he absolutely needed to know. The less someone knew, the less they could reveal when the State caught them.

With its cameras, listening devices, and spies, the State eventually learned everyone's secrets. It was inevitable. No matter how secretive Isaac and the others in his group were, the State's all-seeing eye would uncover their plans. The trick was to be gone before the State could arrange enough puzzle pieces to make sense of things.

The State's men could always make their prisoners talk, even if what they said wasn't true. It was one thing to confess their own involvement—they were as good as dead once they were caught—it was another thing to give up their own parents, their friends, the very people who loved them the most. No one has a choice, though, once the pain starts. It's human nature to avoid such agony. With the rare exception of the monk who sets himself on fire in protest, no one can tolerate the types of pain the State's men have been trained to deliver.

Isaac and the others would count themselves lucky if they were simply doused with gasoline and lit on fire. After a split second of intense pain, they would go into shock and feel nothing. The State's men had no use for such quick and painless methods. If it only took twenty hours to break someone, the torture would last twenty hours. But if, somehow, their devices and their trauma could be withstood, the torture might go on for weeks or months. No doubt there's an even bigger sense of satisfaction in those cases when the prisoner does eventually break. And they always do.

It's not only the physical pain that brings about a person's utter collapse, but the psychological pain as well. A good torturer, someone who has made it their life's work to make people beg for death, will acknowledge that psychological torture is actually more important than nearly drowning someone or tearing their toenails off. When a prisoner is convinced that their parents, their spouse, their children, are in the next cell ready to experience similar pain, they are utterly defeated.

This was why Isaac was happy to be left in the dark. All he had to do was meet with a handful of other men and discuss which events in history were seminal in creating the State.

So when he was told to go to Browning Street at ten o'clock, he assumed it would be another such meeting. Usually, the gatherings were held in someone's basement or in a wine cellar. The State's latest AeroCams could see and hear through walls, so anything said or done in a kitchen or a living room could be monitored. But underground, not even the best microphones could hear what was being discussed. For that reason, the State had passed a law making it illegal for new homes to have basements.

One man in Isaac's group might ask another what he would do if he were only sent back ten years, too recently to stop everything.

Another might theorize what would happen if the other's doppelganger showed up out of the blue, claiming to be from the future. Would you trust him or would you assume it was the State trying to trick you into confessing everything?

Usually, the discussions were more practical, though. The group had compiled a list of all the various ways history could be altered. To stop a single murderer, they could kill both of his parents before he was born. But it was easier and caused less disruption to the rest of the world's timeline if they waited until the murderer was an adult before killing him. The same approach, only on a much more grand scale, would prevent the State from rising.

They spoke of events in world history that had wider ramifications than anyone had realized at the time. Each man in the group understood that these were the episodes they must prevent if they wanted a world where people were still free, where atomic bombs weren't used as playthings.

The group could go on for hours talking about points in history where the country had veered off from the nation it was meant to be to the monster it had become. And yet Isaac and the others continued to meet for the discussions, endlessly cataloging events that could change the course of history. They needed as many ideas as possible because they knew that when time travel did become a reality, if it hadn't already, they would be the ones sent back to alter the past.

Even if they went back in time and prevented a war or an assassination, they would never know if they had changed the course of history enough to prevent the State. Only after they changed history would the circumstances of their present life be altered, but they would already be gone by then. Even if they did go back in time, they would never have a way of knowing if they were successful or not.

After hours of discussing the philosophy of time travel, it always came to this one point.

The Theta Timeline.

4 - HOW TIME ACTUALLY WORKS (THE THETA TIMELINE)

Physicists had long tried to prove the multiverse and parallel reality theories. Time travel was not the only piece of evidence that finally solved the multiverse problem, but it did explain how parallel realities could function.

From what scientists have determined, time is not the straight line they once conceived it to be. Experiential evidence such as memories of the past and expectations for the future tempt us to think of time as a path from Point A to Point B. There is birth and then there is death, but life is not a series of events happening in a line as it might seem. It has been demonstrated that the chronology of our past, present, and future—what we think of as time—is not a line at all, but a fluid sphere with no beginning, middle, or end.

For centuries, Eastern spirituality has taught there is no past nor future, but only the now. Einstein argued that the distinction between past, present, and future is only a stubborn illusion. Both were more correct than they ever could have guessed. Everything that has ever happened in the past, everything that is happening now, and everything that ever will happen, is happening all at once. Or, as physicists explain it: all of time is happening all the time.

In fact, the idea that a time traveler is going "back in time" is misleading. He is not moving backward through a chain of events—what we think of as minutes, years, and millennia. He is merely moving *around*.

Like the universe itself, time is infinite in size. Within its expanding sphere, every possible reality is playing out at the same time, but we are only aware of one of them. There are an infinite number of realities in which the State never arose, and an infinite number in which the State not only formed but is even more extreme than the one Isaac is fighting.

Because we are only aware of one reality, a single dot within the infinite sphere, scientists refer to the world we know as the Theta Timeline, after the Greek letter, theta, which had a mark inside a circle. In terms of time travel, that single mark in the middle of the circle is everything we know about history, giving us our awareness of the past, present, and future.

But outside the reality we call our lives and the history of mankind, every possible action by every possible person is taking place in the rest of the sphere. In one world, a man stays home and reads his newspaper. In another, he goes for a jog and is hit by a truck. Whichever happens, the Theta Timeline adjusts so our consciousness—our reality—is in the center of the sphere. A woman drowns her two-year-old baby in the bathtub, or she doesn't and he grows up to become a scientist who discovers a cure for the next great plague. The Theta Timeline is constantly shifting to adjust to the reality of those events.

But at the same time, there are possibilities we cannot fathom. The man did not go for a jog or read the newspaper, but was a circus clown. The woman never drowned her son, but he died anyway, from eating too much peanut butter. Anything is possible, and the infinite realities encompass every conceivable outcome. What if an election had turned out differently? What if someone was never born? What if a particular war never took place? There are more possibilities than the mind can comprehend.

Going back in time and changing any single action, behavior, or event, no matter how minor, shifts our awareness of the world to a different reality—a change in the Theta Timeline. The shift alters our consciousness to this other life as if we had been living in that reality the entire time.

This is why the effects of time travel are never obvious until after the time traveler has left. After all, the scientists would have grown up reading history books that mentioned a strange series of events or an infamous man who was a perfect match for the person they planned to send back in time. But it's only after the Theta Timeline moves from one reality to another that past events can be put into perspective.

A man could go back in time and murder Christopher Columbus, and the murderer's name could even be the same as the person who will be sent back in time, but the scientists won't become aware that they were enabling Columbus to be murdered until *after* the Theta Timeline has shifted because it won't shift until after they sent him back in time. Only then does what we think of as our history become something other than it was. If time worked any other way, the scientists would have lived their entire lives knowing what the man had done hundreds of years earlier.

But they never are aware of these things until after they send a time traveler into the past. Today, certain historical events only make sense because the Theta Timeline has shifted. The good news is that all the time traveler has to do is move the Theta Timeline to one of the realities in which the State never took power. It's the only way to save the world from mushroom clouds covering the earth.

The bad news, which Isaac is not yet aware of, is that four other sets of time travelers have already disappeared into the past and the State still exists. Something has stopped every single one of them.

5 – SPRINGFIELD

Not only did Isaac and his co-conspirators not know if time travel was actually possible yet, they didn't even know when or where the next meeting would be until the last moment. Even when they were notified, they were told in such a way that the State's computers wouldn't detect a possible threat. When the State scanned the email he had received, it would match the text against a map of the area and register an unremarkable invitation to a sports bar on Browning Street.

The email hadn't used his real name. But it also hadn't used the name he was known by during the meetings.

At the second discussion he attended, an old man had patted him on the shoulder and said, "You will be Springfield."

Isaac never saw the man again, but ever since then, on the few occasions someone did address him by name they called him by the name the old man had given him.

His identity was unknown to everyone he would meet, just as theirs were concealed from him. If the true nature of the meetings became known, a squad of men clad in black armor would burst through the door, assault blasters set to automatic.

If he was ever caught and interrogated, Isaac could reveal everything he knew without divulging anything useful. One of the men had been called Riverford and another had been called Sterling, but he didn't know their real names and would only be able to offer basic physical descriptions. He could confess that two had been Asian, two had been African American, one had been Hispanic, and four had been Caucasian. Basically, he could tell his interrogators that the group was a collection of people you might find anywhere.

At the meetings, the faces varied. He rarely saw the same people at more than two meetings. That was another way the group remained undetected. The State saw everything, and its computers were designed to find patterns of behavior. If they detected the same group of men meeting on a routine basis, everyone in the group was automatically added to a watch list. The software was not infallible, though. In fact, it was common for the computers to calculate a threat, based on tracking tendencies, only to be terribly mistaken. In one case, men with badges and blasters had burst into a classroom full of law students who, ironically enough, were learning about probable cause. The State's calculations did not discriminate based on age: twenty senior citizens died when a group of Security Service officers broke down the door to their retirement home and blasted them away. The wrinkly victims had been doing nothing more than playing checkers, but somehow the monitoring software had identified them as a serious threat to national security.

If they were detected, it wouldn't matter if Isaac and the others were talking about something as innocuous as what it might be like to live in a different century. Just being in a group was enough to become the State's target. The students and the senior citizens had found that out the hard way.

While he showered and dressed, he thought of the practical aspects of time travel—preventing the State from spreading war across the world, stopping them from imprisoning an entire continent of people. Most of all, he thought about how he would adapt to living in a different time.

A man in one of his meetings had said, "If you did appear in a completely different era of history and you were wearing these clothes, you'd stick out like a sore thumb."

They discussed how to blend in and how to adapt to different laws and religious beliefs. They talked about the difficulties of establishing a new life. They would, after all, be appearing out of nowhere without proper identification or proof of who they said they were.

This was usually the point where one of the participants could no longer contain himself and would ask, "What do you guys think would happen if you went back in time and accidently killed the younger version of yourself?"

Eventually, someone always wanted to discuss the paradoxes of time travel. It couldn't be helped: these were the things they had grown up seeing in movies and on TV.

"I've seen pictures of my grandmom when she was twenty. She was smokin'. What if I went back in time, met her, and became my own grandfather?"

"Can we try and stay on topic? We're trying to prevent a tyranny here, not talk about how hot your grandma was."

What they didn't understand was that the realities of time travel negated nearly all of these paradoxes.

6 - THE SO-CALLED PARADOXES OF TIME TRAVEL

If a man went back in time and killed his parents before he was ever born, he would never exist and, thus, would never be able to go back in time and kill his parents in the first place. There were countless variations of this argument.

Or what if Springfield changed history so much that he would never be born? Didn't the fact that he existed at all mean that he would never go back in time and change events in a way that prevented his birth?

The answer to these questions is found in the shifting of the Theta Timeline. All of time is happening at once and, since every possible reality, no matter how absurd, is playing out somewhere, the reality people are aware of is nothing more than an ever-moving target. Any changes in the past simply cause people's current circumstances to transfer to the altered Theta Timeline. Anything can happen because the Theta Timeline shifts to match each possible consciousness. With an infinite number of realities, anything is possible.

This is why paradoxes do not exist in time travel; it's only the current Theta Timeline that everyone is conscious of, and the collective consciousness can shift to match whatever reality the time traveler causes. A man can go back in time and kill his parents because if he does, the Theta Timeline will move to a reality in which he was never born. That does not prevent him, though, from having been born in a different reality, one outside the newly shifted Theta Timeline.

So while there are timelines in which the time traveler was never born, timelines in which he does exist, and still others where he not only exists but goes back and kills his parents, we are only aware of one of those lives. That doesn't mean all of the other realities aren't taking place. In fact, they exist regardless of whether or not we can perceive them. Humans would go insane if they could conceive of all the possible outcomes the universe holds. It's too overwhelming.

Conceivably, there are timelines in which mankind never evolved from simpler creatures, and others in which mankind's evolution produced different bodies than the ones we are familiar with. There are realities in which no one has been sent back in time, and there are realities in which time travel is a form of recreation. Everything is possible as long as it doesn't violate the laws of physics.

What the time traveler aims to do, and what is now known not to be a paradox at all but a shift in collective consciousness, is move the Theta Timeline away from a reality in which the State formed. Maybe one day the State will no longer exist and people will think, "Of course it doesn't exist, this is the land of the free." But that will only happen if Springfield or someone like him is able to go back in time and change the Theta Timeline.

Although sending men back in time was now possible, that didn't make changing the course of history easy. If it were easy, any of the other forty men who had been sent back would have prevented the State. Since there are an infinite number of realities and anything is possible, there are also an infinite number of things that can go wrong.

7 - CAMERAS IN THE SKY

As soon as Isaac opened his front door, he could hear them: the low hum of the AeroCams overhead. The new "silent" version of the flying robotic cameras no longer produced a droning noise like small planes, but with thousands of them in the sky at the same time, they still combined to buzz like a series of live power lines. The noise was a reminder to everyone who could hear it that their movements were being recorded. From the time he left his house until the time he got back indoors, the State was watching everything he did.

The State claimed that having cameras overhead would keep everyone safe. No one liked the idea of being constantly filmed and tracked, but the Ruler reassured everyone that AeroCams had already prevented a dozen attacks. "We can't tell the public the specifics of these attacks," he had said, "but rest assured the AeroCams have been instrumental in saving lives."

When no one was convinced, he added, "Just think of it like the camera in the ATM that makes sure you aren't robbed, except this one flies overhead and keeps you safe all the time."

"Dear lord," Isaac's father had groaned upon hearing

that analogy. That was all it had taken for his parents to turn off the evening news that night.

What people noticed, though, was that crime rates hadn't dropped. There were still robberies. There were still murders. No one was sure what the flying robots were intended for, but the State assured everyone that there had been no more major attacks only because the AeroCams were preventing them.

The Ruler appeared on television and said, "If the public knew how many attacks these cameras had stopped, they would be begging us to put even more in the sky!"

It was around that time that the first rumors started surfacing. People noticed that the AeroCams seemed to be following people who had attended protests before public meetings had been outlawed and people who had spoken out against the State before that had been outlawed too. Drug dealers and rapists were left to do whatever they wanted; the miniature flying robots were tracking a different type of threat.

The Ruler reassured everyone: "These flying cameras have prevented even more attacks than we first realized. Fifty major attacks have been stopped!"

No one dared question how the original dozen was now more than four times larger. If anyone insisted they were being singled out for what they had once said about the State's policies, the number of prevented attacks reported rose again, and the person who complained disappeared.

There were thousands of eyes watching what everyone did and yet there were still as many drive-by shootings and carjackings as there had been before the AeroCams. But if someone went on TV and spoke out against the State, they could be sure the cameras would start monitoring their every action.

When people asked what the point of the flying robots was if there was still as much vandalism and theft as there always had been, the State would say that the AeroCams were only intended to prevent serious attacks. "We would need *millions* of eyes if we actually meant to stop *every* crime."

When another bomb did eventually go off, the State was silent. The cries of indignation picked right back up again. One man, who wore a T-shirt that read "Robots monitor my every movement and all I got was this smoking hole in my city," was arrested and never seen again.

The State responded the only way it knew how: by putting twice as many AeroCams into the sky. The increased robot presence, the Ruler said, would have prevented the latest bombing. Not only that, the additional devices had already foiled a dozen other attacks.

Just in the air over Isaac's apartment building, there were between fifty or sixty such flying robots. As soon as he opened his front door, one of them would split off from the rest and begin following him. His instinct, of course, was to look up and see if one of them really was hovering over him. But the last thing he wanted was to acknowledge an AeroCam. Doing so was one of the State's criteria for registering someone as a person of suspicion. Their logic was flawless: why would you care where the AeroCams were unless you intended to break the law? If Isaac looked up, not only would more AeroCams track his every movement, a squad of Security Service officers would drag him away.

Looking up would be a waste these days anyway. The AeroCams, originally the size of a sedan, kept getting smaller with each updated model. The current version, like the ones flying over Isaac, was no larger than a shoe, which made it difficult to see in the sky unless he had binoculars.

Unlocking his door and getting into his car, he tried to forget about the robots hovering overhead. He took a deep breath and turned the key. The engine started, then the radio. With the sounds of drums and singing drowning out the hum of the AeroCams, he pulled out of the parking spot and began to prepare for the first of the three checkpoints he would have to pass through on his way to Browning Street.

8 - GIVE EVERYONE A ROLE IN THEIR TYRANNY

"Hey, Isaac, what brings you out today?"

The man at Isaac's car window was his next-door neighbor, Fred. Until the previous week, Fred had been unemployed. Neither Jessica nor Isaac knew how long he had been without work or how he had managed to pay his rent while sitting home all day. Over the course of a single summer, he had put on twenty pounds. Both Jessica and Isaac imagined Fred crying himself to sleep each night, a tub of ice cream melting in his lap as he thought of ways to evade his landlord. Now, though, the State was hiring everyone they could find to man the security checkpoints. Everyone, even Fred, could find a job. Shiny black pants replaced the jean shorts that Isaac had seen him in all summer. His stained t-shirt was gone. In its place was a black button-up dress shirt, various company logos covering the sleeves.

"Just going to see the game," Isaac said.

"Ah man, don't even get me started on that. I have to miss it because I'm working." Then, without waiting for a response, his neighbor added, "I'm going to need you to pop your trunk and get out of the car."

It sounded more threatening than it actually was; Fred

was just repeating the commands he had been taught to give each motorist. There had been a time when the authorities only searched someone's car if they had a good reason. Now, it was standard practice before getting onto the highway and entering the city.

Isaac remembered how Fred had originally cursed the new measures to anyone who would listen. "The State is full of shit," he would say. Or, "Freedom? They just want to treat people like freaking cattle." Now that he was gainfully employed, however, Isaac's neighbor didn't seem to think the checkpoints were such a bad idea.

No one receiving a paycheck from the State would be dumb enough to speak out against a new law. Not when their livelihood was at stake. They put their heads down, collected their checks, received their benefits, and kept their opinions to themselves.

All across the country, hundreds of thousands of additional people now had a reason to support the State and whatever security measures it put in place. And that was only the people who worked at the highway and city checkpoints. It didn't include the other, already established, checkpoints at the train stations, bus terminals, libraries, and shopping malls—even golf courses, for some inexplicable reason. There were now millions of people who now had a reason to keep quiet and let the State do whatever it wanted.

Any time people grumbled about the unemployment rate, the State found more places that could use checkpoints. Grocery stores needed them. So did public parks. And since all you had to do was pat people down and make them wait in line, even drug addicts, the homeless, and sex offenders were well-qualified for the job.

Isaac stood in his assigned area and watched as Fred rooted through the open trunk, opening a small tin canister only to find an assortment of tennis balls.

"Just another couple of minutes," Fred called out.

Next to Isaac, a group of men and women, some with children by their sides, all stood in the same area, watching similar inspectors search the contents of their vehicles.

Fred closed the trunk of Isaac's car and moved to the passenger's side door. With a mirror attached to a long stick, Fred inspected the underside of Isaac's car for explosives or other contraband. When that was done, he came back and offered his neighbor a smile.

"All clear. Free to go."

"Thanks," Isaac said. "You still coming over for our cookout next weekend?"

But before Fred could reply, one of the other inspectors, his head still leaning over someone's open trunk, yelled, "Got something here."

The other inspectors all rushed over to the same trunk and began yelling and pointing at a man standing in the waiting area where Isaac had just been.

"Oh that," said the man, his eyes beginning to widen in fear. "That's just my uniform. I'm on my way to a Civil War reenact—"

That was all he had a chance to say before he was thrown to the ground by one of the guards. Without offering commands or telling their suspect to remain still, another guard ran over and kicked him in the stomach. As Isaac put his car into gear, he saw Fred pull out a baton and join the group of guards as they took turns beating the man as he lay motionless on the ground.

Even if he survived his injuries, it was doubtful the man would ever be seen or heard from again. If anyone recorded the beating or mentioned it to the media, they would become the next target. That was why the other men and women who had been waiting to have their cars inspected all put their heads down and gazed at their own shoes. None of them called out for the beating to stop. None of them wanted to do anything that would direct the guard's anger their way. Isaac peered through his mirror at the scene until veering around the ramp to get on the highway.

Then he was on the highway and the security checkpoint disappeared in the distance.

One checkpoint down.

9 – THINKERS

"These people who complain about the checkpoints and the searches—it's only a small portion of the population causing problems for everyone else," the man on the radio said before starting the next song. "Why do they think they know better than their own Ruler? If they would just shut up and go along with what the State says, we could all get along. Why can't they just accept what the State tells them? I do, and look how happy I am."

And with the DJ's two cents out of the way, the next song started.

For as long as there have been men willing to rule over the masses, there have been others who were willing to stand up to them. When Julius Caesar threatened to become a tyrant, a group of Roman senators struck him down. When Caligula made a mockery of the empire, he was assassinated. Not every uprising had to be violent, however. Protests have led to change. Marches have resulted in revolution.

Standing up to the State might have worked before it controlled information and outlawed dissent. If someone were foolhardy enough to appear on television and declare that the State is abusing its powers, they would be found dead the next day, the supposed victim of suicide or a drive-by shooting. Sometimes they would disappear, shipped off to a secret prison, never to be heard from again. When people can be silenced just for wanting a better quality of life, for exposing the lies of their rulers, rallies and pubic debate won't work. A different approach was needed.

The men who saw what the State was doing could only hide in the shadows. Men like Isaac could do little but meet in secret. They were not militants nor revolutionaries. They were idealists. They were people who believed what they saw with their own eyes rather than what they were told to believe. They were people who understood that an idea can be distorted to achieve a goal.

They were scholars, not regressives. They were not afraid of advancement, progress, or technology. They were simply people who thought that citizens shouldn't be frightened into obedience. They were people who understood history and who saw a pattern of the State using fear to further its goals.

They were individuals. They were people who would rather think for themselves rather than accept the groupthink doctrine of why war is necessary or why flying robots and constant checkpoints are critical. They were people who thought privacy was something to be treasured, not a dirty word, not the bastion of a guilty man.

Before the State started rounding up anyone who questioned it, these scholars and historians never missed an opportunity to articulate how the State worked. They pointed out that, over a few short years, a law that would have seemed crazy could be made to look like a necessity as long as enough fear existed. They were people who didn't fall into the trap of blaming one leader or another, but who saw that no matter which Ruler was in power, new reasons to go to war were always found, and new laws to control people were constantly passed.

And that is why the State, when forced to mention them, referred to them as Thinkers. It was intended to be a dirty word, a put-down, as if thinking for one's self was a perverse quality rather than a positive trait.

"These people are dangerous to our country," one of the leaders said during a committee meeting.

"They're inciting the people to violence," said another, even though no one had been provoked to do anything other than to think for themselves.

"These people are trying to turn everyone against us," the Ruler told reporters. "They think life used to be better!" he said with a wry, scoffing laugh. "Don't they know we used to live in an age of terror? Now, everyone is safe as long as they do exactly what we tell them to do."

It was obvious that something had to be done. When simple reasoning could make the State's words and actions look nonsensical, no leader, focused solely on self-preservation, could allow the public to hear the Thinkers' logic. If people believed the quality of life was getting worse rather than better, they wouldn't put up with entertaining the Ruler's whims. That was why the State was so threatened by the Thinkers and why they made sure to use words like *extremist* and *radical* every time the group was mentioned.

The Thinkers told everyone that they should expect more from their leaders, that living in fear of another attack wasn't reason enough to give up their rights. At first, they were ridiculed. But when that didn't deter them from speaking out, the State began arresting them. Someone who encouraged others to expect more of their leaders was weakening the nation's morale. And someone who would do that, the Ruler said, was just another type of enemy.

"These Thinkers," the Ruler said during a national address, "are enemies of our way of life. For the State to keep you protected, we can't have people instilling doubt and fear. Maybe they think the country would be better if we didn't have any security at all and there were attacks every day. Because that's what would happen if we didn't have all of these checkpoints and AeroCams. One thing is clear: we cannot stand by and let these people spread fear and lies. From this day forward, these people, these Thinkers, will be punished to the fullest extent of the State's laws."

The Thinkers became targets. Anyone who sympathized with them or shared their ideas was considered a threat. They weren't even charged with a crime, but were simply whisked away and never seen nor heard from again. There was no opportunity to speak with a lawyer or even loved ones. That was the way the State functioned.

If Julius Caesar and Caligula had cameras in the sky monitoring everyone's actions and words, they never would have been assassinated. Since the State knew exactly what everyone was saying and doing, it knew how to keep itself in power. It was why Isaac and people like him were forced to meet in secret.

The Thinkers no longer tried to convince others that all of the State's wars were initiated under false pretenses and were completely unnecessary—just like their laws. But they also never stopped thinking of ways to stop the State.

Outside of the international scientific community, not much was made of CERN's report that their hadron collider had sent a single subatomic particle back in time. It was only one neutrino and it had only been sent back in time a fraction of a second, but it was proof that time travel could work. The State considered the billion-dollar project a waste of time and money. The public was told to fear the formation of a black hole and the end of the world. The Thinkers, however, knew it was exactly what they had been waiting for.

10 - WHAT'S THE PURPOSE OF YOUR VISIT?

Isaac had been lucky that Fred happened to be the guard at the first checkpoint. No one else working at the State's inspection spots had any inclination to be pleasant. In fact, they often seemed to take pride in how rude and belligerent they could be. Anything someone did to irritate them, even if it was to complain that their genitals were being groped a little too vigorously, was cause to be detained.

The line of people waiting to pass through the next checkpoint stretched around the parking lot where Isaac parked his car.

"Identification," the guard at the next checkpoint said when it was finally Isaac's turn to step forward.

He withdrew his identification card from his wallet and handed it to the man. The guard, fat and sweaty, was wearing the same uniform that Fred and all the other checkpoint workers wore. It even had a yellow insignia sewn onto the shoulder to make it look like they got to wear badges. The man's black pants were rolled up at the ankles to keep them from dragging on the ground. His sleeves hung down past his chubby wrists. The guard, whose badge said he was named "Johnson", wiped perspiration from his forehead before inspecting Isaac's driver's license with wet fingers.

Isaac pretended not to notice how his ID was being handled. If he said anything at all, he would never make it to Browning Street on time. Saying something as simple as "Please, don't do that" was reason enough for a guard to drag someone away and detain them indefinitely. Men sometimes reappeared with black eyes or swollen lips. Some of the women who were detained said the guards told them they could ensure their immediate release in exchange for sexual favors.

The guard swiped Isaac's ID through a reader, then waited a moment as the information processed. A line of people waited behind him, all trying not to let on that they were impatient to get through the inspections so they could continue their lives.

"Hand," the guard said, and Isaac put his right hand into a black box the guard was holding.

If the threat assessor identified any strange chemicals on his person, Isaac would be detained. If it detected an abnormally fast heartbeat, this would be interpreted as a sign of anxiety, evidence that Isaac was nervous he was going to be caught for something. There were rumors that the guards had a button underneath the black boxes that could make it go off anytime they wanted. This explained why so many minorities seemed to be magically identified as possible threats by white guards. It also explained why so many attractive women were detained and taken to secluded rooms where the guards could do whatever they wanted without the fear of being caught on tape.

"Name?" Johnson said.

Isaac wanted to say, "You already know my name. You just swiped my ID, you have all of my information on the screen in front of you." But saying that would only mean trouble. His entire day would be spent in an empty room.

"Isaac Barnhouse," was all he actually said. After waiting half an hour in line as the people ahead of him filed through the same checkpoint, he didn't want to do or say anything that would make this take any longer than absolutely necessary.

"Mr. Barnhouse, what's your purpose for visiting the city today?"

He wondered if people who worked in the city had to say, "to go to my job," every time they went through one of these lines, as if they needed the State's permission to earn money for their families.

"I'm watching the game with some friends."

The black box remained silent.

"Where?"

"Dakota's. 4891 Browning Street."

The threat box did not consider his answer to be suspicious.

Johnson said, "Are you visiting with friends, or with people you've never met before?"

"What does it matter to you?" Isaac wanted to say. "I've told you what I'm required to tell you, now let me go." Part of him was surprised the threat box didn't pick up on his irritation. He wondered if the rumors were true that the boxes didn't really detect anything at all, but only seemed to in order to scare people and give the guards an excuse to pull anyone out of line that they wanted.

What he actually said was, "With friends."

"Awfully far to travel just to watch a game with some buddies," the fat guard said.

But it wasn't far at all. Even by bicycle, it should have only taken half an hour. In a car, it used to take five or six minutes. It only seemed a long way now because of all the checkpoints. The State's trick was that it made every action so difficult and tedious that, after a while, people gave up and realized it was too much of a hassle to do something they didn't absolutely have to do. Instead of spending their day in checkpoint lines, people remained at home and watched television, which only served to make everyone dumber than if they had spent the evening sniffing magic markers.

"Are you a citizen of the State?" Johnson asked when Isaac didn't reply to his previous comment.

From the information on his screen, the guard already knew Isaac was a citizen. There was no point to asking such questions except to teach people that they had to answer every question they were asked if they wanted to be allowed to pass through the checkpoint, no matter how stupid the question was.

"Yes."

The threat box remained silent.

"Have you come in contact with anyone during your drive into the city today whom you didn't personally know?"

While waiting for his car to be searched, he had stood next to a group of people he had never seen before. Just now, he had stood in line, waiting to be allowed through this checkpoint, with people he didn't know. But through all of it, he had only spoken to one person. There had been a time when strangers were polite, when a man would hold a door open for a woman, when two people who had never seen each other before might say hello just because they could. Now, though, when the State arrested someone, they went back through the AeroCam footage to see everyone else that the supposed criminal had spoken to. All of those people were rounded up as well. An entire country of people began refusing to make eye contact with anyone they didn't already know and trust. It was easier to put your head down and not talk to anyone. Subway trains full of people would go from one stop to another in perfect silence. If a man fell asleep and missed his stop, no one woke him because they were afraid they might need to explain why they had been seen talking to someone who was on a watch list.

In the checkpoint line next to Isaac, a man yelled, while being dragged away, "But I only told her that she dropped her wallet." The man must have said he hadn't spoken to anyone, not considering the nicety of helping a stranger as a real interaction. But the AeroCam footage, which had tracked everything he did, saw him say something to the woman on the street, which in turn triggered an alert on the guard's computer. The worst part was that the woman he had spoken to, whoever she was, would now also be picked up by the State's men. All because she had accidently dropped her wallet and a stranger had performed a good deed.

"Just one person," Isaac said.

The guard's brows furrowed. "What did you say?"

"Half an hour ago, in this line, I told a guy that his papers were about to fall out of his briefcase."

"What was his name?"

"I have no idea. I didn't ask."

"You didn't know his name, and yet you spoke to him?"

"I didn't want his papers to blow away."

"You're a real humanitarian, huh?"

Isaac didn't say anything to this. The guards often broke into sarcasm just to provoke a response that would allow them to detain someone. Footage on the internet showed them putting their hands under women's blouses and up girls' skirts. If they complained, they were said to be obstructing an official State checkpoint search and were detained. God only knew what happened to them after that.

The guard's computer did not signal an alert, which meant the cameras in the sky corroborated Isaac's story that he had only spoken to one person he didn't know. Poor old Fred didn't count, not even to the AeroCams.

"You're free to go," Johnson snorted.

Isaac put his identification card back in his wallet and continued forward. Behind him, the line of hundreds of people all took one more step. None of them said anything to anyone else. Probably, all of them were thinking of the lost hour of their lives they would spend in this line, the illusion of safety, instead of being at home with their children and their spouses. The odds were that at least ten of the people in line would be sent to holding cells, even though they hadn't done anything wrong. One of those people would spend the night in jail for no other reason than the fat guard or someone like him was grumpy in his ill-fitting uniform. One or two would disappear and never be seen again, never even being told why they were being dragged away. There was nothing anyone could do; it was the way the State worked.

11 - THE DANGER OF LETTING A MAN LOOK UP AT THE SKY

For the previous meeting, Isaac had been told to arrive two minutes late. This time, he needed to arrive precisely on the hour. It didn't sound like much, but the Thinkers' success came from planning every minute detail of their rendezvous. It was the difference between the AeroCams noting suspicious behavior and going undetected.

Because there was no telling how long it would take to get through all the checkpoints, Isaac had left the house two hours early. Now, though, he was through the final inspection area, the meeting was right down the street, and he was fifteen minutes early. His options were limited. No one knew exactly how sophisticated the cameras in the sky were or what their tracking criteria consisted of. It was possible that just by slowing his pace—turning two city blocks into a fifteen-minute stroll rather than a two-minute straight line—an alert might be triggered. It was also possible that just by deviating from the route he had provided at the last checkpoint, the AeroCams would take note, an alert would be sent, and the Security Service would drag him off the streets. In the eyes of the State, someone who wasn't going directly to where they needed to go was probably up to no good.

After seeing countless people escorted into the State's vans and taken away, Isaac had no idea if there was any intelligent reasoning for who was deemed a threat and who was left to walk the streets without hassle.

And that was one of the many problems with the AeroCams—they didn't allow for the oddities of normal human behavior. The cameras only recorded actions, not motivations, and to the all-seeing robotic eyes, everything could be interpreted as suspicious. A woman walking to meet her friends for drinks could stop suddenly when she saw a dress she liked in a store window. To the State, someone who stopped in front of a store instead of going directly to the destination they had provided was utterly treacherous. A van would pull up and men in black uniforms would make sure she was never seen or heard from again.

A man who reached behind a public trashcan was torn away from his family. There was no doubt he was going to plant a bomb. The man's wife tried to explain that her husband was simply trying to reach for the car keys he had dropped. Before she could, however, the State's men had blasted a hole in his head for resisting arrest.

Another man, arrested for supposedly planning an attack, had done nothing but look up at the sun and the clouds. This was before people realized that the State considered people who looked up at the AeroCams to be the most suspicious of all possible radicals.

"Surely," the man told the judge, "you can remember the days when we watched the clouds drift by in the sky? Is that really a crime now?"

If he thought he would earn sympathy from the State's leaders, he was mistaken. They all agreed: "It's vital to the State's security that this man be found guilty." Why? Because, as they said, "If we let this man go free, everyone will begin looking up at the sky. And if that happens, the AeroCams will have an even more difficult time judging who is acting suspiciously and who isn't."

The man who looked at the clouds was found guilty,

sent off to a secret prison, and never heard from again.

That was why Isaac kept his head down as he took his chances and entered the first bar he saw. The hope was that even if the camera in the sky saw him veer off course from his intended destination, it would register that he had gone into a place of entertainment. Even though all he did was ask for a beer, he couldn't stop expecting to see a group of men rush into the establishment to get him.

He managed to sip his drink without interruption, though. As he did, he noticed that not even the people in the bar would look at each other. Everyone he saw had their eyes turned down toward their drinks, not wanting to be associated with anyone else when the State started making arrests and wanted to find the suspect's accomplices. Even the bartender looked at each customer's shoulders instead of directly at them.

With two minutes left before he needed to arrive, Isaac paid for the drink and went back out on the street. Two blocks ahead of him, he saw another man walking to the exact same sports bar he had been directed to. The man, Isaac knew, would have been told to arrive exactly one minute early. A minute later, Isaac would arrive. He wouldn't do something as foolish as look behind him, but he was sure that if he did, he would see someone else in his group, on schedule to arrive a minute later.

The bar was directly adjacent to an apartment building. The front door to the drinking establishment was only ten feet away from the other door, where people lived and slept. A difficult distance for the AeroCams to judge. Instead if entering the sports bar, he walked a few more paces and went to where he knew he was actually supposed to go.

As was their custom, he expected to get to the front door and walk right in. But a man was there, in the shadows of the apartment building's overhang, out of view from the sky. A wide-brimmed hat cast a ring of darkness over the man's face.

This was not normal.

"Name?" the man said, not bothering to look up at the person he was speaking to. It didn't matter what Isaac looked like, only what he said. Maybe the man didn't look up simply because he didn't want to be able to identify Isaac in a line-up even if his life was at stake.

But a second thought kept Isaac from immediately answering: *What if this man is with the State?* If he was and Isaac gave anything other than his real name, the man would be well within his authority to pull out a blaster and kill him right where he stood. A story would appear the next day on the news about how the shooting was justified because anyone using a fictitious name was obviously a threat to everyone around him.

If he weren't killed on the spot, maybe a group of the State's men would be waiting inside so there wasn't a public scene. If that were the case, the man who had entered the building one minute ahead of him would be a decoy planted by the State to entrap him.

But at the same time, if this man wasn't with the State, if he really was a Thinker, and Isaac gave his real name instead of his code name, he would be immediately kicked out of the group for violating its anonymity rule. As soon as even one other person in the Thinkers knew his real name, he would become a liability.

It was only then, standing there, trying to figure out how he should answer, that he realized the man in the shadows was keeping his hands in his pockets. Probably, he thought, a blaster was there.

"Name," the man said again, fidgeting in his pocket.

While Isaac was trying to figure out if this man was with the State or with the Thinkers, he realized the guard was trying to determine the same thing of him. And if he thought this newest arrival was part of the State, he might pull the blaster out and end the discussion before Isaac could offer an explanation.

Before Isaac could make up his mind, the man added, "Hurry up, you don't want to miss the game," and Isaac knew which side the man was on.

"Springfield."

The man nodded. The apartment building's front door clicked, then opened an inch. Isaac paused at the open door. A stairwell led down to the basement while an elevator led up to the penthouse.

"Down," the man in the shadows said.

As he descended the steps, Isaac saw a sign that said LAUNDRY and knew he was going to where twenty stories' worth of families went to drop quarters into a machine so they could wash their clothes. At the bottom of the steps, another man was standing in front of what looked to be the door to a janitor's closet. This man, although not wearing a wide-brimmed hat like the man on the street, also kept his hands in his pockets.

This wasn't normal either. The Thinkers never had a guard, let alone two. Something was wrong.

"Name?" the man said.

"Springfield."

Part of him was so used to the asinine rules of the State's checkpoints that almost he expected the guard to tell him to remove his shoes and his belt in order to prove he wasn't carrying anything illegal. The guard didn't care about any of that, though.

"Aren't you a little far from home?" the man said.

"I didn't want to miss the game."

The man stepped aside.

Isaac took hold of the doorknob and turned it. From the simple, ugly green door, he had been expecting to step into a small room filled with mops and buckets. What looked like a normal closet door, however, was actually solid metal. Very heavy, solid metal. He had to put his shoulder against it to make it open. Behind him, he was sure the guard had a smirk on his face.

Oh well, he thought, *there's a reason why Thinkers are known for their minds and not their muscles.*

12 - THE PROBLEM WHEN PEOPLE ARE TOO SMART

Not many people cared about a good education any more. Isaac was one of the lucky ones; his parents had ensured he went to a school that still had a good reputation. Looking at the condition of the State's schools, it was no wonder the wealthiest parents were sending their children to other countries to receive their education.

Isaac's tradition, once he had graduated college and was living on his own, was to return to his parents' house each weekend for dinner. While watching the news with his mother and father, one of the State's leaders turned to the camera and said, "We have to be responsible in our spending. We have to pay for all of these new security checkpoints around the country, so we'll have to spend less in other areas."

"I guarantee he's talking about cutting back on education," Isaac's father said.

A month later, the budget was released. The amount of money spent on bombs and planes was once again increased. The portion given to education was once again reduced. The State was spending more on missiles and guns than the rest of the world combined, but the leaders still wanted more. The State's priorities were clear. It was strength and brute force that mattered, not brains or diplomacy.

"Listen," the Ruler said, defending the State's decision, "Nobody cares about education and our youth more than I do. Our children are our most important resource. But we need to be able to defend ourselves from other countries, and we don't have an unlimited budget, so we had to make some tough decisions."

Isaac's mother said, "The State is already trillions of dollars in debt that it will never be able to pay back, but I guess education is the one thing they can't go into further debt over."

Without funds for good schools and good teachers, the State went from being a land of intellectuals to being a populace of mindless adults. In generations past, the State had produced the brightest and smartest kids in the world. After years of neglecting their schools in favor of spending for war, the State's ranking slipped to tenth in the world. A decade later, it was barely in the top twenty-five. Last year, the State wasn't even in the top fifty.

Kids graduated from high school without being able to read. The State could tell the average student that two plus two equaled five and they would believe it, not because they were forced to believe it, but because they had learned that knowing the correct answer wasn't all that important.

As adults, those same people would never be able to question the State's war statistics because they wouldn't know basic arithmetic. They would trust whatever the State said about the economy because they had no hope of figuring it out for themselves. When they heard about the astronomical amount of the State's debt, they couldn't understand its significance. It was exactly what the State wanted; it's much easier to control the population when no one understands the principles of effective governments, economies, or international relations.

It wasn't just a lack of spending that sabotaged the State's education, however. A new law forbid teaching science. Ideas like survival of the fittest and the interdependencies of ecosystems would only lead people to view themselves as independent organisms within a delicate world. And people who understand the laws of nature, the fragility of life, and their place in the universe, are people who know that war benefits no one.

That was why schools were encouraged to forget about Darwin, Fleming, Einstein, and everyone in between. Instead, they were told to teach whatever was fun. It didn't matter what had been proven by physics, mathematics, or archeology. Math and science were replaced with ideology and dogma, and through those means, an entire nation could be controlled.

One teacher told her students that the world was only three thousand years old. An entire classroom of kids grew up thinking the Greek empire was fantasy instead of reality. A professor told his class that humans had once hunted dinosaurs. The State loved this because they understood that misinformed youths inevitably grew up to become misinformed adults—adults that would believe anything the Ruler told them.

No subject bothered the State more than History. When people knew their country's past, they were more likely to become unhappy with the current standard of living. That was why the State made sure that when History was taught, it was revised to suit the Ruler's wishes. The nation's original leaders, once thought of as brilliant and honorable, were re-cast as flawed men, because once they could be seen as flawed, it provided the State with an excuse to change the principles that the nation was founded on.

Smart rulers know that educated citizens only cause trouble, but the State couldn't get away with something as blatant as rounding up and killing the most knowledgeable people. It had worked for Stalin, but in a day of technology and social media, it was too much for even the State to get away with. Nor could they burn books. History had proved that destroying someone's writing only made people want to read it even more. Instead, they made accusations, falsified evidence, made people disappear. Sometimes, people were arrested on the most embarrassing charges the State could think of, solely to cast a blanket of disgrace upon them and to teach anyone else that they too would be humiliated if they thought they knew better than the Ruler did. Others were simply shot in the back of the head and their deaths made out to be suicides.

The State not only wanted a land of people who obeyed their rule, they wanted a population that was too dumb to question any alternative. They encouraged this attitude by acting dumb themselves. The intelligence reports that had led them to war were completely wrong? Oh well, the war is over now. The law that was passed in response to the latest attack doesn't actually prevent future attacks? Oh well, the law has already been passed. Each time the leaders feigned stupidity, it reassured the nation that they were just like everyone else. They were, however, anything but dumb. They were corrupt, they cared more about staying in power than they did governing their people, and they loved war more than peace, but they were not idiots.

"The pen is mightier than the sword," Isaac's parents had told him each night as they watched the news together. He used to believe it wholeheartedly. Now, seeing how the State ruled over the entire world with fear, he wasn't quite as convinced.

Once upon a time, actors and directors had earned notoriety speaking out against societal outrages. Musicians and writers had made their careers spotlighting the injustices of the world. The State, though, understood that people who were too smart for their own good were also too smart for the nation's good, and so it crushed any chance to learn about a better way of life.

"Maybe," Isaac had told his parents one time, "the pen would be mightier than the sword if more people knew how to read and write."

They spoke in these vague back-and-forths because

the earlier version of the AeroCams didn't understand subtleties.

"Honey," his mother said. "The pen doesn't have to be a word, it can be an idea."

She had known, just as the Thinkers would learn, that the State had no fear of a man with muscles. It feared a man with a mind. It feared understanding and conviction.

That was why, when the first neutrino was zapped back in time, the Thinker's didn't view it as a waste of time and money like the State did. The day the news of that experiment was released, the scientists within the Thinkers must have been thinking, *Holy shit! This is the chance for the pen to be mightier than the sword.*

Isaac smiled as he struggled to push the sub-basement's heavy door open. He might have a difficult time opening a solid steel door, but at least he understood that true change was brought about by ideas, not by laws or by force.

13 - A BUNKER

The door that Isaac thought would open to a janitor's closet actually led to another set of steps even further below ground. An old Cold War bunker. There was a time, long ago, when the apartment building's occupants would hear an alarm and rush two levels down into the earth in the hope of surviving a nuclear attack. It was never clear why anyone thought it was better to survive the initial attack only to die months later of starvation in a room filled with rats and human feces, or perhaps to go outside and die a slow death from radiation poisoning. The subterranean room had long been forgotten. From the dust on the steps, only a few prints marking recent footsteps, it appeared that not even the building's maintenance men bothered to go down into the ancient shelter.

With each step, Isaac couldn't help but wonder if any of the other Thinkers found it ironic that a concrete room meant to protect families from atom bombs was now the hiding place for men trying to prevent those bombs from ever being dropped.

At the bottom of the stairs, he finally understood why one guard had been positioned at the front door and a second stationed at the basement. This was not going to be another discussion on the possibilities of time travel. It suddenly made sense why both guards had their hands in their pockets, their blasters ready to be fired if necessary; this was not going to be a discussion at all. This was it. He was going to be sent back in time.

Along the far wall, a line of six men stood shoulder to shoulder. Each wore an identical burlap outfit. Across from them, a group of five men in white lab coats leaned over a pair of laptop computers.

No one asked for his code name. No one said anything to him at all. The men huddled around the computers never turned their attention from the information displayed on the screen. One of the scientists checked his notepad, then walked to a generator of some kind, positioned near the line of burlap-clad men. There, the scientist gave a gentle tug on each cable coming out of the metal box to make sure they were securely connected.

A second box was placed in the top corner of the room, above the first one. Each box had a line of tubing that ran away from it, formed an arc, and then rejoined the metal box. The pair of tubes, one around the men's ankles, the other above their heads, were perfectly in line with each other. The men standing in line were positioned so their entire bodies were within the oval tubes.

It did not resemble what he imagined a time machine to look like. He had envisioned metal chambers filled with energy. Perhaps a ray gun that would be pointed at him. Even a series of electrodes attached to every part of his body as he was submersed in a gelatinous pool of goo. But not something as simple as standing in a basement with cables running around his feet and over his head.

The men in line did not look at the cables encircling them, the boxes, or anything else. Each had a far-off stare as if he was mentally preparing for what would come next.

Only the man who had arrived immediately before Springfield was separate from the others. Springfield watched as the man finished putting on a pair of cheap brown burlap pants. The man's designer clothes lay forgotten on the ground even though they were worth more than a hundred pairs of the burlap outfit he had changed into.

After he was dressed, the man reached into a box filled with canvas bags, withdrew one, nodded to Springfield, then filed in line as the seventh man against the wall. Taking his cue, Springfield immediately began removing his clothes. There was no point to folding his shirt or making sure his pants didn't get dirt on them. He would never see them again. He reached into a box filled with cream-colored clothes and selected a pair of pants that looked like they would fit.

"Make sure they're comfortable. If you're lucky, you're going to be in them for a long time."

One of the men in white lab coats had turned and taken notice of him. But before Springfield could reply, the scientist was already moving to a different part of the room, to the next task of getting the machines started.

Dressed in burlap, a canvas sack in hand, Springfield walked to where the other men were standing, their backs only inches from the cinder block wall. He was the eighth man in line.

Once there, the man next to him nudged Springfield's foot. When he looked down, Springfield saw a shiny cord, not quite metal but also not plastic, looped around each of the other men's ankles. He reached down and tied it around his ankles as well, leaving the surplus for the next men to join the line.

The metal door groaned again and a moment later, the ninth man entered the room. Just as Springfield had done, this man saw the line of men against the wall, saw their clothes, and began changing out of his dress clothes and into his potato sack.

So this is it, Springfield thought. *This is the time.*

The man next to him, as if able to read Springfield's mind, said, "This is the day we make history."

"Or die trying," the man on the other side of him added.

At one of their meetings, such a comment had caused Isaac to say, "Even if we do change the course of history, we'll never know. And even if we change the Theta Timeline, the other, bad timelines will still exist, it's just that nobody will be conscious of them."

He knew what the group must have been thinking after he said it: "Then what's the point to us risking our lives if no one then, now, or ever, will ever care if we're successful?"

At least, that's what he had been thinking.

All of their meetings had been to prepare them for this moment, and yet, now that it was here, he felt like he wasn't the least bit ready. What was the point of discussing time travel when there were so many variables? There were too many unknowns.

He took a deep breath and tried to relax. Standing there, he wished he would have known this wasn't going to be another brainstorming session, that he would be leaving the world he knew. He thought about his parents, sitting in their home watching television, the luxury of being retired and living out their final years in peace. Neither of them left the house anymore because it was easier to stay home than it was to spend their day in an endless series of security checkpoints.

He thought about Jessica, sitting at her job, oblivious to the fact that she would never again see the man she loved. The next time she did see his face, it would be on the news as a suspected traitor. If he had been allowed to know this was the final meeting, he could have at least… what would he have done? Tell her he loved her? He did that anyway. Tell her that when he was gone, she shouldn't believe anything she heard about him on television? She knew that already too. But still, even if his actions wouldn't have been different, it would have been nice to know their final kiss really did mean goodbye. At least then they could have savored it just a little bit more.

His shoulders sank and he let out a long breath. He

knew this was for a good cause—there was nothing better to stand up for than for freedom—but he wished he could have hugged his parents one last time, thanked them for everything they did. He wished he could have taken the picture of him and Jessica off her nightstand and brought it with him so he would have an image of her in whatever new time he was transported to.

And for a moment, his heart almost regretted trying to save the world if it meant his last visit with his parents, his last kiss with his girlfriend, were casual acts rather than treasured moments.

He thought, *What am I doing? I don't even know when I'll appear in history. I don't even know where I'll appear in the world.* And then, again, *What am I doing?*

14 - HOW TIME TRAVEL ACTUALLY WORKS

By its simplest definition, time travel occurs when someone goes from one point in time to another point in time. It could be the difference of minutes, days, or years. Time travel, it is important to note, is only relative to moments in time, not to points in space. Because of this, time travel cannot work the way it has been depicted throughout the years in movies and on television.

The world, in fact, the entire universe, is always moving. Because the universe is expanding at astounding speeds, a time traveler who was sent back one year in time, without an anchor from which to base their travel, would appear trillions of miles away from planet Earth, in the middle of space. Luckily, gravity provides the necessary anchor.

Time travel is dependent on the gravitational force of the body the time traveler is transported from. The apple falling from the tree was vastly more important than Newton could have ever grasped. For humans, Earth's core and the gravity it creates are fundamental to time travel.

That's not to say that travelling back in time is any simpler because of gravity. Even though the planet's gravitational force ensures a time traveler won't appear in outer space, there are still many things that can go wrong. Most notably, because Earth is spinning on an axis, someone can be transported anywhere along the same latitude from where they disappeared.

Earth completes one revolution of its axis every twenty-four hours, which means it's spinning at a rate of 1,040 miles per hour. For the time traveler, this spinning determines where he will appear. If he is on the equator and travels back in time exactly one hour, he will still reappear on the equator, but he will be 1,040 miles away from where he started. If precise calculations were available, a time traveler could be sent back to the exact same spot on the Earth's rotation, allowing him to appear in the very place he departed. It's a pipe dream, though, that scientists could ever become that exact in their formulas; they still can't guarantee what century they will send a man back to, let alone what decade or year.

This is the root of the scientist's biggest concern for their time travelers. Without knowing precisely how far back someone will be sent, the scientists can't calculate where the traveler will appear along the latitude from which they were sent. It's why only thirty-one percent of time travelers are estimated to survive their reappearance.

Why are the numbers so low? Two reasons: water and elevation.

First: Water. Seventy-five percent of the world's surface is water. This means that if you sent a hundred people back in time from random locations, seventy-five of them would appear in the middle of an ocean, sea, or lake. These people would only live as long as they could swim or float. Then they would drown.

The water problem, as it's known amongst the scientists and time travelers, is the main factor for which locations are selected as departure sites. Scientists try to choose places in the world with the highest chance of reappearing on land. The area around the latitude of 34 N, where Los Angeles is, along with Phoenix, Dallas, and Atlanta, not to mention much of North Africa and the heart of China, is one of the scientist's favorite places to travel from. Departing from 34 N, a time traveler has a roughly 56.3% chance of arriving on land. If that same time traveler departed from Johannesburg, South Africa, they could reappear in South America or Australia, but with only a 25.5% chance of arriving back on dry land. 64 N has one of the best chances of success: a whopping 84.2% land-to-water ratio. Time travelers appearing there could arrive in Alaska, Canada, Greenland, Iceland, Sweden, Norway, or Russia. The only problem is that most of the land in Canada and Russia is too far away from civilization, and the climate too harsh for a time traveler to be expected to survive until he could hike south and find a more hospitable environment.

There are some places where time travel will never take place. If someone travelled back in time from the equator, they would have only a 22.1% chance of appearing on land. The nice weather would only be enjoyed until the time traveler's head went under water, never to resurface. With only a 1.5% chance of reappearing on land, departing from Ushuaia, Argentina would be considered suicide.

Elevation is the other factor that decides where scientists select their departure sites, and is the second leading cause of death among time travelers. Except for the spinning of the Earth's axis, a time traveler appears exactly where they departed from in relation to Earth's center of gravity. This means that a man departing from Death Valley in California, far below sea level, and reappearing anywhere else in the world, would either arrive three hundred feet under water and drown, or would reappear hundreds of feet below ground and be suffocated by rock and earth.

But it's not only appearing too low that's risky. If a time traveler were to depart from the peak of Mount Everest, no matter where he reappeared in the world, he would fall to his death. After plummeting thousands of feet, not even landing in water would help.

The average person would be surprised how much

elevation varies from one location to the next. Even in regions without mountains, one town can be hundreds of feet higher or lower than the next town down the road. This means a time traveler might reappear over land, only to fall a hundred feet, shatter both ankles, break his back, and never walk again.

This is why the scientists calculate the average land elevation over each latitude, cross-match that against the ratio of land versus water, and use that as the model for the best departure sites.

The notion exists that time travel is some sort of luxurious adventure. It's not. Time travelers have a higher mortality rate than veterans from any war that has ever been fought. And even if the time traveler does live, there is no way they can ever return to their old life, see their families again, or even know whether their efforts were successful. It's an adventure, but it's the absolute opposite of luxury.

But the time travelers know all of this and they still volunteer. They know there is a very real possibility that they could be transported back in time only to find themselves floating in the middle of the ocean, or go from standing in a dank basement to falling out of the sky.

Every man in line knows the risk is worth it if it means they can prevent the State.

15 - ORDER OF TOWNS

"Where do you wanna go?"

Springfield broke out of his stupor and turned to look at the man next to him in line.

"What?"

The man smiled. "I said, 'Where do you wanna go?'"

"I don't know," Springfield said, trying not to think of appearing in water, surrounded by sharks.

He had been so busy thinking of the places he *didn't* want to appear—in the middle of the Pacific Ocean, no land in sight; five hundred feet above ground, a parking lot rapidly speeding toward his face—that he hadn't given any thought to the places or times he actually would prefer to be sent to. It was like little kids saying which planet they want to live on, or teenagers choosing a celebrity they would most like to bed—it was out of his control.

"I'm Shady Grove," the man said.

"Hi, Shady Grove. I'm Springfield."

Dressed in burlap and holding a canvas bag, the man was identical to everyone else in line. Even though Springfield was holding a bag too, he didn't consider its contents until he wondered what was inside Shady Grove's bag, and then he realized none of the other men had bothered to inspect their bags either. Based on earlier discussions of the things a time traveler would need to have with him, he could guess what the bag contained.

"I'd want to reappear in 1910," Shady Grove said. "New York would be great."

Springfield said, "I guess I'd want to reappear in 1950. Chicago."

The game was usually a lot more fun, but of course it was usually played on a sofa, not while standing where equipment was being hooked up directly above their heads and beneath their feet.

"So this is really it," Shady Grove said. "To tell you the truth, I always thought the meetings we attended were just part of a big setup by the State."

"And you attended them anyway?"

Shady Grove frowned. Springfield looked around him at the other men in the room. What did it say about the men going on this mission if at least one of them thought it was part of a hoax, a way to entrap them, but had still showed up?

As he shifted his weight back and forth, his ankle tugged against the line tied around it, reminding him he was stuck next to Shady Grove and to the others down from him. The ninth man had finished changing into his time traveler's uniform and was walking toward them. When he got next to Springfield, the man reached down and began tying the cord around his ankles just as the others had.

The tenth and final man entered the room. He looked around for a moment, saw the line of men assembled against the wall, saw the scientists huddled by their computers, then went about taking off his clothes and changing into the nondescript outfit. Two of the scientists walked to where the oval ring of tubing looped back into the generator next to the first man in line. One of the two scientists reached down to touch the cable where it disappeared into the generator and the other man quickly smacked his hand away and muttered something no one else could hear.

Without asking, Springfield was sure the man

immediately to his right would be named after a town that followed Springfield in the alphabet. It was too much of a coincidence that all of the men to his left were also in alphabetical order. The only problem was that this confirmed the rumors that other men must have been sent back in time already, and none of them had been successful. He had heard the whispers that four other departures had been conducted, but no one he knew could be sure if it was true or just the fantasies of men hoping to see an end to the State. Standing in line with men named after towns near the end of the alphabet, he now knew the answer.

But that raised other questions. What had happened to the other forty time travelers? Did they all drown or fall to their deaths? Had they successfully made the jump to another time, or had they all died in the attempts? Maybe time travel had made them all deathly sick. It was still a new technology, still vastly under-tested, and there was no way of knowing if everyone standing near the antimatter loop would develop cancer or just fall over dead. If all forty men had failed in changing the Theta Timeline, what did that say about Springfield's chances? And if this group was unsuccessful, just as the others had been, how many more groups would the Thinkers be able to send back in time before the State eventually discovered the capability they possessed, captured it, and used it for their own purposes?

The final time traveler in Springfield's group, somewhat out of breath, grabbed his canvas bag and got in line with everyone else. The man to Springfield's right motioned for the tenth man to look down at his feet. Noticing the cord wrapped around everyone else's ankles, the tenth man tied it around his as well.

Springfield felt a nudge on his shoulder. Shady Grove was grinning as if the entire arrangement was comical.

"It'll be a lot easier if you just keep thinking about where you want to find yourself when this is over. How great would it be if you were transported back to right before the moon landing and got to see it for yourself?"

But Springfield couldn't fantasize about where he would want to appear because when he did, he thought about wanting to be sent back a single day in time so he could tell his parents that he loved them and to make sure they knew they had raised him the right way. The thought made his eyes sting, and he found himself wishing Shady Grove would just be quiet until they all disappeared.

16 - THE DIFFICULTY OF ENDING A LIFE

Isaac was no different from any of the other time travelers. Each of them had a life he was willing to give up. The very nature of time travel—being sent into history with no hope of return—meant they had to be willing to sever all ties with everyone they had ever known and loved.

Growing up, Isaac's parents had never missed one of his Little League games. They had always been there to offer help on his science fair projects. They had instilled in him an appreciation for the arts and history, the Golden Rule, and the value of treating everyone equally. They were, as parents often are, the two people most responsible for making him the person he grew up to be.

They were also the ones, seated on either side of him at the dinner table each night, who explained that there was a difference between what news anchors reported and what had actually happened. Most important, they explained why the difference was crucial. When a television personality reassured his audience that the new, quiet AeroCams would allow people to forget there were little robotic cameras flying all over the sky, his mother had turned to him and said, "Taking away someone's privacy quietly isn't better than doing it with a lot of noise."

During reports of another war, his father would lean over and tell Isaac, "Don't pay attention to why the leaders say they are invading another country. Pay attention to what they do once they get there: they give huge contracts to their friends' companies, or they install a ruler who lets them do whatever they want."

As the news coverage showed explosions and death, his mother would say, "A few of our leaders used to be on the board of directors of the company that makes all those missiles. They still own a large share of stock there. They all just became a lot richer by sending this country to war again."

"What's the war about this time anyways?"

His father rolled his eyes and said, "Supposedly, this time they need to make sure cyber hackers don't bring down our financial institutions."

"That's a new one."

"I guess people were getting tired of hearing all the old excuses."

And that was how he was raised. They taught him about the world, but they also let him experience it for himself. When he said he wanted to study abroad his sophomore year of college, they were happy to drive him to the airport. They never told him if they agreed or disagreed with the things he said because they liked that he was thinking for himself.

That nurturing environment was probably what contributed to his shock when he graduated college, got into the real world, and saw that only one way of thinking was appropriate: the State's way. Everything else was considered dangerous. Sitting in a conference room during his first week of his new job, he made a remark to his co-workers about how everyone should throw in a dollar to bet on the State's next reason for going to war. Everyone stared at him without speaking. Half the room was probably assuming he had been planted there by the State to find anyone who sympathized with the Thinkers. For the rest of the time he worked there, no one spoke to him—not even his boss.

By that time, he was living in an apartment with Jessica, close to the city, but he still went back to his parents' house each Saturday and Sunday for supper.

"Be careful what you say in front of other people," his father warned him after hearing how his son's co-workers had reacted.

"People are scared these days," his mother said. "And when they're scared, they say and do dumb things. Just look at how it was during the Cold War—everyone accusing others of being Communists. Right now, everyone knows if they sympathize with the Thinkers, the State's men will come after them."

Isaac nodded. He wanted to say, "Well, that's not the way it should be. That's not the type of country we should be living in." But how could his parents respond to such a comment other than with agreement?

That was the moment Isaac realized he was a Thinker. It didn't matter if he attended meetings or had a code name. A Thinker was something someone either was or wasn't. All it took to be one, really, was to be able to see what the State was doing and know people deserved better.

He never knew how his parents felt about the Thinkers because he never asked, but they had taught him to be independent, that he didn't need anyone else's approval. He suspected they both would have attended Thinker meetings themselves if such things had been around in their earlier years.

"Mom, Dad," he said, after one of his first meetings with the other potential time travelers, "I'm tired of watching the news each night. The world gets worse every day. I want to be part of the solution."

His parents didn't say anything at first. Maybe they were considering their words in case the AeroCams were directly over their house, recording everything they said. Or perhaps they knew him as the boy who started building a model aircraft carrier with his father in middle school. The model was still sitting unfinished in the attic. And there was the guitar in his closet that he had vowed to master, only to give up on it a month later.

"Can I get more corn or potatoes for anyone?" his mother had said, rising from the table and going back to the kitchen.

And like that, his declaration was left to hover about him without either of his parents acknowledging it.

The images on television changed to scenes of mass destruction over all the places the State had destroyed in retribution for the latest attack on their land. The anchorman used his most solemn voice as he recounted the horrors of the nuclear attack and the millions of missing people. But to Isaac, it seemed odd that for all of the anchorman's supposed distress, he never mentioned the inconsistencies in the State's official report of what had happened—or how much evidence pointed to the State actually being behind the attack.

As if in response, the anchorman said, "And anyone who spreads lies about the State possibly being behind the blast and the devastation on its own people should be shot dead in the streets."

Isaac's father winced. "There was a time when people like him just gave the news and let you make up your own mind without trying to force you feel a certain way about it. I guess those days are gone."

Part of Isaac wanted to mention the Thinkers. But he had only attended a couple meetings; it wasn't like there was much he could really tell them anyway. He didn't even know yet if the things they discussed were actually possible or just fantasies. Most important, he had sworn not to tell anyone else of his participation unless he wanted them to become targeted by the State as well.

Maybe nothing would come of the secret discussions. Maybe his need to stand up to the State would be shelved like his aircraft carrier model and his guitar. But if he did become part of the group, he wanted his parents to be prepared for what would happen. The State's men would arrive at their door. If they thought his parents were hiding anything, both of them would be taken into custody. They wouldn't be allowed to have lawyers. They might be tortured or be taken to a secret prison for the rest of their lives.

He wanted them to know that anything they heard about him on the news would be more of the State's lies. He wished there was a way to tell them these things without risking their safety.

When he did speak, the only thing he said was, "All these people that disappear before the State can find them—I hope their families know they should report them as missing right away. At least then the State wouldn't suspect them of being involved too."

Neither of his parents said anything. They were more aware than anyone that when the State wanted to find traitors, it could create them out of thin air. Their own neighbors, an eighty-year-old couple living out their final years, had been dragged away by the Security Service when they didn't immediately notify the State of their son's disappearance.

"I don't know why anyone thinks they can hide from the State," his father said.

Isaac leaned forward, his elbows on the dining table even though he had been taught not to let them rest there. "Maybe there are ways."

"Oh, Isaac," his mother said, "you know they can get you wherever you go. It doesn't matter what part of the world you go to, their AeroCams will find you."

None of them said anything else. They had taught him to think for himself, to question everything he heard instead of blindly listening to the State or to the people on television. Now that he was the person they had raised him to be, it wasn't their place to doubt him.

If things went well, he would simply never be seen or heard from again. His face wouldn't even be plastered on the television with the label "traitor" underneath it. His parents would think he really had found a place in the world where the State's cameras couldn't find him. If things didn't go as planned, however, then his face would be shown on television as a suspected Thinker, as being part of a plot to overthrow the State.

His father turned back to the television and said, "They say the number of dead on the other side of the world is over one billion, but there's no way of knowing how many more will die of radiation poisoning."

"We're running out of countries to blow up," his mother said.

And like that, the conversation was over. Those were the last things he would ever say to his parents and the last things they would ever say to him. Why hadn't he at least said how much he loved them? Why hadn't he hugged both of them and told them he would make them proud even if they could never understand how? And why hadn't he at least finished that damned model with his father instead of leaving it unfinished for the rest of time?

17 - TONGUES OUT

As the men waited in line, each holding a canvas bag in their arms, one of the scientists turned from the others, put on a pair of rubber gloves, and withdrew a tiny flashlight from his pocket.

Making sure he didn't step on top of or inside the oval tube looping around the time travelers' feet, the scientist walked up to Riverford and said, "Stick out your tongue and say ahhh."

Riverford did as he was told. The scientist pointed the flashlight so it shone inside the time traveler's throat.

When he was satisfied with what he saw, the man in the lab coat directed the flashlight into Riverford's eyes and said, "Follow the light without moving your head."

The light went left. Riverford's pupils followed it. The light went right. Riverford tracked it there as well.

"How do you feel today?"

"Fine," Riverford said.

"No fever? No cough?"

"No. I feel fine."

"Good," the scientist said before moving to the next man, where the routine started all over.

After being allowed to close his mouth and stop

saying "ahhh," Rockville said, "Why didn't you do this when we first got here?"

The scientist continued the health inspection as he spoke. "Would have taken too much time. We're on a tight schedule here. Easier to do all the checks at once."

The next man in line, Rotterdam, followed the light with his eyes and observed, "But we're already in line with each other. If one of us were sick, wouldn't we have already exposed everyone else to whatever we had? If we had something, that is."

This was what happened when too many Thinkers were in one room; everyone questioned everything.

"It'll be fine," the scientist said. "Even if one of you was sick, you wouldn't have had a chance to infect anyone else." And then he added, "Yet."

During Salsburg's examination, he asked if the scientists had ever held someone back from their departure just because they had a cold.

"Not that I know of," was the response.

San Juan pretended to have a cough. When no one laughed, he became serious again and the man in the lab coat finished that checkup as well.

When it was San Lisbon's turn, the soon-to-be time traveler asked if the scientist was interested in performing a full-body cavity search. The scientist smiled, but didn't bother with an answer.

"Are you sure?" San Lisbon said. "These burlap pants are chafing me anyways. I wouldn't mind dropping them."

The scientist made a note in his log, then moved to the next man in line.

It was Shady Grove who asked, "Would you really hold someone back just because they had a cold?"

"Of course," the scientist said, no kindness in his voice.

Springfield could tell that something must have happened during one of the previous departures for these checks to be so important.

When it was his turn for the checkup, Springfield said, "Why not schedule us for a doctor's visit before we come here?"

"Can't risk the State seeing a pattern in ten different men seeing a doctor right before supposedly meeting to watch a game with some friends."

When it was Sterling's turn, the time traveler remained silent.

The scientist seemed surprised. "Don't you have a question or a smart-aleck comment too?"

"No."

Neither did Trenton. The jokes were over.

Everyone had a clean bill of health. The scientist took off his rubber gloves and tossed them in a corner.

But before turning back to rejoin the other men in lab coats, he said, "I know you all want to do a good thing here today, but if any of you lied and don't feel well, the consequences are on you, not me."

Then he walked away.

18 - THE BUBONIC PLAGUE

Originally appearing in the Byzantine Empire during the sixth century, the bubonic plague killed roughly fifty million people. Later, in the Middle Ages, another strain of the same disease, the Black Death, killed more than twenty-five million Europeans. The final death toll was around one hundred million deaths worldwide—somewhere between thirty and fifty percent of Europe's population.

All across the continent, men and women, the young and the old, suffered from swollen lymph nodes and gangrene. Two-thirds of the victims were dead within four days. The plague was spread by rats and fleas, but that wasn't where it originated. It appeared, seemingly out of nowhere, from the mountains bordering Europe, an area which just happens to coincide with the latitude of the first batch of time travelers that were sent back.

There are rumors, perhaps spread by the five scientists who presided over that first departure, that Charlestown was coughing and sneezing the entire time he waited to be transported into history. At one point, he reportedly even had to lean against Alexandria to keep from collapsing. The scientists asked if he was okay. His fellow time travelers asked if he was sure he was healthy enough for the trip. After another round of hacking coughs, he insisted he was fine.

Eventually, the energy generated by the antimatter tubes created enough force that the time travelers vanished. It's easy to guess where Charlestown reappeared: the mountains bordering Europe. And when: during the Byzantine Empire. Sometime after his arrival there, whatever bacteria he had must have mutated with the existing germs of the time. A super virus was created from germs that shouldn't have been around for another millennium. The rest is history.

Looking back, it seems foolish that Charlestown was ever allowed to depart—of course the people from history wouldn't have immune systems that could handle modern colds—but it only seems that way because the Theta Timeline shifted *after* he left. Prior to Charlestown's departure, the scientists had no idea that sending a sick man into history could cause so much death.

In the end, the scientists who risked their lives to save not only an idea, but the entire world from what the State could do, ended up causing more death than they ever could have comprehended. It's why a medical check is performed on each traveler prior to their being sent back in time, and it's why anyone with even a slight sniffle is now rejected.

19 - JOHNNY IS HERE

Springfield's feet had begun to glow. Without his realizing it, the scientists must have powered up the generator. The oval tubes looped around the time travelers' feet and over their heads generated so much light that everything near it was also shining with white energy. When Springfield first noticed it, only the bottoms of his cheap brown shoes were glowing. But then it had crept up to his ankles. Above him, the same metallic glow was slowly descending from the ceiling.

"Any final questions?" one of the scientists said to the line of men.

Springfield wondered what the time travelers were supposed to ask then, moments before departing. Wasn't it a little late for that? If they still had questions now, then God help the entire world. They had already discussed amongst themselves all of the things they might expect upon appearing in a new time. Considering that even the scientists were unsure of when and where any of the time travelers would appear, all Springfield and the others could do was vanish and hope for the best.

Hell, they didn't even know something as simple as whether or not their hair would fall out when they travelled through time, or if their body's organs would fail over time from exposure to the massive energy of the tubes. Those were the things they wanted to know, but those were also the things the scientists could only guess at.

When none of the men spoke up, the scientist said, "Very well," and turned back to the other four men in lab coats.

A new series of calculations appeared on the screen. The scientists scribbled them into notebooks.

Down the line from Springfield, one of the time travelers said, "I hope I get sent back to December, 1962."

No one asked why. Not even Shady Grove, who had been eager to play the game earlier, and whose breathing had now intensified as his feet became engulfed in light. Springfield, looking down the line of men, couldn't be sure which man had said it.

Sterling leaned closer to Springfield and whispered, "That poor bastard is probably going to get sent back to the Stone Age," Then, thinking it was funny enough to warrant recognition, he laughed at his own joke.

"What would that mean for the rest of us?" Springfield said.

Sterling immediately stopped laughing.

The scientists didn't have much experience using the time travel equipment, but they knew the tube around each man's ankles caused a cascading series of departures. The first man in line would disappear a fraction of a second before anyone else, then the next man, and so on down the line. Trenton would vanish last. And with each sequential disappearance, each man would be sent back further in time than the previous man. It meant that if someone in the line were sent back to the Stone Age, everyone after him would be sent back even further.

One of the scientists called out, "Final checks," and the other men in lab coats inspected the cables, generators, and computers to make sure everything was okay.

The scientists had just finished their last round of

inspections when a two-way radio next to the computers emitted a burst of static. In the short amount of time Springfield had been in the room, no one had used a two-way radio or a cell phone. Using either was an easy way for the State to listen in on anything that was being said in the room. If a radio was being used now, it could not be a good sign.

Then there was a transmission. "Johnny is here. I repeat, Johnny is here."

It sounded like the man under the overhang who had ushered Springfield off the street and into the building. The man didn't have enough time to release the transmit key before the gunfire started. A series of shots sounded through the radio as if they were only feet away from the Thinkers. It only lasted a split second before the radio went silent again, but everyone in the room could hear the sounds of war breaking out two stories above.

The State knew their location and were coming to get them. They had been foolish to think they could keep their plans secret forever. It was a miracle they had gone undetected for as long as they had.

20 - THE STATE KNOWS EVERYTHING

A government that trusts its people is powerful only if the people also trust their government. A government that does not trust its people is only powerful if it knows exactly what everyone is doing at all times.

This was why the State listened to every phone call and monitored all internet activity. It was why they had AeroCams tracking everyone's movements. It was a necessary precaution, they said, to keep the public safe from radicals. It was, however, a necessity only to keep themselves in power.

Everyone was told the State's actions were solely to identify threats to the people, but it wasn't long before citizens speaking out against the State were the ones being targeted. If someone said privately that the leaders were out of control, they were branded a Thinker and arrested before they could spread their opinion. If a reporter planned on covering the dissent, the State found out about it before the story was finished and the reporter disappeared.

No amount of surveillance was enough, though. They began tracking everyone's keystrokes on their computers. They passed a law that assigned everyone a State-issued internet ID. It became illegal for people to put black tape over their laptop and cell phone cameras. It wasn't specifically stated in the law why this was needed, but everyone knew the State had access to everything those cameras saw and didn't like it when people took that access away.

When the house of a suspected Thinker exploded, investigators said it was due to a gas leak. They said this even though a video posted online showed what appeared to be an AeroCam firing a rocket at the home.

A man suspected of being a Thinker was charged by the State with embezzling money. After posting all of his financial records online for everyone to see, it immediately became obvious that he hadn't broken any laws. The next day, a gunman walked up behind the man, shot him in the back of the head with a blaster, then darted off. Miraculously, the State said none of their AeroCams had managed to record the incident even though it happened right on the courthouse steps. The gunman disappeared without being heard from again.

Once the State became afraid of its people, nothing would ever make the leaders feel safe again.

21 - THE DIFFICULTY OF ENDING A LIFE – PART II

As soon as the first blast sounded, Springfield began thinking of Jessica. Poor Jessica.

Above them, on the street, an endless barrage of shots rattled off, pausing for a second, then resuming. Each time the gunfire picked up again, a different vision of Jessica burst into his mind. Jessica telling him she loved him. Jessica burrowing her face into his shoulder, trying not to let on that a sappy movie was making her cry. Jessica kissing him awake in the morning. Jessica. Jessica.

She had no idea she would never see him again. While he was in a Cold War bunker preparing to travel through time, she was at work, unaware that the man she loved was getting ready to be sent into history. The realization made him rub his eyes in frustration.

She hadn't even known for certain that he was a Thinker. Part of being a Thinker was not trying to convince others to share your views. People had to decide for themselves whether the State needed to be stopped. Trying to convince others that one set of ideas was better than another was exactly how the State had grown into a monster in the first place. Not to mention that Thinkers were people who thought for themselves and couldn't be persuaded.

Because of that, he had never been sure if Jessica considered herself a Thinker. He suspected she did, or liked to think she did. She had commented about the State always looking for excuses to go to war. She groaned each time another set of laws told them what they could and couldn't do. Maybe while he had been attending meetings with one set of Thinkers, she had been attending meetings of her own.

Another burst of blaster fire sounded, a small explosion far off, more blasters, a brief pause, then so many shots that it sounded like the entire army must have been brought in.

And still, all he could think about was Jessica. Had she believed him all those times he said he was going out to watch a game with friends? Or had she known not to delve into anything that might deal with the Thinkers?

Another round of blasts, followed by Shady Grove nudging him and saying, "I wanted to give my wife a proper goodbye. But if she knew I would be underground, tied to nine other men while a shootout was going on above me, I doubt she would have given me an appropriate send-off."

Springfield looked down at the other time travelers. Were they also wishing they could spend a few more minutes with the people they loved?

Looking down at his feet, he noticed the glowing light was up to his shins. Above him, the same light was creeping down toward his head. In that moment, he was reminded of the five-year old version of himself who had cried because he didn't want to leave his parents for his first day of school. Except now he was almost thirty, heartsick with the knowledge he would soon disappear without ever seeing Jessica again.

All he could do was vanish and hope he changed the world for her. At least then she wouldn't have to see the people she loved being dragged away by the State. As a teenager, she had watched as her brother was escorted out of their house, never to be seen or heard from again. They had said he was a mastermind hacker who stole billions of dollars. But he hated computers, barely even used one. The real reason he was arrested was that he had been seen wearing an anti-State T-shirt. She still had no idea if her brother was dead or sitting in a secret prison.

She had seen how a family in her neighborhood was shunned by the rest of the community after being falsely accused of being Thinkers. No one wanted the State to come after them next, so after that, even people who sympathized with the Thinkers turned against them. Fear had made the family outcasts.

Sterling looked down the line of men before saying, "There was a time when people were told that governments should be afraid of their people. Not the other way around. But somewhere along the way, that message got distorted."

"I hear ya, buddy. I hear ya," Shady Grove said in a way that gave Springfield the impression the man hadn't actually listened to the words at all. The blaster fire above them was too distracting.

Springfield wondered how he could leave someone who had already seen so many other people disappear from her life. But he knew, too, that if he managed to shift the Theta Timeline, she could grow up in a reality where no one was ever taken by the State. He lost her if he left. The world lost its humanity if he stayed.

He hadn't discussed the State with her very often because all it did was upset both of them. As soon as either of them mentioned it, they realized life wasn't meant to be spent having all of their words recorded, all of their actions catalogued to be used against them at a later time. How was it even possible to fall in love in a world where the State erased entire countries from the map just to keep people distracted?

Outside, sirens began to blare, adding another layer of chaos to the shots and the yelling. It was amazing that a single man could hold the State off from entering the building.

"Can we get this show on the road?" Trenton said, but no one answered him.

Springfield reminded himself that this was what he had signed up for. He had volunteered, not been pressured. He was the one who had decided it was better to try and change things. Why, then, with the intense glow having reached his knees, gunfire continuing outside, was he now having so many doubts?

How could anyone sit back and watch war after war, each one worse than the previous one, and not want to make a difference? If someone were to say, "Raise your hand if you would risk your own life so that billions of other people can live," how many people would actually dare to keep their hand down? Why then was Jessica the only thing he was thinking about right before he disappeared?

The standard approach in all the movies he had seen, when someone was going away and knew they would never return, was for them to either make their loved ones think they were dead, or to end things as if they were breaking up. That way, at least, the other person would have closure and be able to move on with their life. But he hadn't even told her he was a Thinker, let alone that he would be vanishing.

After this was all over, she would see his face on the evening news, a caption saying he was an enemy to the State. They would never say he was a man trying to return the world to a place where wanting privacy didn't mean you had something to hide, it simply meant you were an individual. There was no telling what story they would come up with for him—he was trying to blow up a city, he was trying to steal everyone's money—but they would come up with something in order to discourage everyone else from standing up to them. In the end, whatever he was accused of would just be an excuse for the State to send more cameras up into the sky, add more security checkpoints, or explain why everyone would need to start wearing tracking devices. Day after day, she would be told the man she had loved was a traitor. How long would it take for doubt to creep in and for her to believe what they said?

It would have been easier if he had just said things

were over between them, that he was unhappy in their relationship, but he never could. He loved her more each day, not less. Each time he thought there was nothing to smile about, she made him chuckle. When someone was loved like that, it wasn't fair to send them away wondering what they had done wrong. She would have been left to feel that if she had only been a little prettier, a little less imperfect, or a fraction funnier, then maybe things would have worked out. Had he fallen in love with someone else? Could she have made him stay? She didn't deserve those torments. There was no one who deserved love more than she did.

"Someone has to do this," one of the men in line with him said, almost yelling. It was clear the other time travelers were having the same doubts that Springfield was having. The same man added, "If everyone expects someone else to stand up, no one ever will."

"Amen," someone else said.

Jessica had asked him one time, "Do you think one person can change the world?"

He hadn't had a response. He wished she could see him now and know the answer was a resounding yes.

He had thought about telling her, one time, that there were an infinite number of other realities where every possible outcome was playing out. There were an infinite number of lives in which they would never meet, and an infinite number in which the State would never take power. But he hadn't said those things. It would only make her ask why he was telling her that. Nor did he mention that if any number of events in history had been altered, they would be living in a completely different world. A world where she could grow up with her brother. A world where neighbors weren't shunned by society for questioning their leaders. And while she might not know him in some of those other realities, she would have her rights. She would have her freedom. Both were worth more than any one relationship.

That very morning, as she got dressed for work, she had told him she loved him and he had said the same in return. But when it came time for her to leave, it was almost as if she could sense something was going to happen because she asked, "You'll be here when I get back, right?" She never said things like that.

"Of course. Get going so you aren't late."

But still, she held onto his arm as if he would vanish right there if she let go. She opened her mouth to say something, then closed it.

"I'll be here when you get back," he had said.

"We'll watch the rest of *The Great De-evolution* when I get home?"

"I don't know if I want to see the rest."

"But we've already watched half the season."

He kissed her, said again that he would be there when she got home, and then she left.

An hour later, he had departed as well. If he had realized then that the meeting at Browning Street wasn't going to be a discussion at all, but *the* meeting, he would have said a hundred more times that he loved her.

Blaster fire was destroying everything above them. He realized then, two stories underground, his legs glowing, that the last thing he had ever said to Jessica would be a lie. He wouldn't be home when she got back from work. He would never be home again.

He hoped she could forgive him for that.

22 - YOU KNOW WHAT TO DO

A second voice came on the two-way radio: "Johnny is close. I repeat, Johnny is close." As if the time travelers and scientists couldn't hear everything going on above them. Springfield assumed it was the second guard, waiting in the basement, the final line of defense to hold the State's men back from entering the room they were in.

Anything said on the radio would be monitored by the State, but with the shootout going on above them, they were past worrying about being discovered. The already frantic scientists became even more rushed in their movements, racing back and forth between computers, cables, notebooks, and generators, ensuring everything was working as planned.

Don't rush the calculations, Springfield thought. *I don't want to end up being sent back millions of years.*

It wasn't worth telling the scientists this, though. They had more at stake than the time travelers did; they had to stay behind and be subjected to the State. It was only a matter of time until the first guard was dead and the second was putting forth whatever type of defense he could muster. The scientists knew they only had a few minutes left before they were taken away and tortured, maybe killed, maybe thrown in a small room for the rest of their lives. Even with the chance of appearing in the middle of the ocean, the time travelers were the lucky ones because they were getting away.

Once the time travelers were gone, the scientists must know they would be facing a miserable end. And yet Springfield was sure they had planned for this possibility. They seemed to have a contingency plan for everything.

The ten men looked up and down the row at each other, then at the steel door. The barrage of blaster fire on the street above them seemed endless. Even through the thick metal, two flights of stairs, and tons of concrete, the shots sounded like they were right next to them. Their quiet city had been transformed into a war zone.

Two of the scientists argued over a series of numbers displayed on the screen.

"It will work."

"It won't."

"Trust me, it will."

The time travelers didn't ask what the two men were arguing about. Above them, what sounded like a concussion grenade went off. The scientist who had been skeptical gave up and let the other man proceed with his calculations.

The rest of the scientists were yelling now as well, not because they were panicking, but because they needed to in order to be heard above the violence above. The five men in lab coats all knew their fate was sealed, knew it was a matter of time until the State's men came through the door. None of them seemed to mind what would happen to them, though. It was better to stand up for what they believed in than to live in misery and degradation.

It was inevitable that it would come to this. The State had too much surveillance, too many agents walking the streets pretending to be unhappy with the Ruler while trying to infiltrate the Thinkers. Although he doubted it, Springfield couldn't be sure that one of the men in line with him wasn't one of the State's spies. As for the scientists, if they had in fact sent back four other sets of time travelers already, it was probably a pleasant surprise that they had made it this far. He could only hope there were other teams of scientists who knew the technology the way these men did so the battle could be continued.

"How much longer?" one of the time travelers said to the scientists.

None of the men in white turned from what they were doing to provide an answer.

"I'm not afraid to die," Shady Grove said. "But if I do die today, I'd rather it be from falling out of the sky than being blasted against a wall like a common criminal."

Springfield said nothing. Neither option sounded pleasant.

There was a series of explosions. A pause in the gunfire. When it resumed, the shooting sounded even louder than before. Maybe the guard at the door had rigged the entryway with explosives, his final effort to keep the Security Services from gaining entry. Or maybe an AeroCam had shot one of its missiles into the doorway and the guard was now nothing but chunks of bone and blobs of flesh.

Whatever it had been, Springfield guessed the first guard, the man at the building's entrance, was dead. The State's men had moved into the building, made their way down the basement steps, and were in a shootout with the second guard.

"You all know what to do," one of the scientists said to the line of time travelers, telling them rather than asking. Without waiting for a response, he rushed back to the computers and began running more numbers through the calculations.

The glowing white light was up to their hips. Above him, all he could see was light, and he assumed his head was already engulfed in the descending energy.

"Prepare for departure," another scientist said.

Springfield had no idea how he was supposed to prepare for what was going to happen. All he could do was remain standing where he was and not let go of the canvas bag. Thinking that perhaps he had forgotten some last-minute instruction, he turned to Shady Grove to ask if they were supposed to do something special when the departure announcement was made. Before he could say anything, though, Shady Grove shrugged and gripped his bag even tighter.

The light was not only higher, but had intensified so much that his feet seemed to have vanished into the gulf of energy. His thighs glowed as if made from pure light.

The curious part of Springfield was tempted to move his toes outside the glowing tube just to see what would happen. He didn't dare move, however, lest he be sent back in time with the tips of his toes missing.

The light at his legs and head was perfect brilliance, making it appear more yellow than white now. And yet it didn't hurt his eyes or make him squint. A steady hum began filling his ears. Even through all the blaster fire going on outside the steel door, the humming was so loud that it seemed to be coming from within his head. He looked at Sterling to his right and Shady Grove to his left to see if the other time travelers heard the same noise, but both men only stared at the door and the sound of chaos outside it.

One of the other scientists came running over to the line of men. "None of you have metal or electronics on you, right?" When none of them replied, the scientist yelled, "No jewelry, no rings, no cell phones, right?"

All ten men nodded. For Springfield, at least, the humming was so loud, drowning out even the explosions, that he doubted the scientist would hear anything he had said in response.

"Well, at least one thing is going the way it's supposed to," the scientist said before running back to the other men huddled around the computers.

As subtly as he could, Springfield rubbed his wrists to make sure his watch and keys were on the other side of the room. Out of the corner of his eye, he saw Shady Grove doing the same thing.

23 - THE TUNGUSKA EXPLOSION

In 1908, a massive explosion destroyed over eight hundred square miles of land near the Podkamennaya Tunguska River in Russia. Eight hundred square miles is a lot of land. It's roughly the same size as New York City, Chicago, Baltimore, and Atlanta if they were all put in a big circle together. In terms of Russian wilderness, it's equal to roughly eighty million trees. From the vast area of destruction, officials determined the force of the explosion was equal to one thousand times that of the atomic bomb that was dropped on Hiroshima, Japan in World War II. In more modern terms, it was equal to four nuclear bombs of the kind that the State would one day secretly detonate on one of its own cities.

The Tunguska explosion was felt well beyond the actual blast radius. Houses crumbled to their foundations. Windows were shattered. The earth shook as if a massive earthquake had occurred. If a similar blast had taken place in the Pacific, tsunami warnings would have no doubt immediately sounded.

Witnesses outside the blast radius said they saw an incredible burst of light followed by what sounded like a drawn-out boom of thunder that lasted for minutes. Over the next few days, the night sky continued to glow as if it were haunted.

Some people said it had to be a meteor, but no crater was ever found. Others tried to say the explosion was due to a comet made of ice. This was more likely because the ice would have melted in the atmosphere, thus explaining the lack of a hole in the ground.

But whatever had caused the devastation at Tunguska had not only made it through the lower atmosphere, it made it all the way to the ground. Traces of materials that weren't known to exist on earth were discovered. This made some people say the blast was due to a crashed spaceship. But only very small traces of chemicals were found, a pocketful at most, certainly not enough to be the remains of an unfortunate alien crew.

A handful of people said a meteor burning in the Earth's atmosphere could fuse with chemicals already present on our planet and produce nature's version of a hydrogen bomb. This, however, is not scientifically possible.

Black holes have been blamed, but the laws of physics say this even more impossible than a naturally occurring hydrogen bomb. Even Nikola Tesla has been blamed for the event, as he is given credit for everything mysterious that occurred during his time.

What the people constructing these wild theories had never noticed was that the affected area of Russian wilderness fell into a latitude of Earth with a 64.9% land-to-water ratio. They certainly hadn't thought to map out which other places on Earth share the same latitude. And most of all, they would have no way of knowing the Thinkers would one day use Anchorage, Alaska as a departure site to send men back in time.

Ten men would line up in a row, each dressed in heavy clothes and each carrying a burlap sack filled with supplies. As the scientists worked to get the time machine ready, as the hum began sounding in the time travelers' ears, the men shifted nervously back and forth. But particularly one man. Because amongst those ten time travelers setting out from Anchorage, one had chosen to ignore the instructions he had been given.

Only a select few men know what really caused the Tunguska explosion. What they know, which no one else could possibly understand, was that an explosion of that magnitude is what happens when an electronic device reacts with the antimatter forces that are transporting someone back in time. The scientists still aren't sure which of the ten time travelers it was, but whoever it was, he died before his mission could ever start, and his burial ground is a charred patch of eight million trees.

All because he thought he knew better than the scientists and could ignore their warnings.

24 – GOODBYE

There was another burst of blaster fire, two screams, then a momentary silence. The time travelers knew what this signaled: the second guard was dead. The heavy steel door was the only thing left between the State and the time travelers. No door, not even one of reinforced metal, would provide much of a delay for men carrying explosives and everything else the State had at its disposal.

For the briefest of moments, all five scientists stopped what they were doing and looked at the bolt that kept the door locked from the inside. The moment only lasted a fraction of a second, but all of the time travelers noticed it—the scientists knew their fates were sealed. If they were lucky, they would be killed on the spot. If they were taken away, there was no telling how long they would be tortured. And because no one could withstand the methods the State employed, none of the scientists would be able to withhold what they knew about time travel.

The State would finally understand what the Thinkers were capable of. When they did find out, the entire world would have bigger concerns than nuclear bombs decimating its landscape. The leaders would do what they always did: create their own time machine and find a way to use it as a weapon. And once that happened, the State would never be stopped.

They knew one thing and one thing only: how to turn existing technology into a way to inflict suffering and continue their rule. It hadn't had any hope of learning how to harness nuclear energy, but once Einstein and his peers laid the groundwork for how to trigger atomic fission at the flip of a switch, the leaders knew they had a beautiful new toy at their disposal. The same would apply for time travel. Until it was a reality, the State laughed it away. But as soon as the fantasy came into existence, the leaders would stop at nothing to get their hands on it. There would even be fighting over which agency controlled the technology.

As if the scientists were thinking this exact thing, one of them asked the others, "Has the safeguard been turned off?"

One of the other scientists nodded.

To be sure there was no confusion, the first scientist said, "We need to make sure it doesn't occur until after the men have been transported."

Another said, "The fail-safes have been cancelled. The machine will exceed safe limits."

The other three scientists continued entering lines of numbers into the computers while this conversation was taking place. None of the time travelers bothered to ask what would happen once they were gone. They could guess the Thinkers knew it was a matter of time until the State raided one of their departure sites. And they knew, when that happened, that they would need to destroy every bit of proof of what had been taking place there.

Springfield envisioned that the room he was currently standing in would become nothing more than ash and smoke, including the scientists. And once again Springfield found himself hoping there were other Thinkers who could recreate the machine and continue sending men into the past until someone managed to shift the Theta Timeline and prevent the State from rising.

For once, the chances of surviving the actual time-travel departure didn't seem quite so bad. Of the men standing to Springfield's left and right, three, maybe four, would survive reappearing in a new time and place. At least they had a chance, though. None of the scientists were going to be alive when this was over.

For their part, none of the scientists seemed concerned about their impending doom. None of them tried to persuade the others that there was an alternative. The complete and utter destruction of everything and everyone in the room was the only possibility. No man of conscience could let that power fall into the State's hands.

If it did gain the power, the Ruler would claim that the State was the only nation responsible enough to possess time travel capabilities. No other country, no other person, would be allowed to create a time machine except the State. Anyone caught trying to construct one would be eliminated.

But instead, the room would be turned to dust. The computers would be gone. The calculations and the oval tubes—all of it would be gone.

Of course, the public would never be told what had really happened in the room where Springfield stood. Even after an explosion occurred and the room was destroyed, the only thing people would see on the news would be a story that a group of Thinkers had been foiled in their plot to hurt the public. There would be no mention that these supposed radicals were men trying to return the country to what it had been. People all over the country would be told that the dead were nothing more than scum who had betrayed their own country. Every station would have the same story because it was the story the State wanted to have reported.

The humming grew even louder. How was that possible? Springfield didn't know. Maybe the bright light had descended enough to engulf his entire head. The noise was so encompassing that it felt as if it were coming directly from his brain. Closing his eyes did nothing to help reduce the jarring vibrations in his head. In fact, it seemed to get louder, flowing through him as if his entire body was shaking. Everything below his hips was blotted out by bright white light.

One of the scientists stopped what he was doing, turned to the line of men, and said, "Remember, the future depends on what you do today." A quote from Gandhi before they departed.

But the humming was so loud that Springfield couldn't be sure that was really what the scientist had said.

From the other side of the door, someone began to yell. Even above the humming of the time machine, the yelling and the pounding on the door was audible. The scientists didn't acknowledge it.

Trenton yelled toward the door, "Kiss my ass," then laughed in a maniacal fashion, his way of coping with the stress of the situation.

A split second later, the metal door blew off its hinges and flew across the room, coming to a stop three feet away from where Trenton was standing and only inches away from where the glowing oval tube wound around his feet before returning back to the generator. Springfield hated to think what would have happened if the door had crushed it. He had a vision of the time machine malfunctioning, leaving the ten men exactly where they stood, no hope of changing the future.

The realization also struck him that if there were realities for every possible event in time, there was a reality in which the door had not only landed on the glowing tube, but damaged it enough that Springfield would soon be dead, along with everyone else.

Only one of the scientists stopped his work when the door blew off. The other four ignored the smoke and continued their scribbling and calculations.

That one scientist turned and, looking at the time travelers, mouthed, "Good-bye."

He might have actually said the word, but over the loud hum in his ears, Springfield wasn't sure. Without waiting for the time travelers to offer their own goodbyes, the man in the white coat pressed the Enter key on the computer he was standing in front of, then stopped working.

Through the smoke, men in black armor began filing into the room. Each had a plastic type of body armor that protected them from blaster fire while allowing unobstructed movement. They did not, as Springfield thought they might, have their assault blasters firing as they entered. Instead, they made sure no one was pointing weapons at them, then stood aside as their squad leader entered.

The leader, also dressed in all black, looked at the time travelers, then at the scientists, then back at the time travelers. This only took a second. All he would likely take away from the scene was that a line of men were engulfed in light. He wouldn't have any way of knowing they were about to vanish. The only other things he saw were the cables running around the room, a generator, a couple computers, and the scientists. The man's frown showed that his assessment of the area offered nothing but confusion.

There were a lot of things Springfield noticed in those final seconds.

He noticed that none of the men in black armor wore official State uniforms. They were most likely a private contracted group of killers, trained to look and act like an army, but without any of the inconveniences of needing to obey a military code of conduct. Such armies had been instrumental in the State's wars, so much in fact that the State had started using them at home as well. Every agency had their own pack of mercenaries they could dispatch whenever they needed.

The State loved them because the contractors were free to be as ruthless as they wanted, and none of the horrendous things they did could be directly tied to the leaders. The men were nothing more than machines that killed without consequence. On the few occasions that videos of their brutality were posted to the internet, the Ruler could say the death squads weren't officially part of the State and could wash his hands of the matter.

The Security Services leader walked over to one of the scientists and asked a question. Apparently, he received an answer he didn't like. Without saying anything else, he withdrew his hand blaster and shot the man in the head. The shot was barely audible over the noise. The scientist dropped to the ground, the grotesque sounds of his ligaments popping and his skull bouncing off the concrete floor also eclipsed by the powerful humming.

Springfield suspected the squad leader had asked what was happening in the room, heard the answer, and thought it was a joke. Not liking it when he wasn't taken seriously, he had reacted the only way he knew how.

"Come here," the team leader yelled at the first time traveler in line.

Springfield couldn't actually hear the words over the humming in his head, but he could decipher what had been said by reading the man's lips. Riverford didn't move, however, only stared back at the squad leader without stepping away from the oval tube.

"No thanks, I'm fine where I am," Riverford might have said.

The squad leader leveled his pistol at Riverford's face, then thought better of pulling the trigger. In a group, it was easy for each man to display stubborn bravado. Taken to secret prisons and tortured, the men would quickly break and tell everything they knew.

The squad leader shouted orders to his men, then began speaking to another of the scientists. Having received their instructions, two of the men with assault blasters began motioning with the barrels of their weapons for the time travelers to move away from the glowing light and lie down on the ground. When none of the Thinkers did as they were told, the men in black looked confused. They weren't used to people who refused commands while having a blaster pointed at their face.

The scientist who was speaking to the squad leader shrugged, then pointed to the metal box where the cables received their power. Springfield saw a shift in the mercenary's demeanor. Whether it was because he had also noticed the refusal of the men against the wall to do as they were told and realized more was going on than he first suspected, or if he finally realized the first scientist hadn't been joking in his response to the man's question, the squad leader finally seemed to understand that he and his men were in extreme danger. Without hesitation, the group's leader shot another scientist in the head. Then another. The two bodies lay crumpled on the floor next to the first.

On cue, the men with assault rifles went into action.

Looking to his left, Springfield saw seven of his fellow time travelers looking impatiently at the light that was surrounding all but two or three inches of them, each wondering how much longer it would take to disappear. There was glory in dying for what you believed in, but he could tell from the faces of the men down the row from him that they would rather die having had a chance to start their mission than to be filled with blaster holes and bleed to death on a concrete floor before the mission ever began.

When his eyes shifted to his right, he expected to see the same look on Sterling's and Trenton's faces. What he saw instead was Trenton's forehead explode in a burst of red and black as a blaster shot a hole through it. Pieces of the Thinker's brain scattered across the cinderblock wall behind them. Pieces of his face, along with splatters of blood, covered Sterling's shoulder and cheek.

Sterling had just enough time to see his fellow time traveler's death, then look to his left, take comfort that Springfield and the others were still standing next to him, all as determined as he was. Then his face exploded as well.

All of this happened in less than one second. Springfield couldn't help but do the exact same thing: he knew he was next in line to be shot, and so he looked to his left, knowing the other seven men would still be by his side, would still have a chance to save the country. Instead of a line of seven men, however, he only saw five. Riverford and

Rockville were also dead on the ground.

He saw a scientist say something else to the squad leader, then smile. From the leader's reaction, Springfield could guess what had been said. The Security Services leader barely took the time to shoot the scientist in the head before dashing toward the same doorway that he and his men had appeared from. The room was going to be destroyed before any of them could get out of the old bomb shelter.

Springfield almost expected Shady Grove to nudge him and say, "What a shame that none of us will get to go on the journey."

He turned to hear this comment from the man who had provided running commentary since the two of them had been standing against the wall. But Shady Grove was gone.

They got him too, Springfield thought. But when he looked down at the ground, he noticed Shady Grove was nowhere to be found. Neither were San Juan or San Lisbon. Only half of Riverford was still there—the half that had been lying outside the glowing oval tube after his dead body collapsed to the ground.

Oh, of course, he thought. The two sections of glowing light, one from the ceiling and one from the ground, had finally connected. The men down the row from him were gone.

At the doorway, the mercenaries were pushing each other out of the way so each of them could get to safety first, all of them blocking the way for everyone else. Realizing there was a bottleneck, one of the State's men dropped his assault blaster and charged at Springfield. Maybe he was going to tackle him, or perhaps he merely wanted to escape the impending explosion by going wherever the Thinker was going.

None of that mattered to Springfield, though. Because when he blinked he was no longer two stories below ground. There were no assault rifles pointed at him. No one from the Security Services was rushing toward him. The loud hum was gone. All was quiet.

It was terribly bright. But not from the glowing tubes. It was sunlight that was hurting his eyes, making him squint. In front of him, he saw only fields of trees and grass.

He was in another time.

PART TWO – THE PAST

"The past is never dead. It's not even past."
William Faulkner – Requiem for a Nun

25 - GETTING ORIENTED

No one knew exactly what to expect from being sent back in time. The scientists had warned the time travelers that they might suffer from headaches or temporary loss of equilibrium—the time-traveling equivalent of decompression sickness. There were urban myths that the hair on a time traveler's head would turn white or that all of their body hair would fall out. None of this was true, however. The sun did hurt Springfield's eyes, but that was only natural after being taken from a basement two stories under ground to an incredibly bright day.

Other than having to squint, he didn't notice any side effects at all. There was no vomiting or motion sickness. His memory was intact. It was amazing that his body could be transported from one place in time to another without his brain or any other part of his body reacting to the change.

Memory loss had always been one of his unspoken fears. Having had two grandparents who suffered from Alzheimer's had made him terrified that the same might happen to him one day. Each night, after another meeting with the Thinkers, he experienced nightmares in which he was transported back in time, only to open his eyes and find that his memory was gone. He would be in a strange place without any idea how he had gotten there. He would try not to panic, but the nightmares always ended with him screaming as he was dragged away to an insane asylum. He had never mentioned the dreams or their underlying fear to the rest of the group, but it always lingered in the back of his mind as a possible explanation of why none of the other time travelers had succeeded in their missions.

But looking around at the sun-filled sky, having appeared on solid ground, his shoulders and back collapsed with relief. There was rarely a spot on the planet that was exactly the same elevation as another place, and yet he hadn't fallen to his death. Nor had he appeared under the earth with no way to free himself. Even if he had departed and reappeared from the Grand Canyon, his fate could vary wildly. In one spot, he could be standing on the edge of a chasm. Just one foot further, though, and the ground would be two hundred feet below him. Luck was everything, and his had been impeccable.

Not everyone would be so fortunate, though. At least three of his fellow time travelers had been killed before they could depart. That left seven men. Some of them were at that very moment either plummeting to their deaths or treading water in the middle of the ocean. If the survival rate was roughly thirty percent, it was likely that only one other time traveler in Springfield's group might have a chance at stopping the State.

But even as he accepted that possibility, he couldn't help but smile at the fields and hills in front of him. At first glance, the ground didn't seem very uneven. Only when he forced his eye to draw a flat line across the stretch of hills did it become apparent how drastic the elevation changed from one spot to another. He could have arrived a hundred feet to the left and wound up ten feet below ground, in the middle of a hill. He would have died without being able to move a finger or take a breath. Likewise, if he had appeared above the bottom of the hill, he would have fallen three stories before hitting the ground. After breaking an ankle or shattering a leg, he would have been stuck out in the open. As soon as night came, a wolf or panther or whatever else was out there would circle him until it was sure he was an easy meal.

The openness of the world in front of him was amazing. All around him was a land full of possibilities. For as far as he could see, there were no buildings. No people. No AeroCams. But he also had no idea what year he had arrived in. Nor did he have a guess for where along the 38 N latitude he had reappeared.

As much as the sight of green hills made him want to go skipping, whistling to the birds and dancing about, the memory of dead scientists gave him pause. The scientists hadn't sacrificed themselves so he could enjoy the scenery of a land without robotic cameras flying in the air above him. He shuddered at the memory of Sterling's and Trenton's heads exploding, mere feet away from him. Bits of skull and bone had sprayed the cinder block wall behind him. Those final bloody images from his own time would haunt him for the rest of his life. But they also offered a reminder of why it was so important to change the Theta Timeline.

He also knew, from seeing half of Riverford's body remaining on the concrete floor, that half of a body would appear somewhere in time and no one would ever know where it had come from, who it belonged to, or where the other half was. It might end up being blamed on a serial killer or maybe a drug cartel. But whatever explanation was accepted, no one would ever know the real reason that a middle-aged man's legs and hips were found while his torso and head never were.

26 - DEAD BODIES APPEARING OUT OF NOWHERE

Ever since humans began documenting death, they have recorded cases of unidentified bodies being found. The phenomenon is not isolated to one country or part of the world. Many of these instances, the ones that will never be solved, share a common trait: the body was dressed in burlap. These are the bodies of two types of time travelers: those who appeared in water, drowned, and washed to shore, and those who appeared in the sky and immediately fell to their deaths.

In 1908, in Northern Algeria, a team of archeologists found the remains of a human body possessing all of the traits of a *Homo sapiens* male. The only problem was that the researchers were excavating in an area that was thought to predate modern man. The archeologists were looking for clues as to how the transition from *Homo erectus* to Neanderthal had occurred. The last thing they expected to find was a skull with teeth that had obviously received the care of an orthodontist. There were no other similar remains nearby, nor other signs of modern human civilization to explain why the body would be there. The archeologists were baffled, and the mysterious skeleton ultimately led to a host of misconceptions regarding how prehistoric man migrated through the world.

On Tuesday, June 6, 1944, tens of thousands of Allied soldiers stormed the beaches of Normandy. Complementing these amphibious landings were thousands of paratroopers. The chaos during the invasion was unimaginable. There were bombs, guns, and explosions everywhere. Dead bodies littered the beach.

But during the peak of the madness, more than one hundred paratroopers reported seeing the same thing: a flash of light followed by a screaming body plummeting toward the earth without a parachute. Officials explained away these stories by saying an explosion had caused the flash and that the falling body was just one of the many paratroopers who hadn't survived the jump. But to their dying days, every soldier who witnessed the bizarre event insisted that the burst of light was something other than an explosion caused by anti-aircraft artillery. German weapons, they said, did not create light that lingered in the sky. And, they insisted, the man falling to his death was wearing light brown clothes while everyone who jumped from Allied planes wore various shades of green.

In 1951, a body washed ashore on the coast of France with no identification. In the days leading up to the body's appearance, no ships had been sunk, and no captain reported any members of his crew as missing. However, residents of a nearby French village had reported seeing a bright flash of light in the sky just two days earlier. Unfortunately, this was incorrectly attributed to lightning. To this day, the body remains buried in an unmarked grave near the French coast.

In 1972, a body was found between Death Valley and Las Vegas. Almost every bone in his body had been broken. Medical examiners correctly determined that the body had fallen out of the sky, but they mistakenly concluded that it was a theatrical killing by a casino kingpin. When questioned about this specific corpse, one casino owner burst out laughing and replied, "If I did kill him, why would I waste time stealing his clothes and dressing him in burlap before I threw him out of the plane?"

These are not the only cases. One body was thought to be an additional victim of a notorious Canadian serial killer. One was chalked up as a mentally ill Russian man who had drowned himself. Another was simply classified as "unknown" in the hope that information might one day become available that could offer additional insight on the case.

Roughly thirty percent of time travelers survive their reappearance. The rest are left to coroners, reporters trying to get their big break, and confused villagers to try to figure out what happened.

27 - ANOTHER FLASH OF LIGHT

Everywhere Springfield looked, there were only hills and trees and grass. There was no sign of a river or ocean. Unfortunately, there also was no sign of civilization. For as far as he could see, there were no buildings, no houses, no shopping malls. Not even a sign pointing to where those things might be found. A horrifying thought crossed his mind again: What if he had been sent back *thousands* of years in time, had risked his life for nothing?

He knew the scientists sent time travelers back in cascading depths of history. It was the best way for the Thinkers to ensure they had men working toward the same goal in as many different periods of history as possible. The problem was that the science of gauging how far someone was sent into the past was still mostly theoretical, and where the first man might appear and how much of a gap there would be between each subsequent traveler was largely a guessing game. There was no telling if Springfield had been sent back a few decades or a few millennia. Maybe even before man ever started walking the planet.

A lot can be processed by the human mind in a short amount of time. All of this—his assessment that there were no side effects to time travel, his appreciation that he had appeared on solid ground and not water, recognizing that there were no signs of civilization within sight—all took place in a single second.

In the next moment, it happened: another burst of light in the sky.

His first thought was that it must be a residual effect from his own arrival, the same way people reported seeing flashes of light following the Tunguska explosion. That thought was quickly replaced by terror. A man, dressed in the all-black uniform of the State's death squads, fell out of the sky.

The State had already found him. But how? Did they have their own time travel capability after all? Was it even more precise in its ability, able to send men to an exact moment in time so they could hunt down any Thinkers who were attempting to change the Theta Timeline? Was that why the other time travelers had failed, because the State sent their own men to kill each Thinker?

Then he remembered the gunman who had been rushing toward him right before he vanished in time. The State didn't have its own capability to travel in time. Springfield was just unfortunate enough to have one of their men jump into the portal in the exact same spot where he had been standing.

He saw the man fall twenty or thirty feet before disappearing behind a hill. Just seeing the black uniform again was enough for Springfield's knees to begin shaking.

"Son of a bitch," he muttered before turning to run.

If he wanted to live, he needed to get as far away as possible from that man. But before he could take a single step, something tugged at his hand. Confused, he turned to look at what could possibly be calling for his attention. It was then that he noticed the bush next to him. It was ten feet tall, filled with twigs and branches. He had appeared only inches from it, and one of its smaller branches ran straight through his palm.

He had been lucky enough to appear on dry land

instead of drowning in the middle of the ocean. He had even been lucky enough to arrive at ground level so he didn't have to fall from the sky the way the State's man just had. But that was where his luck ran out.

Like a puppet, the branch, about an inch thick, moved anytime he moved his arm. It grew out the main body of the sturdy bush, and right through the place where a fortune-teller would predict his future, leaves poked out of the other side of his hand.

If he had appeared a foot to the left, his chest and vital organs would have merged with the tree. He would have had twigs poking out all over his body, branches obstructing the flow of blood. His arteries and major organs would have pieces of wood running directly through them. Any movement he made would have caused the branches inside his body to tear his organs and blood vessels. It would be a sickening way to die.

If he had appeared ten feet further ahead, he would have died inside the trunk of an even larger tree, his hands and feet sticking out, the only proof that he had ever been there.

Instead, he only had a single branch poking out through his hand. But it was enough to keep him stuck in place. He tried to pull on it, but the pain was excruciating. He could just as easily have a wooden stake driven through his hand and be asked to tear it out by himself. Thinkers were educated men. They were historians and avid readers. They were not used to the unbelievable pain of wresting foreign objects out of their own bodies.

He and his fellow time travelers had discussed every imaginable scenario—appearing in water, dying instantly inside a mountain—but Springfield had managed to experience one of the few things the Thinkers had never thought of: being only partially stuck to an object, not enough that he would die, but enough that he most certainly was stuck.

The State's man was out there somewhere and

Springfield couldn't hide. It wouldn't take long for the man in black, trained at hunting and finding people, to track him down.

In addition to never discussing being partially stuck to an object, the Thinkers had never considered the possibility that one of the State's men might also be sent into history.

For the second time in a matter of seconds, Springfield took a deep breath and said, "Son of a bitch."

28 – ASSUMPTIONS

The less he looked at his hand and the branch sticking through it, the better. It wasn't going to be pretty, but he had a plan. At least he thought he had one.

With his free hand, he gripped the branch where it met the trunk and forced it back. He could feel the wood straining in the middle of his hand as he was trying to snap it. If he tried to break it off any closer to his skin he risked the branch splitting in the middle of his hand. Splinters would gouge the veins running to his fingers. Infection would spread. He might even die if a chip entered his blood stream.

The branch groaned and creaked. With only one hand to work with, he struggled to get enough force to make a clean break. But finally, it snapped away from the rest of the bush and crashed to the ground, pulling his arm down to the ground with it.

Three feet of the branch still stuck out the back of his hand, and the side with the leaves still poked out through his palm. But at least he could take it with him while he started hiking away from the second flash of light. He could worry about the remainder of the tree while he got away.

Without another thought, he picked up the sack that the scientists had given him and began walking.

Periodically, the limb would bang against another tree or get caught in other vegetation. Each time this happened, it tore at his flesh and sent waves of pain coursing through his forearm and up his shoulder. As he walked, he snapped away tiny twigs that were sprouting out from the end of the branch. One by one, small bits of wood, along with green leaves, fell to the ground behind him. Eventually, the branch went from looking like a baby tree to a small stake.

If I run into Dracula, he thought, *I can just smack him on the chest and kill him.* But his joke didn't make him feel any better.

After the stick was smooth, he broke segments away until only six inches worth remained poking out the front of his palm and another foot out the back of his hand. It wasn't ideal, but compared to being stuck to the tree until he starved to death or was found by the man in black, he could accept it.

He walked and walked, but didn't see any signs of human life. A pair of impossibly fluffy grey rabbits watched him with wide eyes until he got too close, then disappeared into the brush. Birds chirped all around him, some yellow, some black, and a few red with spots of brown. A chipmunk scurried past his feet. But still, no people.

He kept looking over his shoulder, expecting the mercenary to come running up from behind. The man in black was never there, however. As he descended one of the endless stretches of hills, he opened the burlap sack to see exactly what it contained. The scientists had provided him with ten protein bars, a small blanket, and a water pouch with an internal filter. That was all. Everything else was up to him.

Time travelers were fluent in multiple languages. They were historians. They were trained to understand human psychology. But they knew nothing about surviving in the wild. They understood the principles behind catching animals for food, but understanding something and being able to do it are completely different things. They knew that some mushrooms are edible and some are poisonous, but they would never trust their own life on their ability to distinguish between the two. This meant that he had to make the ten protein bars last long enough for him to find civilization.

Continuing up the next hill, he looked back at the place where the second flash of light had burst in the sky. He had no idea if the man in black had survived the fall, but he assumed as much. It wasn't as if the man had fallen hundreds of feet. A paratrooper would be trained to survive a hard landing, which is what a two-story fall would amount to for a professional killer.

There was no way for Springfield to know if the State's man would be smart enough to figure out which direction he would need to travel in order to pursue his target. If the assassin didn't understand the Earth's rotation relative to geography, there was a chance he could start walking in the opposite direction and never find his target. If that was the case, Springfield could stop and rest his feet, which were already beginning to ache. He could even unwrap his first protein bar. Maybe even take some time to find a sharp rock and carve away another section of the branch in his hand.

Of course the man in black knows which way to go, he thought. He's been taught how to find his target and get back to base just from the position of the stars in the night sky.

Underestimating the mercenary, even for a moment, would mean his death. He could never forget that. And because of it, he didn't stop for rest.

As he crossed another series of hills and valleys, he tried to remember exactly how long it had been between the time he appeared, standing next to the tree, and when the second flash of light had signaled the man in black's arrival. The immediate shock of being transported instantaneously from one place to another had made him think of everything except how long he had been standing there. But it couldn't have been very long if he was able to make out the assassin's black uniform, complete with its shoulder insignia.

Two seconds? The Earth is spinning on its axis at 1,040 miles per hour. If it had been two seconds, the man would have fallen over half a mile away—much too far for Springfield to see the yellow patch on the killer's shoulder. Could it have only been a single second?

He concluded that the man in black was probably a quarter of a mile behind him. If it came to a foot race, Springfield would surely lose. A trained mercenary would have no problem chasing down a time traveler, even if Springfield did have a head start.

At least with the trees all around, the hills everywhere, Springfield was sure he was out of sight. The man in black would have to find his trail first, then follow it without veering away. That would take time. Springfield had no idea how much time, but it was the only hope he had of getting away and beginning his mission.

At the top of the next hill, he scanned the distance for any sign of the assassin, but again saw nothing. Back in the basement, right before disappearing, it had seemed like the killer was coming at him in slow motion. Probably, his senses had been overwhelmed. Shock will do that. His confusion upon noticing that the men to his left had disappeared, illustrated that he must not have been thinking clearly. If guns hadn't been firing all around him, it would have been obvious that the other time travelers had already disappeared into the past. Instead, he had stood there, dazed, as the man in black charged at him.

If Springfield's departure had been planned for two seconds later, it would have been too late. The mercenary would have tackled him against the cinder block wall, knocking him out of the oval loops and glowing light. He would have been stuck in the very reality he wanted to escape. But only for a second. Because after that, the scientist's self-destruct mechanism would have triggered and the entire basement would have turned to smoldering ruins. One second. That was the difference between him dying on the concrete floor and surviving in a new time.

One second could change everything.

29 - THE MAN IN BLACK

The assassin remained seated on the ground. He knew the Thinker was out there somewhere, but the trees and hills blocked too much of the surrounding area for him to get a sight on his prey. If he could see his target off in the distance, he would race across the field and kill him in a matter of minutes, no matter the terrain. No amount of begging would keep the time traveler from dying a brutal death in the middle of... wherever they were.

But instead of starting off without a plan, the Security Service's hit man considered his options. He had no idea where he was—couldn't even fathom that he might need to be asking the question, *when he was*—but he could see from his surroundings that they must be in an extremely remote location. Not an AeroCam in the sky! Indeed, they must be very far away. Unlike Springfield, the assassin was comforted by the lack of other people nearby. No one would be coming to save the time traveler; the man in black could take his time.

It was his job to do the State's killing, not to make the plans for them, but he couldn't help but be concerned at this latest development. The Thinkers knew how to teleport from one place to another? He guessed that was how they managed to keep eluding the State, no matter how many laws were passed to restrict the population's movements, no matter how many cameras and checkpoints were created to track when and where people could go. Except for monitoring thoughts, the State had complete knowledge of what everyone did. And yet the Thinkers found ways to walk undetected amongst the public, to continue meeting in secret. Once he got hold of the Thinker, the assassin planned to keep him alive long enough to get answers.

The problem now was that he wasn't sure how soon he would have that opportunity. He didn't have to look at his ankle to know it was going to slow him down. At least for the next few days. Even through his boot, he could see the swelling becoming more pronounced.

All of his training told him to tuck and roll into a fall. It had become a basic instinct, like adjusting his blaster's scope to compensate for distance and wind. But none of his training had taught him that he might go from trying to subdue a target two stories below ground to falling thirty feet from the sky into a vast expanse of fields and trees.

He was already on the ground, searing pain shooting through his ankle, before his brain could accept that he was no longer in the old bomb shelter. Even though his swollen ankle was proof of his fall, he simply didn't trust his own eyes or process what had just happened. Only a moment earlier he had been running toward a man, the sound of yelling drowned out by a loud hum. Then the Thinker that he was running toward seemed to disappear. Right after he jumped into the light as well, he was falling, surrounded by daylight, thudding on the ground with a groan. With a little more warning, he would have responded appropriately—tucked his chin, kept his elbows in tight to his ribs, rolled as he landed— but being teleported, or whatever had just happened, was too disorienting for his training to kick in. That was why he had landed with a sickening crunch.

It was the kind of noise that would make a professional athlete drop to the ground and call for the team doctors. It was the type of pain that caused normal men to hobble around on crutches for a month. To the man in black, however, it was just another annoyance, another reason to kill the Thinker for putting him in this situation.

The man in black was on uppers, though, and these made the pain an afterthought. The State had learned early on that death squads killed even more indiscriminately if they were on amphetamines. If it wasn't for the pills that he had taken, he might have been more alarmed by the swelling under his boot. But since he was still twitching from the rush of chemicals, his focus was on mutilating the Thinker's face with his bare hands. The thought made him grin like a child.

He tried to stand up and get a perspective of his surroundings, but one step and his ankle forced him back down on the ground. It wasn't the pain that made him stop. If he had to, he could still dart across the field with his limp. He sat back down because he knew if he didn't address the injury, the internal damage could get worse, eventually leading to an infection that might kill him. He didn't mind dying, the State would ensure that his family lived in comfort for the rest of their lives, not to mention the hero's funeral he would be given for hunting down a traitor, but he didn't want to die before killing the wretched Thinker.

It seemed like a waste of time to take off his boot and inspect the injury, mostly because he already knew what was wrong. And anyway, once he took the boot off, he would just have to put it back on again. But applying pressure could help control the swelling, so he pulled off the boot and tied a bandana tightly around his ankle.

Sitting on the grass, hills all around him, he considered his options. He didn't hear any gunfire, meaning it was doubtful that anyone else from his team was nearby. Now that he thought about it, he didn't even hear the remnants of the explosion that his team leader had said was coming, didn't smell the residue of blaster fire in the air following the shootout.

A few minutes had gone by and still there were no AeroCams in the sky. This was the only thing that truly had him concerned. What part of the world could they be in where the State's cameras weren't recording everything?

He would never admit it to anyone else, but even through the amphetamines, he felt overwhelmed with everything that had just happened. In one moment, he had gone from being part of a team that was raiding a Thinker stronghold, to being in the middle of hills and fields. The city was gone. There was no sign of human life. Even for a trained killer, for someone who spent his entire adult life learning how to survive in harsh environments, he was at a loss to explain what had just happened.

Without a radio, without AeroCams in the sky, he had no idea how to contact his superiors. He assumed he was on his own. There was no way of knowing if anyone from his team had survived. And even if they had survived, they were probably still in the basement, not wherever he was.

He didn't even have his gun. He would never know how lucky he had been to drop the weapon right before lunging for the Thinker. Nor would he know how lucky he had been that he didn't carry any electronics on him. If the squad leader had charged into the portal with his portable radio, millions of square feet of land would have instantly been reduced to charred remains.

His missing weapon wasn't his only concern, though. He was also without any provisions for surviving in the wilderness. Granted, he could easily build a shelter and catch his dinner, but it would take valuable time that would be better spent tracking down his target.

To have any chance of success, he needed to get moving. That was his top priority. He pulled a strand of paracord from a pouch on his belt. Along with a thick piece of wood on either side of his foot, it would act as a makeshift ankle brace.

But when he reached down for the knife on his hip, he noticed it was gone. Confused, the assassin scanned the ground. Three feet away from where he had fallen, the knife's rubber handle was poking out of a pile of leaves. But when he grabbed it, he noticed the fancy metal blade was gone. By itself, the handle was useless. He tossed it back onto the ground.

Fortunately for him, every other part of his uniform was made of high tech plastic, more resilient than any metal. Besides providing better protection, the plating also weighed less than traditional armor. He laughed at the memory of the Thinker's guard on the street, wearing one of those bulky, old-fashioned Kevlar vests. It had no chance of protecting him from the State's assault blasters.

He smiled at the memory of the guard's expression when he had realized his left arm had exploded away from the rest of his body. He had to hand it to the man, though: most men would have given up after seeing their forearm fly ten feet down the sidewalk and collide with a trashcan. But with the one arm he did have left, the guard had begun unleashing a barrage of grenades. That was when another hundred shots had chopped the man to bloody, unrecognizable pieces.

The man in black had the feeling he would need to recall these heart-warming images frequently if he was going to keep his sanity for the next couple of days. There was no telling how angry he would get once the amphetamines wore off and he didn't have additional pills to keep him high.

Without a knife to cut the paracord, he found a stone with a sharp edge. Then he broke both pieces of wood until they were the same length—each long enough to run from the bottom of his foot, up to his knee. With them in place, he set about tying the contraption together. It wasn't the best ankle brace, but with the supplies he had, it would have to be enough.

He pushed himself to his feet, tested his ankle, and nodded. Every step he took would be awkward, but at least he could get moving.

He knew which way the sun was moving across the sky, knew that if the Thinker had appeared just before him he would probably be somewhere to the East. He had no idea, though, how far away the Thinker would be. But knowing the general direction was enough. He would find his target eventually. With that in mind, he took his first step. Then the next.

The hunt had begun.

30 - THE UNKNOWN

Springfield had only been walking for two hours, but already his legs were tired and his feet were beginning to drag over rocks and fallen tree limbs that ordinarily wouldn't have slowed him down. But still, he kept moving. He hoped that the mercenary had fallen too far and wouldn't be able to pursue him, but he didn't dare risk his life by stopping to rest.

Somewhere out there, the life he had known was still going on without him. He thought of his parents watching the news, the first reports of a supposed attack that would no doubt lead to yet another excuse for war and for more laws. He thought of Jessica going through her day, everyone avoiding her because she had been the girlfriend of one of the men whose photo was plastered all over television. Those were the thoughts that kept his feet moving—he had to stop the State.

When he had first started hiking, he felt the need to look over his shoulder every few seconds. Each time, he expected to see the man in black running him down, ready to slice his neck. However, after two hours of walking, glancing back a thousand times, he found himself checking less and less often. Every five or six minutes, his paranoia would kick back in and he would be sure that the assassin must be approaching. If he were taken by surprise, the last thing he would feel was one hand over his mouth and another driving a blade across his neck from ear to ear. There never was anything behind him, though, except birds and chipmunks.

While he wasn't looking off in the distance at where he had just come from, he ate one of the protein bars from his bag. Even something as simple as opening the wrapper was turned into a struggle because of the stick poking through both sides of his hand. Each time he tried to place his thumb and forefinger on the wrapper's edge to rip it open, the stick pushed the protein bar away from him. Finally, he growled and used his teeth.

As if scanning for an enemy and staying nourished weren't enough, he also tried to figure out where and when he might be. He knew from the sun's position that he was walking east. That much was easy. But there was nothing around to tell him what he really wanted to know. The mountains in the distance provided his best hint. There were only a few ranges across the 38 N latitude, but he couldn't tell if the peaks he was seeing were part of the Rockies, Himalayas, or Alps.

The mountains were his only clue. Everything else was unknown. The same lack of indicators to let him know where he might be, also limited his knowledge for *when* he might be. Without signs of civilization, even a single building or a lone person, he had no way of knowing if he had been transported to one of the few remaining places mankind hadn't spoiled, or if he was standing in what would one day, maybe a thousand years from now, become Denver or Dayton. He could be in the remote hills of Afghanistan or China or Switzerland just as easily as he could be standing on what would one day become Kansas City or Philadelphia.

"This is just great," he said as he walked. But then, just as quickly, added, "You've only been out here for two hours. Don't start talking to yourself already." Then he chastised himself for scolding himself out loud.

If he had survived the raid and the slim odds of

appearing on land instead of water only to be sent back a thousand years, everything he had done would have been a waste. His parents would never be free of the State. Jessica would spend the rest of her life going through checkpoints, being groped by professional molesters. He might even be standing on what would one day become a place where people were forced to show their identification just to get to work. He might even be right down the street from where he would one day say goodbye to Jessica for the last time. The entire world offered not only a history, but also a future that he couldn't know.

If he had been sent back a thousand years in time, he would have no choice but to spend the rest of his life trying to grow and hunt his own food. He would have to create a workable shelter for himself—another thing he had read about, but never actually tried to do. He would be like one of the first settlers except that they had each other and he was alone. Not to mention that they knew how to survive in the wild, while he was used to driving a car to the grocery store anytime he needed food. He would have no chance of altering the Theta Timeline. He would be away from the people he loved. And it would be for nothing.

To top things off, it seemed he would spend the rest of his life looking over his shoulder, making sure the man in black wasn't there. If they had been transported back in time too far to make any relevant changes to history, he hoped he could convince the mercenary to put aside his hatred for Thinkers and leave well enough alone. He doubted the assassin would go for it, though. And even if the man did shake Springfield's hand and say there was a truce, he had a suspicion he would still wake up one night with a blade at his throat.

No, he had to assume the man in black would come for him, no matter where they were in time. Even if they were transported to the Jurassic Age and could be ambushed by dinosaurs, the hatred and propaganda that the mercenary was indoctrinated with would be enough for him to kill a Thinker.

Even if it meant he was killing the only other living human on Earth, the assassin would do what the State had taught him was his duty to his country.

A relentless killer. Not knowing where he was in time. Not seeing his parents or Jessica ever again. All of these ideas combined to make Springfield's legs go weak. And before he could steady himself, he fell to the ground and began to cry. No matter how many times he rubbed at them, his eyes clouded over with more tears until, finally, he no longer tried to wipe them away but gave in to loneliness and fatigue.

"How did I get myself into this?" he said, but of course no one was there to offer an answer.

When he was done feeling sorry for himself, he pushed himself back to his feet and began walking again. He had hoped he would find an earlier version of the same world he just left, but seeing the world around him, he knew he was more likely to happen upon Mesopotamia and the Hanging Gardens of Babylon, the still-lush wonder of the world before it was forgotten to time. He began walking again anyway, wishing the entire time that he could face the difficulties of establishing a new life the way the scientists had envisioned, rather than being alone in the wilderness without knowing anything at all.

31 - THE DIFFICULTY OF ESTABLISHING A NEW LIFE

A time traveler doesn't simply appear one day and change history. He wouldn't have the resources to alter the Theta Timeline in a meaningful way. Instead, he would get a job, preferably one with the government. After that, it would be a matter of building a new life, gaining friends and influence, and gathering power. It would take time to gain favors and accrue wealth, which would be critical in one day buying people's services.

To best accomplish this task, the Thinker's judged that the perfect place in history for their time travelers to appear was the early-to-mid twentieth century. Before that and it would be difficult for them to do much that would prevent the rise of the State. Any later than that and it would be too difficult for the time traveler to establish an identity in his new life, get a job, and gain influence. A man who spends his life as the principal of a middle school is admirable, but someone who goes into law and is eventually appointed to be a federal judge will be in a vastly better position to prevent the rise of the State.

If a time traveler appeared before the twentieth century, he would have no problem claiming to be a shipwrecked sailor or a lost outdoorsman. Without universal electronic records to make it easy for people to verify identities, a time traveler could go to a courthouse and claim someone else's identity as his own. It was even possible that he could pick a random obituary, travel across the country, and claim that there must have been some mistake since he was, obviously, still alive. Or he could say his original birth certificate had been lost in a fire.

Anyone who has ever researched their family tree knows that people used to disappear from public record only to reappear years later, or they might disappear forever without even a record of death. It was how crooks used dead people's names to vote as many times as they wanted, but it was also the time traveler's best way for appearing in a new era and building a life for himself.

The problem with arriving too late in the twentieth century, or any time in the twenty-first century, was that it became more and more difficult to appear out of nowhere and start a new life. Courthouse fires could no longer be used to explain away the lack of a birth certificate. No matter where the time traveler went, electronic documents would be available to contradict his claims. A courthouse clerk would lose his job if he approved a request for new identification to someone who showed up without any proof of who they claimed to be.

In an age when the average person could pay a couple dollars to find out every detail about anyone they wanted, a time traveler couldn't very well show up and say he had just drifted in from another part of the country. Fingerprints would be needed to validate the claim. These, of course, would not match anyone on file. The time traveler would be taken to a room where he would have to explain why he was trying to pass himself off as someone else. His new life might even start with some time in jail until the cops figured out what to do with him.

The time traveler could say he was suffering from amnesia and didn't know who he was. That would at least earn him concern instead of suspicion. However, there aren't many influential jobs available for men who walk out of the desert or a national park one day, claiming they have no memory of who they are. The amnesia story might allow him to establish a new life for himself, but he would never get promoted to the rank of General or have a seat on a corporate boardroom if his early years were a mystery.

The average person has no idea how many people are missing in the country. At any given time, there are thousands of men and women whose whereabouts are unknown. Some will eventually be discovered as decomposed bodies found by hunters in the wilderness. Work crews at construction sites might uncover a body here and there. But most will never be found. Some of these people are runaways who want to be left alone. Some are people who sit on a sidewalk each day, as thousands of people ignore them on their way to and from work. A few are merely clerical errors caused by someone typing too quickly, the wrong person labeled as deceased while the person who actually died is never heard from again. These things happen.

In a country where so many people are missing, the time traveler's best chance of making a new life for himself is in claiming amnesia and letting the authorities match his face against those missing people who resemble him. Out of the thousands of possibilities, at least ten or twenty will share a few physical traits with the time traveler. After that, it's a matter of learning about each person's life until one of them sounds familiar. "Sounds familiar" is slang for an identity the time traveler would like to inherit as his own for the rest of his life.

That was how it was supposed to work. The social services worker or other local official, thumbing through a stack of 8x10 photos with key information paper-clipped to each photo, and asking if "any of this rings a bell."

With luck, the time traveler would hear of a man who went missing three years ago off the coast. A millionaire banker perhaps. That sounded nice. But suppose the man also had a wife and three kids. Not good. A time traveler might be able to game the paperwork system and maybe even the insurance companies, but he would never be able to fool a wife and three kids into believing he was their missing relative, especially when they were happy spending the dead man's fortune.

"I'm sorry, none of that sounds familiar," the time traveler would reluctantly say.

The authorities would go through this routine, giving nuggets of information about each life, hoping it might jog the amnesiac's memory. They would have no idea the time traveler is analyzing the same information for the best new identity.

After getting his second-hand identity, it's a matter of reclaiming the life of a man who probably fell to his death, got lost in the wilderness, or was attacked by a mountain lion. The time traveler would return to the dead man's job—not a single employer would refuse someone their old job because they had been declared dead prematurely.

To anyone else, the time traveler would seem to be just another person. Except instead of coaching Little League or refereeing soccer games, he would be trying to earn promotions and enter social circles as quickly as possible. That way, by the time one of the Thinker's primary objectives did come around, he might have the influence required to change the course of history.

It wouldn't necessarily have to be a high-ranking appointment within the government. Even being a college professor might work. He would get the opportunity to teach hundreds of college kids about the dangers of authoritarianism, explain how the natural cycle of rule meant that democracies naturally turned into tyrannies, and tell them how to detect the transition. He would even remind them that no matter how many times people might laugh and say, "It could never happen here", those people were insulting history's ability to repeat itself. And, he would remind them, every other time a tyranny had risen from democracy, there had always been people who said it couldn't happen to *them*. Famous last words.

If he told enough kids, and if he was persuasive in what he said, his students might go out into the world with their degrees and with an awareness of how they could keep their freedom. Maybe one of them would eventually become a senator and remember his history professor's lectures each time he voted against new ways controlling the population. Maybe a student would become a lawyer and one day argue against the endless security checks on every street corner.

And then, when the time was right, he would give up that life and begin to focus on forestalling an event from taking place, something that would eventually lead to the State's formation.

Those were the problems Springfield wanted to have—dilemmas of which life to lead, which event in history he should change—not how he should survive in the wild, how he should evade a trained killer. He wanted to worry about creating a new identity, not about spending the rest of his life in a world devoid of civilization. He had heard rumors of other men being sent back too far in time, and nothing of what he had heard offered encouragement now.

32 – NOSTRADAMUS

It wasn't that the Thinkers forgot to discuss the possibility of being sent back too far in time. In fact, they loved the topic because it conjured images of all the prehistoric science fiction they had read as boys.

A worst-case scenario was being sent back in time tens of thousands of years, before any traces of what could be considered human civilization existed. *Homo sapiens* has been on the earth for two hundred thousand years, but only very recently mastered plumbing and electricity. If a time traveler was transported back to before the Chinese invented paper or the Germans invented the printing press, what would he do with the rest of his life? The only answer the Thinkers could come up with was that they would give up on having any chance of changing history and lead as normal a life as possible. There was too much time before the State would form to do anything else. They might as well settle down somewhere and make a family.

As part of a community, they would live out the rest of their lives as hunter-gatherers, nomads, or farmers, however the rest of the people around them survived. Half of all babies would die before they were one year old. A third of all women would die while giving birth. Men would die from war or disease.

If this became the time traveler's new reality, they could always become an educator in the village and teach the importance of freedom to as many kids as possible. Maybe the children would one day teach their own sons and daughters the same lesson. The idea might even spread to neighboring tribes and then to other lands. Over hundreds of years, the message would reach faraway lands—it was important to stand up for yourself when someone tried to control you, and that if a government can have total power over its people it will do horrible things to keep that control.

It was one thing to educate as many people as possible and hope the message persisted through history. It was quite another thing to create specific warnings for future generations—an active approach to stopping the State. And it's why many of the Thinkers in Springfield's discussion group became convinced that Nostradamus wasn't a French seer at all but a time traveler just like them.

Is it a coincidence that Nostradamus's specified birthplace in France is on the exact same latitude as one of the Thinker's previous departure sites? Doubtful. Even more telling is that everything that's known about Nostradamus's early years was learned from the seer himself. He was the one who said when and where he was born. There was no proof other than his word that any of it was true. What was he supposed to tell people, that he was from the future and needed to warn everyone about the great dangers that lay ahead? So he told everyone who his parents were (even though there was no record of them either) and where he was born.

What the time travelers could not agree on were Nostradamus's predictions. Was he trying to warn future generations of the world they would one day live in? Were his lines about fireballs in the sky and death plaguing the masses actually talking about the wars the State would wage on the rest of the world? Were prophecies that had been interpreted to be about World War I and II and about the creation of the first atomic bomb actually about the State's reign of terror?

Or was the seer, frustrated with being sent back too far in time, just writing down random predictions that could be interpreted however people wanted, just to mess with everyone's head? The few people who met Newcastle before he disappeared into the past agreed that he was an arrogant prick who considered himself smarter than everyone else. It would be very easy to see him sitting around in sixteenth century France, bored and looking for something to amuse himself with. What better way for a smug asshole to get a cheap laugh than at the expense of future generations, who would never stop trying to make sense of everything he had written?

The chance that Newcastle took is why time travelers are now asked to respect the rest of history and not make needless changes to the Theta Timeline. If the rise of the State has taught the Thinkers anything, it's that history should be honored, not be made into a punch line.

And it's why, anytime a Thinker gets too excited about being sent back in time and possessing knowledge of a future that no one else will have, someone else in the discussion group tells him to "quit being such a Newcastle" and to get back to more practical matters.

33 - NOT THE DESIRED SIGNS

As he walked, Springfield continually rubbed his palm where the branch was poking through. Even when he looked over his shoulder for signs of the man in black, his index finger and thumb ran in circles around the stick. Other than making it hard to make a fist, the foreign object didn't seem to be affecting him much.

On his way up another hill, he tried twisting the branch, thinking that if he could get it to spin inside his palm, it might become easier to pull out. But turning it even the smallest amount felt like thousands of splinters being injected into his palm. On his way down the other side of that same hill, he tried to work the branch forward, out of his palm, but any pressure to slide it in either direction caused excruciating pain. Eventually, he became resigned to it and left it alone.

As a child, he had needed to have eighteen glass chips removed from his hand after a car accident. Riding in the backseat of his parents' car, seeing a minivan careening through the intersection, he had put his hands out in an involuntary defensive reaction. As if a kid's little hand could ward off a two thousand pound projectile. The doctor who removed the glass said that Isaac's natural reflex had probably saved his eyes from being sprayed with glass. Instead, the doctor removed the pieces from the boy's palms, tiny pieces, one after another, each piece clinking into a trash can. After eighteen clinks, the doctor stitched up the cuts and sent Isaac home with his parents.

A month later, his hand was like new again. Only a series of fancy scars proved anything had happened, and the pink lines impressed all of his friends more than any new toy ever could.

Unfortunately, twenty-one shards of glass had lodged in his hand during the accident. The doctor had found most of them, but a trio of pieces remained under his skin, undetected.

A year after the accident, after playing baseball with friends, he took his glove off and saw that his hand was covered in bruises. That summer, the same thing happened every time he played neighborhood ball. Months later, as the year's first snowfall covered his parents' driveway, one of the pieces of glass finally worked its way through his skin—such a tiny chip that he would never have guessed it could turn his entire hand purple. Over the next year, the other two pieces worked themselves out of his hand as well.

Since his body had rejected the foreign objects back then, he hoped it would do the same thing now. His concern, though, was that if it had taken an entire year for tiny pieces of glass to work themselves out, it might take a lifetime for the wood sticking out his hand to be expelled.

At least the branch in his hand diverted his attention from his current predicament, including the complete lack of human civilization. He had walked and walked and walked, all without any indication he was headed in the right direction or even that any direction might be better than any other. If he had been transported back hundreds or thousands of years, it wouldn't matter where he went or how far he forced himself to go. For that reason, the embedded stick was a welcome distraction.

All he could see were mountains, hills, forests, and fields. Still, he could not discern which mountain range he was looking at. Nor was there any sign that he would find people who might be able to help him. Worse, it was still his first day in his new time and he had already eaten three protein bars. There were only ten in the bag and he knew he should be careful about how quickly he ate them, but he couldn't help himself.

He had a limited amount of food. He had no idea where he was, or when he was. He had a stick in his hand, and maybe a mercenary following his trail. He was tired and his feet hurt. He either had to stop walking and start building a shelter, which would give the assassin a chance to catch him, or he would have to keep moving and do without a shelter, which, if it rained, could mean disaster for his health.

Not knowing what else he could say, he mumbled, "Son of a bitch," and then, "Maybe I should've spent a little less time learning foreign languages and world history and a little more time learning how to survive out in the wild."

As if in agreement, a nearby bird chirped twice, then flew away.

For the first time, he cursed himself and the other time travelers for sitting in a room to brainstorm every aspect of going back in time rather than practice how to make fires and shelters. And he cursed himself for thinking a 61.5% chance of being transported to dry land was actually a reasonable number. It was better than the 56.1% chance that the previous batch of time travelers had been given, but he was quickly learning that better than bad wasn't quite good enough.

He also cursed himself for going along with the mission at a point when time travel was still so new that the scientists had no idea which part of history they were sending men back to. He would have gone eventually, of course. The monster that ruled his country had to be stopped, but why hadn't he waited until he could at least be given an estimate for how far back he would be sent?

At the top of the next hill, he had a clear view of the surrounding area. Part of him didn't want to look. He was afraid there would be still more uninhabited landscape. The other part of him, the part that couldn't sleep the night before Christmas, couldn't wait to see smoke rising from a chimney or a man walking his dog. All he saw, though, were more trees and grass. The hills were monotonous—one after another—and he couldn't tell how far he had walked or how far the same landscape continued in the distance. It might be two miles or twenty or two hundred.

Only two options existed: lay down and quit, or keep walking. With this thought in mind, his feet once again carried him across stretches of hills and fields. He walked to the top of two more crests, but each time the same view presented itself.

The sun was starting to go down over the western horizon. It wouldn't be long before night came and he was stuck in the wild without a shelter. Other than birds and little rodents, he hadn't seen any animals, but that didn't mean they weren't watching him from the trees, waiting for him to stop moving.

He groaned. Too tired to go any further, his shoulders collapsed toward his knees. His bed would be the cold, hard ground. Letting out a sigh, he patted the grass and the dirt to see exactly how uncomfortable it would be. It was amazing how little protection the burlap outfit offered from the ground. A pebble jabbed into his back. When he tossed it away and repositioned himself, two more stones presented themselves under his hips. When he tossed these away, three more stones were in their place.

The blanket would offer a small amount of cushion, but he suspected it would get cold during the night and he would need to pull it over his body.

Closing his eyes, he couldn't help but wonder what Jessica was doing right then. If time was linear, not even her parents would be alive yet, maybe not even her great-great-great grandparents. But relative to the timeline he had just left, she would probably be getting home from work and find the apartment empty.

Was she sitting in their living room, looking at the furniture and the framed pictures of the two of them? Was she trying to figure out which parts of her life could remain the same and which parts would be changed forever? Was she being visited by men in dark suits who asked the same questions over and over?

"Did you know your boyfriend was a Thinker?" they would ask. After writing down her response, they would follow it up with, "Give us the names of anyone else he might have associated with."

Maybe a small part of her had always suspected things would end up this way—she would be relieved that she could finally get on with the rest of her life. She was probably wondering where in the world he had gone. The news reports would label him a traitor and say his burned remains had been found smoldering in the destroyed basement. Or maybe she had heard whispers of time travel herself and was now trying to imagine him in a better time. For her, there was only the now. She would never be sent back in time the way Isaac had. And that meant sitting on their sofa in an otherwise empty apartment, thinking about what she would do the next day and the day after that.

34 - SEXISM AND TIME TRAVEL

Until fairly recently, most civilizations treated women as indentured servants or second-class citizens. The majority of religions reinforced this concept by teaching that women should be subservient to men and shouldn't be allowed to hold the same roles as their male counterparts. There was almost nowhere a woman could go where she could be considered equal to a man, and each time men found a new role or responsibility they also found a new way to hold women back from the same opportunity. Men were allowed to vote while women had to fight for the right. Men were CEOs while women were expected to be their secretaries. Women who worked the exact same jobs as men brought home smaller paychecks.

So maybe it shouldn't have come as a surprise that, when the Thinkers were planning how they could most effectively alter history, they decided early on that only men would be allowed to take the journey. There are two interesting aspects about this decision. First, the men-only requirement had nothing to do with the Thinkers being sexist. And second, the scientists and sociologists within the Thinkers that first came up with this rule was itself formed of an equal number of women and men, all of whom agreed on the requirement.

The reasoning was similar to the argument for why women weren't initially allowed into active combat roles in the military. Most male soldiers are killed on the battlefield by an enemy who just wants to see them die. If captured alive, they might be tortured until they provide any useful information. Then, they are shot or hung. But a female soldier goes through a completely different experience. Enemies try to avoid killing women on the battlefield so they can have a prize after the battle is over. Female soldiers are sometimes even nursed back to health by their captors just so they don't die too soon and can be passed around amongst the enemy. They might not be shot in the head after providing information, but they might wish they had been. Generals, many of whom had daughters of their own back at home, did not like to consider such things, and so women weren't allowed to fight.

Sadly, human history has proven itself to be even more unfriendly toward women than modern war. Sent back in time, with no idea where or when they might be transported to, there is almost no chance that a woman would be able to make a life for herself before falling victim to men.

If the scientists could guarantee that a time traveler would only be sent back in time two or three decades, women would be relatively safe. But even then, their chances of climbing the corporate ladder and gaining positions of power would still be less than that of a comparable man. Given that the scientists still couldn't predict where or when a female time traveler might be transported back to, the risk was too great that she would appear in a time when women were punished for wanting to go to school or when their desire for independence would be considered insulting to men.

The Thinkers' scientists and sociologists agreed: there was already a high probability that a time traveler would either drown in the middle of the ocean or fall too far out of the sky (or both). Adding the additional criteria of needing to be transported to a time and place where society respected the well-being of women was too unlikely. An entire row of female time travelers, lined shoulder to shoulder against a concrete wall, could very well be sent back in time without any of them having a chance to change history.

Maybe, when time travel technology improves, women will be able to take part in the same missions as their male counterparts. But for now, they are faced with yet another way in which the history of the world, a history of intolerance and closed-mindedness toward the fairer sex, denies them the same opportunities as men.

35 - STRIKE ONE

The sun was already above the trees when Springfield opened his eyes. Disoriented, he looked around for someone or something to explain where he was. In the distance, snow-capped mountains loomed. Closer to him, hills were dotted with trees and bushes. He had actually expected to open his eyes and find himself in bed, Jessica next to him. Confused, it took him a moment to remember why he was on the ground, surrounded by rolling fields.

If Jessica had been next to him when he woke, she would have asked what was wrong with him. No matter how comfortable their mattress had been, he tossed and turned every night. She would wake every morning looking like she had barely gotten any sleep, all because she had been stirred awake twenty times by his movements. But out on the field, lying on top of rocks and dirt, he hadn't woken even once. Not only that, but he had slept through the first signs of daylight. Judging from the sun's position, it was already close to noon.

Even with the midday heat already making his tongue stick to the roof of his mouth, he was shivering uncontrollably. Bringing his shoulders to his chin did nothing to stop the shaking. His teeth chattered until, like a simpleton, he let his mouth hang open so he didn't chip any of them.

Nothing made sense. Where was the man in black? And why, assuming he was out there somewhere, hadn't he found Springfield while he slept out in the open? Out in the open, like an idiot. The worst thing he could have done was to sleep without a shelter, and that was exactly what he had done. It was possible that he had been so tired from hiking the previous day that he hadn't been thinking clearly. Fatigue had given way to sickness. The chattering teeth and disorientation upon waking up proved that much.

He tried to sit up, but instead of his body moving, the entire world seemed to shake and spin. When he lay still again, the world stopped gyrating. Even something as simple as rolling over on his side made him feel like the world was falling apart. His hands and body wouldn't stop shaking.

Something tickled his lips. Without thinking, he rubbed his hand back and forth across his mouth. But when he brought his wrist away, it was covered with dirt. He rubbed his chin. Dirt came away from there too. Confused, he wiped one cheek, then the other. Both times, black dirt smeared his skin. He looked at his filthy hands as if they were complex math equations he was expected to know.

My eyes must be playing tricks on me, he thought.

This idea was reinforced by one of the bits of soil moving across his palm. He watched it with a slight grin, fascinated that a grain of dirt would be considerate enough to leave his skin without needing to be washed away. But when he closed his eyes, then opened them again, the dirt was still there, still moving.

Instead of being alarmed, the thought simply came to him that maybe he wasn't hallucinating after all. A voice in the back of his head told him that what he was seeing had to make sense, but he couldn't think clearly enough to understand how it could. Another piece of dirt began moving across his fingers. Then another. The voice in the back of his head, persistent as always, told him dirt didn't crawl. But shivering, maybe delirious, he had no idea if it was the voice or his vision playing tricks on him.

It wasn't until one of the pieces of dirt bit him that the voice suddenly cried out in pained triumph: *I told you so! Dirt doesn't move!*

Ants. He was covered in ants. They were on his face, in his mouth, on his clothes, all over him.

He had no idea if they were the kind that could kill him or if they were the same annoying but harmless ones that used to ruin his picnics with Jessica. The pure shock of realizing he was covered in little bugs, poisonous or not, made him stumble to his feet and yell. Later, he would have no memory of whether he had been screaming actual words or just gibberish.

He was able to take two steps before the world began spinning again. When it did, he fell back on the ground. Still screaming, he scrambled back to his feet. Both of his hands smacked at his face, brushing ants away everywhere he could find them. He didn't realize it at the time, but in his carelessness, the piece of wood, still sticking out of his hand, drew bloody scratches across his cheeks and forehead each time he brushed more bugs away.

There were too many of them. His clothes were covered. After stumbling and standing one more time, he tore his shirt off. When he went to do the same with his pants, the spinning world threw him straight onto his face. Without thinking, he reached out to brace himself. A pulse of searing pain drilled through his hand where the stick drove through his palm. With one pant leg off and the other still on, he cried out in agony like he never had before. It didn't even enter his mind as he bellowed that if the man in black was nearby he would now know exactly where his target was.

The one good thing from his outburst was that he was no longer shaking. Probably, when the adrenaline died down, the shivers would start all over again. For the moment, though, it was nice to have fairly steady hands, even though nothing else—not even the ground beneath him—was motionless anymore. Even the sky was spinning. He crawled to the nearest tree and sat with his back against it.

His fellow time travelers would be ashamed if they could see him in his current condition. One of the supposed saviors of the future had his pants half off and bugs all over him. Men had willingly put their lives on the line. More than half would die before they could even begin their mission. And here he was, in only his underwear, jumping and stumbling and screaming like a complete idiot.

That was his last thought before he passed out.

When he opened his eyes again, the sun was going down over the western horizon. He was covered in sweat. Without clothes and already sick, he wouldn't survive the cold night. Already, he was having trouble thinking clearly. He faded out of consciousness again. Back in. Back out. When he opened his eyes the next time it was the middle of the night.

During one of his moments of lucidity, he thought, *they were only ants; I really shouldn't have been so careless and yelled out like that. I never even got to start my mission. The State will go on forever without half the country ever knowing how enslaved they really are.*

And then, as if on cue, a hand reached through the darkness and grabbed his shoulder.

And then he was unconscious again.

36 - THE ILLUSION OF FREEDOM

The greatest trick the State ever pulled was convincing half the population it was still free. They believed it each time the leaders went on television and said, "These new restrictions are to keep you safe." And they believed it when the personalities on the evening news said, "Of course you're still free." These people didn't like waiting in checkpoint lines or having cameras monitoring their every movement any more than the rest of the population, but they accepted it because they chose to believe what they were told.

For these people, life was tolerable if they kept their head down and did as they were told. They put their fingers in their ears if someone said the State used war as an economic tool. When they heard someone say they were no longer living in the same country their parents had known, they repeated the line they heard so often on television and accused the speaker of being stuck in the past.

At one of the thousands of checkpoints, a man refused to be patted down, saying he shouldn't be treated like a prisoner. He was quietly ushered away and never seen nor heard from again. To the Thinkers, it was proof of everything that was wrong with the State. But to the half of the population that believed what they were told, the man had simply been a troublemaker and deserved whatever punishment he got.

"If he would have just followed the rules, they wouldn't have had to arrest him," these people said.

A woman was found dead in her hotel room the morning after going on television and speaking out against the State's use of AeroCams with infrared cameras to spy into people's homes. The Thinkers, seeing that she had been shot in the back of the head, was covered in bruises, and had a broken nose, said it was obvious that people were no longer free to question their leaders. The other half of the population saw the same death, offered a nervous laugh, and said she had probably suffered from depression.

It was vital to the State that they keep as many people as possible believing they were free. Because with half the population not understanding their predicament, there would never be a revolt.

It's true that even in the State people still had an official list of rights, touted by the Ruler as proof that his people were still free. This comforted the half of the population who believed their leaders. But for the Thinkers, it was only a reminder of the place they used to live in.

The faces on television loved to say things like, "Have you ever known a dictator who allowed people to say whatever they want? Of course we're free." What they didn't mention was that exposing the State's lies was punishable by death. Posting images of the innocent people the State had killed also resulted in death. Reporting on the ways the State was breaking international law was punishable by life in prison. If someone exposed corruption within the State, they could plan on disappearing and never being heard from again. If they complained about one of the State's laws, they were said to be inciting violence and would also disappear.

The people who believed in the State's illusion shrugged their shoulders and said, "Don't these people understand the State would leave them alone if they just minded their own business?"

Privacy was still a concept that people understood, but the State's courts had ruled that every possible kind of intrusion was justified because it protected the people. The threat of attack, whether real or imagined, from abroad or from home, gave the State all the excuse it ever needed to be able to search people and spy on them whenever they wanted.

"It's for our own protection," the personality on television said. "I really don't understand why people are complaining. Can't they see the checkpoints stop future attacks?"

When a man came forward with official documents exposing the checkpoint program as a way not to capture radicals but to control the population, half the people within the State were genuinely confused. "But they've prevented hundreds of attacks."

When it was proved beyond a doubt that the pat-downs and questions weren't actually preventing attacks, these people said, "Well, I guess they still make me feel safe."

When arrested, the State's citizens still had a right to a fair trial. Unless they were considered radicals. For the people who trusted what they were told, this was a comforting reassurance. For the Thinkers, it was the realization that anyone could be considered a threat. The State had only to declare you were a radical and—poof!—you were. And if they said it, there was no trial, no access to a lawyer.

The State was adamant that it needed to protect its people. That meant, the Ruler said, not treating radicals the way they treated everyone else. At the press conference where this was announced, a reporter raised her hand.

"Yes?" the Ruler said.

"Why not?"

"Why not what?"

"Why can't you treat radicals like other criminals?"

The Ruler laughed as if the question was a joke. The next morning, the reporter who had asked it was found dead of what was declared to be a drug overdose. All the fingers on one of her hands had been broken, the people in the room next to her had heard screaming, and there was a trail of blood in her hotel room where her body had been dragged from the bed to the bathtub. But it was obviously a suicide.

Half the country shrugged and said, "She probably did kill herself. She was obviously depressed if she was jaded enough to ask our Ruler a question like that."

A man who used his blog to question the State's latest war was declared to be a radical. That night, the leaders lined up to tell an array of cameras, "Of course he was a radical. Questioning the State's motives is just a way of trying to incite a revolution. And what's more dangerous than that?"

Thinkers saw a troubling trend. But the other half of the population was angry with the man for questioning the State and thought he deserved what he got.

Every once in a while, the State chose to make an example out of someone rather than kill them or make them disappear. This was done with a fabulously drawn out trial that would prove their guilt. But these people were never tried for the things they actually said. The State would find the most humiliating charges it could think of as a way to destroy the reputation of anyone who pointed out its corruption or lies. A successful businessman, who said the leaders should all be sent to jail, was suddenly known to be a child murderer. A college professor, who taught about the dangers of State, was charged with being a necrophiliac. The non-Thinkers tuned in to the 24/7 coverage of the trials to see if justice would prevail. For the State, it always did.

At the end of each trial, the leaders pushed each other out of the way in order to be first in line to speak to the cameras. "This trial just shows how we need additional laws to protect the people so the same thing doesn't happen again!" one said. "I plan on introducing legislation tomorrow morning that will put a hundred new laws on the books!" another said.

This, of course, made half the people feel very safe, and the other half, very scared.

37 - BLURRED VISION

Springfield's eyes opened. The sun hurt his head and he had to squint so much that his eyelids flickered shut again. Almost nothing could be seen. The little he could make out consisted of the outline of a man moving next to the remains of a campfire. Squinting from the sun, he could only tell it was a man and not an animal because of the way it moved—walking two steps, bending over, picking something up. Everything else was a green haze.

His head swirled and he groaned. The figure stopped what it was doing and turned toward him. Springfield was fascinated that the man in black, after finally catching up to him, hadn't murdered him right away, but was content to make a camp and relax.

Maybe the mercenary didn't understand where they were and was waiting for Springfield to explain everything—why there were no AeroCams in the sky; how they went from the sub-basement of an apartment building to a vast stretch of hills and trees—before doing away with him. It was doubtful the man in black had any idea this was a one-way trip. If the State didn't realize time travel existed, the assassin probably still thought they were transported to another part of the world and would eventually be found by the

AeroCams. Only after he tortured Springfield into telling him everything he knew would he understand the truth.

Springfield didn't mind the thought of death. That had been demonstrated just by agreeing to vanish into a random time and space, knowing there was less than a forty percent chance he would appear somewhere where he could actually survive. What he did mind was the thought of being tortured needlessly. No matter how useful the information may be that he could tell the man in black, which in turn would surely earn him the reward of a quicker, less painful death, it would be information that was utterly useless to the State. The assassin didn't understand that, though, so Springfield would die a gruesome, agonized death and it would all be for nothing.

Not only did the mercenary not realize he was in the past, he also wouldn't know that once someone went back in time, it was impossible to return to the time they had come from. After he got done torturing Springfield, he would realize that nothing the time traveler had said would actually help him.

And even if the man in black could get information back to the State, what could Springfield say that might help them? He didn't know anyone's real names, only their aliases, and those men were all gone to other parts of history now as well. He had no idea how the time machine really worked. He didn't even know the nicknames of the men in white coats, let alone their real names. The few code words he had overheard—Atlas, Costello, Dusklands, Timbuktu—had probably already been picked up by the State's vast array of surveillance. There was nothing he could be tortured into revealing that would make any difference at all.

The worst part, though, was that there was nothing he could say that would convince the man in black of this. And even if the mercenary did believe that torturing his captive was useless, Springfield had the suspicion that a grisly death would occur anyway. It would take place just because the man in black had nearly died in the basement. It would happen because the assassin would now have to live the rest of his life in a different time and place than his friends and family. And, Springfield thought, it might happen simply because killing Thinkers was the only thing the assassin knew how to do. There was no better way to feel powerful than to make others feel powerless. That was what drew so many of the State's men to their jobs.

He remembered something one of his teachers had once said: there is nothing stronger in life than someone's survival instinct. The same remark had been reiterated by one of the other Thinkers in what turned out to be their final group discussion.

The man had looked at the others gathered in a circle and asked, "If the State ever does catch us, do you think we'll want to die so the torturing stops, only to find our survival instinct keeps us struggling to live, no matter how much we want the pain to end?"

Springfield didn't want to find out the answer to the man's question.

His temples hurt. When he lowered his head back to the ground, he realized he was resting on a small bushel of grass instead of dirt. Maybe the man in black was starting his routine by being the good cop. After the two of them were friendly for a while, the bad cop would make his appearance. That was Springfield's last thought before drifting off to sleep once more.

When he stirred the next time, he noticed the blurred figure immediately stand up and walk toward him. The moving black silhouette suddenly came into focus.

It wasn't the man in black at all, but a native.

All at once, Springfield experienced overwhelming joy and sadness. He wasn't sure if he should laugh and wrap his arms around the man, or cry and warn him that a killer would surely have seen the campfire and was no doubt going to murder them both.

He tried to say, "We have to leave this spot right away or we're going to die." But even as he spoke he realized he was slurring his words. And even if he had been speaking clearly, there was no chance at all that this man, part of a tribe on the other side of the world, would understand English.

He tried to form his words again, but "We have to leave this spot or we're going to die," sounded more like, "Eee ave ohh eave eh ot eih." He knew how dumb he sounded, but no matter how hard he tried, he couldn't make his words any clearer.

"Son of a bitch," he tried to say, but it came out as, "Un of ah ich," and that made him groan with despair.

The last thing he saw before he passed out again was the tribesman kneeling over him, looking very confused.

I don't blame you, Springfield thought. *I'd be confused too.*

And then everything was darkness again.

38 - THE VISIT

Jessica wasn't surprised when the State's men came to question her. Her only shock was that it took so long. As soon as she got home the day before, saw Isaac wasn't there, then heard the news reports of a shootout with a group of ultra-radical Thinkers, she knew the State would show up eventually.

With the AeroCams recording the actions of everyone on the street, the State immediately knew the names of all the men who had been in the basement, along with each person's known friends and family. There was no telling if the Security Services would drag her away just for dating a Thinker. They had done worse with less of an excuse. It was possible she would be taken to a secret prison and left there for years, long enough for them to determine if she really didn't know more than she was letting on. At that point, they were just as likely to let her go back into society as they were to kill her and claim she had committed suicide.

It was a shock that they hadn't shown up at her job. She wasn't complaining, though. Most employers would terminate someone if the State showed up asking questions about them. In the eyes of those managers, not getting rid of someone who the State was interested in was reason enough for them to fall under suspicion too.

In fact, the State's men hadn't visited her at all that first night. She had spent the entire evening sitting on the sofa, numbed by the knowledge that she would never see the man she loved again, all the while waiting for the knock on her door. Late that night, when they still hadn't shown up, she brushed her teeth and got in bed. It was the first time in two years that she would be going to sleep without Isaac next to her. Although she thought it would make her feel better if she did, she couldn't cry. Disbelief refused to allow tears too soon. But they would come—both the tears and the State's men.

As she laid in bed that first night, she wondered if he and all the other Thinkers really were dead, as the news reports had said, or if that story was just a cover. Was the man she loved alive? If so, was he being transported to one of the State's many secret prisons? Or had he never been in the basement at all? Nothing she had heard on the news could be trusted because they were simply reporting the story as it had been told to them by the State. There were no photos of his body in the rubble. Until she saw proof, she liked to think he was out there somewhere.

Already, the leaders were on television calling for action: "We need to have laws in place to prevent this sort of thing. A shootout in our streets? An explosion? Obviously we need new laws if we want to prevent the same thing from happening again."

That was all the news really told her. She reached for the remote, turned the television off, then spent the rest of the night staring at her ceiling.

That was the first night. The second night, there was a knock on her door.

This is it, she thought. She had half a mind to say something corny from a movie, something like "What took you guys so long?" just so she could see their response before they took her away.

But before she was out of her bedroom, she heard a

door open, a greeting, and a door close, and she realized it had been someone knocking on her neighbor's door.

She walked to her bedroom window. On the streets below, a line, hundreds of people long, was taking two steps forward, pausing, then taking another two steps forward as people filed through a checkpoint. Above them, AeroCams circled, recording everything that was going on. With their swirling, constant movement, she couldn't count how many there were. Probably hundreds. And thousands more recording the rest of the city.

How could life go on like this? It wasn't so much that Isaac would never walk through the door again, although that didn't help things. It was the fact that if the State's men hadn't shown up already, they might never knock on her door. That didn't mean she was safe, though. It simply meant she might go to sleep one evening and never wake up. One of the State's men would enter in the middle of the night and stick a needle in her arm. She would be dead before she could make a sound. The news reports would either explain to the public that she had overdosed on drugs or had a history of depression and had finally killed herself.

Her parents, Isaac's parents, her co-workers, would all read in the paper that she had been a drug addict for many years and had finally gone too far after the news that her boyfriend was a radical Thinker who was involved in the senseless bombing of an apartment building. She thought about leaving a note for her parents to let them know that if anything did happen to her, it wouldn't be what they heard on the news. That tactic was pointless, however. The State would find the letter, destroy it, and leave one of their own in which she apologized for turning to drugs and for loving a dirty radical. If she tried to write an email, the State would intercept it before it could be delivered to the people she loved.

She didn't know anything about what Isaac had done, but she doubted they would believe that. Once the State was afraid of its people, it suspected everyone was secretly against them. They saw a man's actions and because they tracked everyone's movements and words, they assumed everyone next to him had been in on it with him. Everyone had the potential to be a radical—the average person just needed to be pushed into the role so they could more quickly be removed as the threat they had been all along.

That was what she thought about as she closed her eyes. Sometime around three o'clock in the morning, she drifted off to sleep. When her alarm woke her in the morning, her eyes begged to remain closed. Even without looking in the mirror, she knew they would be puffy and bloodshot.

If she called her boss and told him she didn't feel well, it would only make her look more suspicious in the eyes of the State. If life didn't continue, no matter what tragedy someone suffered, it was considered proof that the State had rightfully considered someone a suspect. She spent all day in a haze of fatigue and sadness, constantly looking over her shoulder for the men from the Security Service to drag her away.

But that night, as she sat at home and watched the continuing coverage of the Thinker's attack on the apartment building and the videos of the Ruler explaining how the incident proved the need for more checkpoints and AeroCams, the knock finally came.

A second knock sounded just as she was getting to her door, but once again she realized it was her neighbor's door and not her own. Something about the knock made her remain at the peephole so she could hear what was happening.

Through the fisheye, she saw two men in dark suits facing her neighbor's door. Just as one of the men was about to pound for the third time, Jessica's neighbor opened the door and was facing them. The girl was shocked into silence. The man who had been knocking seemed more annoyed that his hand was interrupted than he was happy that the door was finally open.

"Jessica Redfield?" the other man said.

"No," her neighbor began, "she's—"

But the two men pushed the girl inside her apartment and closed the door behind them.

Poor girl, Jessica thought. But going over there and trying to tell them they had the wrong person would only make matters worse. Once the State's men started something, they either saw it through to the end, no matter how wrong they were, or they started killing people.

On the bright side, for her neighbor at least, the two men had knocked on the door instead of breaking it down. People had come to expect certain outcomes based on the way the State announced themselves. If they broke the door down without waiting for a response, everyone inside the dwelling would be killed, and the State would say this was justified because they had encountered some form of resistance. If they made contact and the occupant was unwilling to let them in, they broke the door down and the same result ensued. It didn't matter if they had arrived simply to question someone; once they experienced any hint of resistance they were trained to act accordingly. But if they arrived and knocked on the door, there was only a fifty-fifty chance of things turning violent.

There was nothing Jessica could do except wait at her sofa and hope the men realized their mistake before they took her neighbor away to prison or killed her for claiming she wasn't who they said she was.

It wasn't surprising that they had knocked on the wrong door. The State didn't want an educated populace, and so it had made sure there was no money to provide qualified teachers to educate the masses. Some schools were closed all together, forcing twice the amount of kids into crowded, unruly rooms. Pushed through the system, students graduated without being able to read or write. But what the State didn't realize was that these youths would one day grow up to become the State's workforce. The result was administrators who were lucky if they could read the reports they were given, personnel who didn't understand basic math, and, in

Jessica's case, officers who questioned the wrong people because they wrote down the wrong address or misread the correct one.

It started off with SWAT teams showing up at the wrong house, breaking down some innocent person's door, and shooting their dog when it barked at the intruders. The dog-killers, of course, were never punished for invading the wrong home and killing the family pet.

But then it escalated. A drone was sent to the wrong home, blowing up the neighbor of a suspected Thinker instead of the man the State had actually been targeting. An entire innocent family was killed. Instead of trying to justify why they thought they could kill anyone they wanted, the State blamed the unfortunate event on faulty software. This, the leaders felt, cleared the State of any wrongdoing.

It became routine for the State's goons to raid suspected Thinker strongholds, only to find a senior citizen's book club in progress. If any of the old people complained, a man twice their size either gassed them with pepper spray or tasered them until they were having seizures.

One of the State's death squads, ordered to use "maximum force" against a suspected internet hacker who was responsible for leaking the State's secrets, accidently gunned down a random mother and father while their two children looked on in horror. This was blamed on the existence of two different streets with the same name. As if that was all the justification the State needed for its behavior.

What the State didn't understand was that every time they gunned down a suspected radical they created two more. The man who saw his dog gunned down went from supporting the State to rooting for the Thinkers. The children who watched their parents slaughtered at the hands of a death squad would one day join the Thinkers. The neighbors of the family who watched a missile fly out of the sky and blow up a house would see what the State was capable of and stop believing what the Ruler said on television.

Eventually, Jessica's neighbor's door opened and the

men walked back into the hallway, never apologizing for forcing their way into the wrong home. They looked at the address in front of them, then knocked. With a deep breath, Jessica reached out and turned the knob.

"How can I help you?" she said as she opened her front door.

The two men stepped past her, into her apartment. The days of asking permission to enter were over; the State did whatever it wanted. One of the men immediately disappeared into her bedroom to look around. The other officer directed her to sit down on the sofa.

"What can you tell me about Isaac Barnhouse?" the officer asked once they were both seated.

"I saw on the news that he died in an apartment explosion yesterday."

"Yes," the man said, his brow furrowing. "We know that. That's not what we want to know."

"What would you like to know?"

"Have you been in contact with him since then?"

"Since he died in the apartment explosion?"

"Yes."

"How could I?"

The officer frowned, unsure of how to deal with the question. The State wanted to know the real whereabouts of the men who had disappeared, but their official story was that all of the Thinkers had died in the explosion. If the State's surveillance heard the officer admit the official story wasn't true, a different set of men could just as easily come for him.

"Just answer my question."

"No, I haven't been visited by a man who died in an explosion."

"What did you know about your boyfriend's acquaintances?"

"Not much. I'm sure you know more from all of your tracking. I just lived with him."

The man's jaw clenched, then he said, "And you haven't seen him since yesterday?"

"Since he died in the explosion?"

"Yes."

"No, I haven't."

It went on like this for a few minutes. Eventually, the other officer came back, satisfied that there was nothing of interest in the apartment. Later, she would discover that two pairs of her panties were gone. If that was all they took, she considered herself lucky.

Hopefully, she thought as she closed the door behind them, *that will be the last time I ever see them.*

And just like that, the State's men were gone.

She returned to the sofa, where she cried and laughed at the same time. She cried because the visit from the State's men made it official: Isaac was out of her life forever. Somehow, she would have to continue on without the person she most loved. But she laughed, too, because Isaac hadn't been in the basement when the explosion occurred. Not only that, he wasn't at one of the State's secret prisons or else the man in the suit wouldn't have been asking all those questions. It wouldn't make Isaac return to her life, but somewhere out there, the man she loved was still alive, still fighting against the State. After this visit, she was sure of it. And that made her laugh most of all.

39 - TO BE FOLLOWED OR NOT TO BE FOLLOWED

A series of nightmares kept Springfield whimpering and pleading through the night. In one dream, he was surrounded by fire while an unseen chorus sang beautifully sad music. At the same time, hands reached out of the darkness and tore flesh from his arms and legs. The flames were too high to jump over. The hands followed him wherever he went. No matter how much he cried, no one would come to help. The singers continued their melody as the hands ripped his skin away.

In another dream, he was tied to the ground while a pair of giant cyclops stood over him, arguing with one another over which would get to eat him. One of them kept flicking the piece of wood in Springfield's hand, annoyed that it was tainting an otherwise sumptuous meal. The other cyclops grumbled and banged two large stones in a series of loud clacks.

In the last nightmare, Springfield was standing in the same field he had first appeared at. The man in black never fell out of the sky. Something even worse happened, though: Springfield somehow knew that no matter what he did, rather than preventing the State, he would only make it worse. He saw it forming before he was ever born. Saw his father being taken away to a secret prison. Saw lines of men shot where they stood because it was quicker and easier to kill them than it was to pat them down and ask them questions. There was Jessica, brainwashed by all the propaganda she was raised on. Anything he did would only end up making their lives even more miserable, create an even more tyrannical and brutal monster.

When he woke up, he was once again lying in front of a small fire. But he was no longer in the field where he had been. Now, he was in what appeared to be a hut. The black smoke from the fire wafted out through a small hole in the roof. Someone was either asleep with their back against the hut, or they were watching him in the darkness of shadows. With only the small fire offering light, he couldn't tell if it was a man or a woman keeping an eye on him. Knowing that would at least tell him if he was a prisoner being guarded or a sick man being cared for.

The man in black would be there soon. The smoke rising in the air would be impossible to miss. The thought came to him that he should warn whoever was in the hut with him. If the assassin wasn't already there, planning his attack at the camp's edge, he would be soon. And when he did get there, there would be hell to pay. Probably, he would kill the entire tribe just for harboring a man who, in the future, would be considered his enemy. The villagers wouldn't have any way of knowing that was what they were supposedly doing. That wouldn't matter to the killer, however.

As much as Springfield wanted to warn the figure in the shadows, neither his lips nor his tongue would move. When he tried to sit up, his body wouldn't stir. There was nothing he could do but close his eyes again and hope that when he opened them next, the man in black wouldn't be standing over him.

He was close to sleep, in the grey area between sleep and consciousness. A wishful thought came to him that the man in black might be dead. Maybe the fall from the sky had been too far after all. Or maybe, because he jumped into the time portal instead of standing still, his body wouldn't function correctly. His organs would begin to fail and he would be found dead by the same tribe that had discovered Springfield.

Or maybe the man in black would somehow discover how far back in time they had been sent and would know that not only was there nothing Springfield could do to change the course of history, but that they were now just two men—two men who were more similar than they were different. Away from the world they had both known, they could become anything and anyone they wanted. With his survival skills in the wild, the assassin could live off the earth in peace and quiet. There were men who would like nothing more than that. However, Springfield doubted the mercenary would be one of them.

Springfield had met people who sympathized with the Thinkers, and he had known people who believed everything the State said. He had also spoken with people who were indifferent to both the Thinkers and the State and just wanted to live their life in peace and quiet. But he had never met a member of the Security Service, the State's private army. They were trained to look and act just like soldiers, but got paid twice as much to be twice as ruthless. He had the impression they were thoughtless machines, killers who were shown a series of faces by their handlers and told which ones to capture and which to kill.

It wouldn't mean anything to the mercenary if he was in a different time and place. A mission was a mission. Everywhere Springfield went, the man in black would be right behind him, trying to murder him. Finally, the man in black would kill him. He would end up just like the man who had gone back in time to stop John F. Kennedy's assassination.

40 – JFK

Kennedy wasn't originally supposed to be assassinated in Dallas. This is a fact. In a previous plot, the President was supposed to be shot in Chicago. When that attempt didn't work out, he was supposed to die in Tampa. Both times, even though men were in place, ready for an ambush, the plots fell apart at the last minute. It was only the third attempt, the one everybody knows about, that was finally successful.

The men who were involved in the Chicago and Tampa attempts offered a variety of reasons that their plans fell apart.

"A cop showed up," one of the men said. "Right before the President drove by, asking why I was in a building where I wasn't supposed to be."

Another rolled his eyes and said, "The room I was supposed to get set up in was locked. What are the chances that the same door I checked the previous day would have a deadbolt on it right before I needed to set up my rifle?"

Both men agreed that it was almost as if fate was trying to foil them, but conspiracy thinkers don't believe that at all. These people say the men who were hired to carry out the first two shootings weren't hindered by destiny—they were merely low-level thugs, not professionals, and that was why they bungled the hit. There are also people who believe some men are protected from above. But even protected men can only be saved so many times before not even the heavens can keep them alive. These are the people who think it wasn't a coincidence at all that the cop arrested one of the shooters for being where he wasn't supposed to be, and another was kept from his vantage point by the unexplained appearance of a deadbolt; God or fate or whatever people wanted to call it was protecting the President.

The Thinkers know something else, though. They realize the Chicago and Tampa attempts had nothing to do with fate or hitmen who weren't up to the mission. What they know is that one of their time travelers saved the President on two different occasions, only to fail the third time. They surmise that the Theta Timeline originally had JFK dying in Chicago. The nation watched in horror as grainy footage of the President's motorcade showed him being shot, not near the grassy knoll and the book depository in Dallas, but two blocks away from Wrigley Field. But then a Thinker caused a timeline shift and the footage changed.

There were supposed to be four gunmen set up in abandoned factories in Chicago, just like there were in the later attempts. Each assassin would be positioned along the motorcade route, which they knew ahead of time even though it was supposed to be a closely guarded secret. But then the phone rang at the police station—the Thinker alerting them that suspicious-looking men were up to no good. The President's motorcade was able to pass through the city without incident. In some other timeline, Kennedy still died in Chicago, but in the Theta Timeline, he left the city in perfect health.

The plotters, unsuccessful in their first attempt, began making plans for how they could assassinate him at the next stop in his journey. Once again, four shooters were positioned along the route that Kennedy's motorcade would take, this time in sunny Tampa. But once again, someone called local authorities and alerted them to suspicious men carrying what looked like rifles into warehouses and factories. Some of the empty warehouses were deadbolted shut. A string of people—all of whom had ties to the CIA and the mafia—were detained by the police, but all were eventually let go. Although the second attempt also failed, there is another a timeline out there in which the President died in Tampa. Because of a time traveler, though, it's not the reality we are aware of.

The men involved with the third attempt, the one that would end up being successful, were all later quoted as saying they had to pack their bags and rush off to Dallas with little warning. The powers that wanted Kennedy dead never thought the first two attempts would fail and they were desperate to kill him as soon as possible.

This hastily planned mission was successful, but failed in its secondary objective to support the official lone-shooter scenario. If the men had the same amount of time they were used to having to prepare for their kills, they could have carried out the mission without leaving any clues as to what had really happened. They would have found a way to limit the number of witnesses who contradicted the lone-gunman theory, and they would have been able to carry out the killing without making it obvious that a single shooter could never have made all the shots on his own. In short, they wouldn't have made it so obvious that the official story was flawed.

Rushed or not, though, JFK was removed from power. Our Theta Timeline shifted from him being assassinated in Chicago, then to being shot in Tampa, to finally shifting one last time to Dallas—the location we now take for historical fact.

What happened to the time traveler who managed to prevent the shootings in Illinois and Florida? Why couldn't he prevent the Texas shooting as well? Somewhere along the way, between Tampa and Dallas, something must have happened to him. Maybe the people behind the assassination attempts were able to track down his phone calls to the police. After getting a description of the caller, they would have been on the lookout for him. His body likely ended up in an alligator-filled swamp outside Tampa. Or perhaps his body was found the day after Kennedy's death, in a dumpster two blocks away from the book depository.

Either way, the time traveler was unable to prevent the third shooting and Kennedy subsequently died. It's likely that even if the Thinker had prevented the third shooting, there would have been a fourth attempt, a week later, in Ohio. And if that one had also been foiled, another attempt would have been scheduled the week after that, in Massachusetts. The time traveler would have spent every waking moment following JFK, always on the lookout for men lurking in the shadows.

There's no way of knowing how long the President's assassins would have organized failed attempts before Kennedy finally realized there were powerful men who wanted him dead. Maybe it wouldn't have mattered even if Kennedy had known they were out to get him. Ultimately, the time traveler delayed the event that he had been sent to stop, but he couldn't prevent it from happening all together. Our current Theta Timeline is proof of that.

What point is there? Springfield thought, barely conscious. *Even if I do something that changes our history, the State will still find a way to take power.*

And with that, he passed out again. The same nightmares he had been experiencing since being sent back in time immediately started haunting him once more.

41 - NOT A DEMON, JUST A MAN

It was already light out by the time Springfield was able to prop himself up on one elbow and think clearly again. His head no longer ached and the world didn't seem to spin when he turned to inspect his surroundings. Even the sunlight, which he expected to hurt his eyes, was a welcome sign.

Most of the ground was smooth dirt, but underneath him was a thin bed of grass, compacted together to offer a tiny amount of cushion. Maybe that was also the tribe's way of repelling ants. The walls surrounding him looked like a combination of mud, clay, leaves, and twigs.

Most of the sunlight was coming through the same small hole in the roof that had allowed the smoke to drift up into the sky. Additional light sneaked through a flap that served as the door. The flap, partially open, also allowed a morning breeze to wash over him. The cool air against his lips reminded him how thirsty he was, but searching the hut's floor, he found no trace of his bag or the water pouch that had been inside.

The thought returned that he might be a prisoner. If they found him in the fields outside their village, they might have mistaken him for an invading army's scout. Of course, no scout would be dumb enough to sleep on an ant mound, out in the open, but he couldn't rule out the possibility they considered him a threat.

The light from the entrance dimmed. When he looked up, he saw someone leaning inside to check on him. When the tribesman saw Springfield was awake and sitting up, he yelled in a language the time traveler didn't understand.

I'm fluent in English, French, Arabic, Russian, and Mandarin, Springfield thought. *But of course I have no idea what this guy is saying.*

If he stood up straight, he would poke through the top of the roof and ruin their shelter. Instead, he pushed himself to both feet, bent over like a hunchback, and shuffled out into the daylight.

The incomprehensible yelling resumed. He had no idea what the word meant, but he could tell from the way the guard held a three-meter long staff toward his face, its metal blade almost touching his cheek, that the man was not telling him a joke. Just that fast, Springfield forgot he was thirsty. After living through a shootout, an explosion, and a swarm of ants, he had no desire to die from a misunderstanding. He did what it seemed the guard was telling him to do: he stopped right where he stood. The warrior's spear was long enough that even from yards away, the metal tip was only inches from Springfield's face. Although no larger than a razor blade, the spear's point could split him open from throat to belly.

He raised both hands, palms facing out, to show he meant no harm, but this only enraged the tribesman even more. The warrior screamed at him again as he moved the spear's blade from Springfield's mouth to the hollow of his neck.

"Okay, okay," he said, and slowly sat back on the ground.

By this time, there was yelling all over the camp. Several tribesmen had emerged from their huts to see what was happening. Some carried spears similar to the one being leveled at Springfield, while others carried knives. A group of women and children spied the proceedings from the corner of a far hut. At least they weren't aiming weapons at him too, he thought. But when he looked in their direction, they ducked out of sight and the angry warrior stepped between Springfield and the spot he had been looking at.

Three more warriors joined the first. The four men circled Springfield, each with his spear constantly held at the time traveler's head or neck. Strangely enough, they did not seem any less aggressive toward him now that he was on the ground with his hands held out toward them. They seemed to expect him to put up a fight, even though he had just woke up from a long illness and was sitting—unarmed—on his ass.

No amount of learning history, reading classic literature, and keeping up on world politics could have prepared him for a confrontation with four warriors who wanted to kill him for no discernable reason. There was nothing he could do other than show them he meant no harm, but each time he held his hands out to them, it seemed to fuel their fury.

As the four men whispered in their native tongue, probably debating whether they should get it over with and slice him apart, an old man called to them. Reluctantly, the four warriors took a step back. Then another. The old man said something else and each warrior lowered his spear. They remained there, letting the old man walk between them so he was right in front of Springfield. Each tribesman had only taken two paces back, but with their long spears now lowered, Springfield realized each man was more than ten feet away.

"I don't mean any harm," Springfield said, but the old man only frowned.

The guards seemed to take these words as threats because each of them gripped his weapon tighter.

"*Je ne veux pas dire du mal,*" he said in French. Still no reaction from the man.

He tried again in Mandarin. Nothing.

Then in Russian.

175

The old man nodded.

"*Bbi nohnmaete?*" Springfield asked. *You understand?*

The old man nodded again and replied in Russian steeped in a thick accent Springfield couldn't identify. "They think you demon."

The man was missing most of his teeth, and the ones he still had were yellow and small. His lips were covered with more wrinkles than Springfield had ever seen before. That, along with the man's diminutive size, made him seem much older than he probably was.

Springfield couldn't help but break into a big smile upon hearing words he could actually understand.

Again, in Russian: "Why do they think I'm a demon?"

The old man pointed to his own palm, then to Springfield's hand. It was only then that the time traveler remembered the branch sticking out of his hand. He touched it now, instinctively, and was shocked to find that it no longer protruded out of either side of his skin. It was smooth. Someone, while he had been unconscious, must have sanded it down. The piece of wood was still in the middle of his palm, but it was now flush with his hand so that if his eyes were closed, he would only know which part was his flesh and which part was wood by the absence of sensation.

"Not a demon," Springfield said. "Just a man."

The old man nodded and translated his guest's Russian into the language that everyone else in the tribe understood. Everyone gathered around to hear what the old man had to say.

The warriors didn't seem convinced. They let their spears touch the ground, but none of them loosed their grip on their weapons. And none of them took their eyes off the time traveler in case he made a sudden move.

"How did tree in hand?" the old man asked, pointing to Springfield's palm.

"It's a very long story," he said and smiled.

The old man smiled back. "I have much time."

The two men spoke in broken Russian. Springfield

didn't ask where he was in the world. Nor did he ask what year it was. These were the two things he wanted to know more than anything else, but instead he asked the old man about himself and his village.

42 - WHAT TO DO AND WHAT NOT TO DO

The Thinkers were smart enough to realize that if they went back in time without any forethought as to how they should act once they got there, they would end up dead, or worse, in an insane asylum.

They wear plain burlap pants and shirts because it's the most generic outfit they could come up with, allowing them the best chance to fit in with other societies throughout the world, regardless of when they appear in time. Something else might make them stand out, though: their questions.

The time traveler doesn't automatically know what year he reappears in. He has to find out somehow. But how would people react to a man who walks up and asks what year it is? If a newspaper isn't readily available how else is he supposed to find out where he is in history? No one would be blamed for calling the police if they were approached by a man wearing burlap rags who wanted to know what decade he had been transported to. Surely, in modern society, such a person would be declared incompetent. The time traveler would risk his life to stop the State, be lucky enough to survive the reappearance, only to spend the rest of his life in a padded room.

To prevent that, the Thinkers came up with the

following rules:

1. *Do not ask anyone what year it is.* This is the easiest way to let people know you aren't where you belong or don't have all of your marbles. Instead, get them talking about current events until you can figure out what broad period of history you are in. Thinkers, by their very nature, are historians—you can't appreciate the world you live in and know if it's better or worse than previous generations unless you know your history. So ask questions, learn what key events have just occurred, and then go from there.

2. *Do not ask where you are.* This is only slightly less alarming to people than being asked what year it is. Instead, figure out what language people are speaking in order to narrow down the possibilities of where you might be. Look at landmarks and styles of architecture. Pay attention to the laws of the land to see what type of government the people follow.

3. *Do not wear clothes that make you stand out.* This is why time travelers are transported in burlap shirts and pants. Granted, you don't see anyone walking around New York City wearing burlap clothes, but the outfit can easily be confused for the rags a vagrant might wear. The possibility of being confused for a homeless man in modern society is better than appearing in the seventeenth century in blue jeans and a fancy shirt. No amount of lying would convince people that you belonged there. But likewise, if you are only sent back fifty years in time wearing something outlandish like a Civil War uniform, you might as well save the police the time and energy and send yourself to the mental hospital. If you appear in the Gobi desert, it doesn't matter if you are wearing blue jeans or a suit, no one would risk their own life in the scorching wasteland to help a stranger wearing odd clothes. You would die of dehydration in your fancy outfit.

Plain clothes, preferably simple material (unless you are departing from above 50 N latitude and need something heavier) are the most universally accepted outfits a time traveler can wear.

4. *Do not take any materials back in time with you unless they*

have been pre-approved. Scientists are still trying to determine what materials can pass safely in the time machine and which cannot. So far, the list of items that cannot be sent into the antimatter portal include anything metallic, but especially electronics of any nature. Advanced polymers and anything emitting a radioactive signature, even at levels safe for human exposure, can also react strangely with the antimatter machine and affect whether a time traveler appears safely in the past.

5. *Do not travel back in time if you are sick.* The Bubonic Plague has already been mentioned. Poor Charlestown had no idea his virus would turn him into history's greatest killer; he was only concerned with trying to prevent the State. But there is also the story of King Tut's tomb.

For a long time, people thought the tomb was cursed because everyone who went in eventually died of a mysterious sickness. It wasn't until researchers, wearing chem suits with breathing masks, went in and took air samples that they realized there wasn't a curse at all. The tomb was filled with germs that man hadn't been exposed to yet. A time traveler had been there. Inside the tomb, his germs had thousands of years to mutate with the germs of the time. The result was a new strand of super-germ. The immune systems of the people entering the long-sealed tomb, couldn't defend against the modified viruses. And so "the curse" killed them.

The bottom line? If you don't feel well, don't go back in time.

43 – CHETNIK

"My name Chetnik," the old man said as best as he could in his accented Russian.

"Springfield," Isaac said, patting himself on the chest.

Conversations between them were not easy. Every once in a while, Springfield would say something and the old man would look completely baffled as if his guest had randomly added in a comment about his mother. It was very possible, after not polishing up his Russian for so many years, that Springfield was confusing his consonants and changing the meaning of what he was trying to say. It only takes a slight pronunciation mistake to turn "I come in peace," into "I roam in meats."

It was also possible, as much as he didn't want it to be, that he was so far back in time that Chetnik's Russian was the equivalent to old English, technically the same language that Springfield was speaking, but vastly different over the centuries.

Using a combination of words and gestures, though, the men were able to understand each other for the most part. It took a while for the four warriors who had been circling Springfield to put down their spears and go about their business around the village, but they eventually did.

He learned that the old man spoke not only the local tribe's language and Russian, but a third language as well. The third, like the first, was unknown to Springfield, but it sounded vaguely similar to Arabic. Chetnik offered what Springfield guessed was a greeting in each of the three languages. In turn, Springfield said hello in Russian, then English, French, Arabic, and Mandarin.

Chetnik, it turned out, had been the trader for the tribe before growing weak in his old age. When other tribes or travelers came through the area looking to buy and sell their goods, Chetnik helped negotiate fair prices and quantities for both sides. Over the years, the role had exposed him to various languages.

"You trader also?" Chetnik said, trying to determine why Springfield might be in the area.

"Not trader," Springfield said. "Traveler."

"Traveler?"

Another word that Chetnik had never been exposed to before; someone who moved from place to place for no better reason than they could.

"I journey."

But the old man had no concept of what this meant. He was familiar with other groups arriving at their village and then disappearing, but for him, when someone went from one place to another, it was to survive or to exchange something they had for something they didn't have. For a man who spent his entire life with his tribe in the exact same spot on Earth, sightseeing was an idea Chetnik could not fathom.

"Hand what happen?" Chetnik said, pointing to Springfield's palm and to the piece of wood that was now smooth against his skin.

Springfield thought about all the possible things he could say. From the way the warriors reacted to the wood in his hand, it was obvious he needed a good explanation.

"Bad man did this to me," he said.

Chetnik's response was not what Springfield thought

it would be. He expected the man to be concerned about some mystical villain who could somehow insert parts of the earth into his victim's bodies. But Chetnik was more confused than anything else. The old man reached over and took Springfield's hand between his own fingers, then asked how a man could do that to someone else without causing any blood or injury.

He flipped Springfield's palm over and pointed to the other side as well, saying, *"Het Tpabmbi,"*—*no injury*—over and over.

"The man is evil," Springfield said. "He can hurt you in ways other men cannot."

The old man accepted this in silence, nodding with sadness.

"Many men can make great evil. Very sad."

"Yes," the time traveler said. "That's very true."

As he sat with Chetnik, watching men and women happy to chop wood, cook food over open fires, and weave clothes and baskets, he began to appreciate the simplicity of their way of life. He briefly entertained the idea of becoming part of the tribe, living out the rest of his days with these uncomplicated people. In a few years, his hand would be completely healed—the piece of wood having been covered by skin or rejected by his body. Only a scar would remind him of what he had gone through before arriving at this place. The same four warriors who had thought him dangerous and wanted to strike him down would each laugh with him at the memory of how threatened they had been by a simple stick. It would be a happy life. Sitting in the grass with Chetnik, it was the best life he could possibly imagine for himself.

Just as quickly, though, that image was replaced by the man in black coming into the village, finding Springfield and killing him, then killing everyone else as well for no better reason than they had nursed an enemy of the State back to health.

"I need to warn you," Springfield said. "The bad man

may still be looking for me. If he comes this way, he won't stop until he finds me and kills me."

Chetnik shook his head in acknowledgement, but did not seem concerned. Springfield thought the old man would be more alarmed at the thought of dark magic and demons taking the shape of men. Maybe the old man had confidence that his warriors could handle anyone or anything that came close. Or perhaps Chetnik's dealings with so many other groups of travelers had shown him that people were generally kind no matter who they were or where they came from. Interacting with various types of people had made the trader more accepting of the differences between cultures, whereas the younger warriors had yet to see much outside their village and were troubled by things they didn't understand.

"Aren't you worried?" Springfield asked the grinning little man. "This evil person, he is very dangerous. No one is safe."

Chetnik gave a polite chuckle.

"Warriors," the wrinkled man said simply, pointing to where four men had circled Springfield, eager for permission to cut him down.

He thought to argue, to insist that the man in black's ability to kill was better and more vicious than anything Chetnik might have seen before. Not wanting to irritate his host, however, he remained silent.

That was when Chetnik pointed at one of the tribesmen, who was walking from one hut to another, and said, "Hunter find you in field."

It took Springfield a moment to realize Chetnik was pointing to the member of his tribe who had found Springfield as he lay sick in the middle of nowhere and had saved his life.

"How did he find me?"

"He say you dance and yell like crazy man."

He must have seen me when I was wiping the ants off my face, Springfield thought. But what he said was, "How long had he been watching me?"

"You pass other village," Chetnik said.

The old man marked a circle in the dirt, then held his hands up in the air to signify the circle represented the village. Then he drew another line roughly corresponding to a stream Springfield had been following and two more circles further downstream.

"You pass two other villages."

"That's not possible," Springfield said. "I didn't see any houses or people."

The old man smiled. "Villages make look like earth. You walk past two different. Hunter follows."

Springfield groaned. He had been in what he considered to be a life or death situation, looking for any sign of other people, of any sign of human life at all, and he had walked right past two other sets of huts. If the future of the world depended on his ability to make his way out of the wilderness, everyone would end up with one of the State's blasters at their head.

"Warrior find wood in hand. Think you demon. Want to cut."

As if to clarify, Chetnik gestured with an invisible knife. However, instead of simulating cutting the branch out of Springfield's hand, he pretended to cut Springfield's heart out of his chest. After all, that would be the sensible way to kill a demon. It had been sheer luck that Springfield's last conscious moment hadn't been waking up with a warrior's knife in his chest.

"I'm glad he didn't," Springfield said, rubbing his palm again. "I was just sick."

"Very sick," Chetnik agreed. "Some wood poison to man. You lucky." Then, pointing to the smooth piece of wood remaining in Springfield's hand, added, "Not poison that kind."

Maybe luck was with him after all. He easily could have appeared next to a different type of tree, one that was toxic to humans. The veins in his hand would have become enlarged and purple before ultimately turning black. Necrotic flesh would have engulfed his hand and made it look like he was wearing a dark leather glove. The rot would have created an ungodly stench, spread up his arm until he died from sepsis. Yes, the piece of wood in his hand was annoying, but at least his body didn't seem to care that it was there.

"Thank you for sanding it down," he told Chetnik.

"Sand?"

"Make smooth," he said, and the old man understood this.

"The less evil in you, the better."

Springfield agreed.

Chetnik once again took Springfield's hand between his own and lightly rubbed his fingers from flesh to wood and back again, the way children would when fascinated with something new.

The old man gave a light chuckle before saying, "Even after save life, warriors want hand off."

To illustrate the point, Chetnik offered a chopping motion that let Springfield know he was lucky to still have the hand at all.

The tribe's leader added, "Good-feel-man think different. He say open hole allow more demons inside."

"That's probably true," Springfield said, not because he was mocking Chetnik or the tribe's beliefs, but because an open wound of that size would allow the invisible demons that Springfield knew—bacteria—to get into his hand and make him deathly ill.

It wasn't preferable to have a piece of wood in the middle of his palm, but at least having it there meant he didn't have an infected wound.

"What you do now?" Chetnik said.

"What?"

"What you do? Where you go?"

"Oh, that. Begin traveling again. Keep walking."

He thought to ask Chetnik for a map, but he knew that if the man understood Russian the last direction he would want to continue walking was east. The next thought caused his lungs to struggle for air. His hands started shaking.

If he needed to be walking west, he would have to go back in the direction he had just come. It didn't discourage him that he would have to retrace all the miles he had walked. No, he trembled because walking west would mean he would have to walk toward the place he had last seen the man in black.

The thought was so unappealing that he actually considered continuing east until he got to the Russian or Chinese coast. He would have to find a way across the Pacific Ocean before his mission could start in earnest. This didn't make sense because the mountains he had seen during his hike probably were the Himalayas after all. He would never make it through the range alive. He was just scared and fear was making him think the wrong options were the right ones.

Only then did he remember the canvas bag with his supplies.

"Did the warrior carry my bag too?"

Chetnik nodded and looked over toward one of the small huts near the middle of the village. Maybe Chetnik's home.

"I give back," the old man said, standing up.

And with that, Chetnik brushed the dirt off his legs, and walked to the hut where Springfield's bag had been stowed for safekeeping. Left alone, Springfield watched the women and children doing their daily chores. Everyone seemed perfectly content. Half the children would probably die before they were teenagers. The tribe probably didn't eat much on the days the hunters couldn't catch food. Yet none of this seemed to matter to any of them. Other than being scared that a strange man had appeared with what seemed to be a tree demon growing out of his hand, they seemed completely carefree.

He thought again of remaining there and making a life for himself. There were no AeroCams recording everything he did and said. There was no fear that doing or saying the wrong thing would earn him the label of traitor. He would never have to see someone he loved scream in terror as the State's men dragged them away. But it was the same voice that had told him to walk east if that meant he could avoid the mercenary that was now telling him he could quit hiking and stay where he was. That voice was not to be heeded. That voice would lead to one thing and one thing only: Springfield letting down his parents and Jessica, the people he loved more dearly than anyone else, the people he needed to save.

Chetnik returned with the bag.

"Everything here still," the old man said, and Springfield nodded without checking its contents.

"What do now?" Chetnik asked.

The time traveler thought about asking for food or water to take with him. But he already knew there was a stream along his route and the filtered water pouch would provide him with all the water he needed. Anyway, whatever food they gave him would spoil before he had a chance to eat it.

"I go now," he replied. "Before the evil man finds me here."

Chetnik frowned. "Evil man come here, then warriors."

But even if the warriors were able to kill the man in black, they wouldn't be able to do so before losing a good number of their own men. The entire tribe would be weakened and it would be Springfield's fault.

But just then, right as Springfield was standing and stretching his cramped legs, a man ran over to Chetnik, yelled a series of words, then ran off. A group of men gathered at one of the huts. Each retrieved a long spear and slapped each other's chests.

"What's going on?" Springfield asked.

Chetnik turned back to his guest. "Village," he said, pointing to the circle in the dirt representing the first village Springfield had passed. "Destroyed. Everyone dead." Then he pointed to the second circle, the closer village, and added, "Under war. All dying."

"Under attack? By who?"

Chetnik looked off in the distance as if he was going to cry, then said, "Alone man. All black." Then he walked away.

Springfield was left there, by himself, to think about exactly what that meant.

44 - PARENTS OF A TRAITOR

Isaac's parents were prepared for the knock when it sounded at their door. From the pair of recliners they almost always sat on, they looked at each other, took a combined breath, then glanced at the framed photo of their son which still hung on the living room wall. Isaac's father stood and went to the door. There was no point to looking through the peephole; they knew it would be the Security Service.

"Hello," he said to the two men dressed in suits and standing on his welcome mat.

Uncomfortable with niceties, one of the men answered with a barely audible "hello" of his own. Neither man waited to be invited inside. Both were already approaching the recliners as Isaac's father closed the door behind them.

"Do you gentlemen have a search warrant?" he said, much too softly for either man to actually hear; he didn't want to ruin a nice day by being taken to prison.

One of the men waited in the living room, in between the recliner that Isaac's mother was still sitting in and the empty one that his father would soon reclaim. The second man had already vanished, off to their bedroom or anywhere else he wanted to go.

"Judy Barnhouse?" the man said to Isaac's mother.

"Yes."

"And George Barnhouse?"

"Yes. How can we help you?" Isaac's father said.

The man frowned, not liking the fact that he had been asked a question, even if it had been rhetorical and merely to show good manners.

"Have you heard from your son since Thursday?"

"I don't understand," Judy said. "He was in the explosion. How could we hear from him?"

The State's man squinted, then chuckled. He hadn't asked a dumb question. It was the Thinker's mother who showed her stupidity by answering the way she did.

There was no look that could keep a mother from asking about her son, though. If her boy was alive, she needed to know: "He wasn't in the building? Is he alive? The news said he was killed in the blast."

George leaned over and put a hand on her arm. With that single touch, she went silent.

"You do realize I'm the one asking the questions, right?" the agent said.

That was when George realized the man had never given them his name. Neither had the agent upstairs. Not a good sign.

"You monitor everything we do and say," George told the man. "Surely you know we haven't talked to him."

"Of course we know that," the Security Services agent said, amazed at the asinine things average citizens said.

But the agent and the time traveler's parents were at the same impasse Jessica had come to. The man wasn't allowed to admit that their son's body hadn't been recovered from the sub-basement. That would be admitting that the official story wasn't true, and would be reason enough for the State to suspect the agent of being against them.

The man repeated his question: "Have you had contact with your son since Thursday or not?"

Judy leaned forward. George held his breath.

"No," she said. "We haven't seen our son, who was blown up in a building on Thursday, since Thursday."

The agent leaned forward and wrapped his hand around her throat. He didn't choke her, he merely wrapped his giant fingers around her neck and let them rest there. There would be no marks, but it immediately worked in shutting her up, let her know he could crush her windpipe and get away with it.

"There's no need for that," her husband told the agent. Then, to his wife, he said, "It'll be okay, Judy. Everything will be all right."

The agent's hand returned to his side.

"You folks are lucky we don't take you in and charge you as being Thinkers."

"What would make you think we might be?" George said.

"Your son was one. He had to learn it from somewhere."

Neither of Isaac's parents said anything. The beauty of claiming an invisible enemy was that anyone, with a single word, could also become that enemy.

The agent said, "Have you ever heard him use the alias 'Springfield'?"

"Springfield?"

"Yes," the man in the suit said.

"Like the town?"

"Yes."

"No," his father said. "Our son was never big on nicknames."

The State's man flinched. Just that, the father of a Thinker belittling the little bit of intelligence they did have, was almost enough for the agent to knock George silly.

But just then, the second man came back with his hands empty. "Nothing."

Isaac's parents might discover some money missing from their dresser, perhaps a piece of jewelry gone, but at least they could be fairly certain that Judy's underwear would be left alone. If they did notice that money or jewelry were missing and they were dumb enough to report it, they were sure it would be these same two men who would return to file the report. And when they did, the agent who had wrapped his hand around Judy's throat wouldn't be so kind.

The first agent stared at both of Isaac's parents for another few seconds, eyeing both of their faces as if imagining how nice they would look with broken noses and black eyes, then said, "If you hear from your son, contact us immediately."

The State was always watching and listening—the comment was merely to remind them that being proactive was the difference between receiving the State's sympathy for being the unfortunate parents of a dirty Thinker, or being viewed as Thinkers themselves.

The pair of agents left, leaving the front door open behind them. Isaac's parents remained seated, staring at each other in silence. Neither of them said it, but they knew they were both having the same thought: if their son had been a Thinker like the State said he was, they had never been more proud of him than they were at that moment. Someone needed to stand up to what was happening.

45 – MADNESS

Everywhere Springfield looked, people were darting from one hut to another. A little girl, by herself at the edge of the village, wiped tears from her eyes, until a young man, maybe her brother, picked her up and carried her to the arms of a woman who was wider than she was tall. Once he saw that the girl was quiet and protected, the man grabbed a spear and joined a group of warriors who were assembling by the far huts. A horn, crafted to sound like a bird's call, trumpeted through the village. Three women, all with thinning and uncombed hair, looked on with fear while their younger counterparts organized supplies for the warriors. Chetnik stood and watched the entire scene without comment.

If there was something Springfield could have done to help them, he would have. He doubted, however, they would want his help even if they needed it. Instead, he stood and watched the village's response just like Chetnik.

The thought crossed his mind that he should leave the village as quickly as possible, just start running and not look back. But unless he wanted to run toward the Pacific Ocean, exactly the opposite direction he needed to go, he would run right into the man in black.

Chetnik was staring at him. Not at him exactly, but at

his hands. That was when Springfield realized he had been running his fingers over the smooth piece of wood in his palm. Did Chetnik see the injury now and wish the hunter had cut Springfield's heart out after all? Did he see the stick and begin to believe that the time traveler was the demon that his people had suspected him of being? The old man frowned and returned to watching the warriors assemble before heading off to combat.

People were rushing this way and that. Everything seemed to be happening in a blur. Inside the sub-basement, everything had seemed to take place in slow motion when he had been the one to face the explosions and gunfire. Even as the steel door had exploded off its hinges, as mercenaries in full body armor rushed in and began gunning down his co-conspirators, everything had seemed to happen at a crawl. Why, as he faced the assault blasters, had time seemed to almost stand still, devoid of sound and smell, while the exact opposite occurred when a group of villagers that he had never met before readied themselves to face death? Except for the infernal humming, the basement had seemed quiet. Now, all around him, noises clashed with each other. A woman, watching her son holding his spear, moaned with sorrow. Children cried. The campfire crackled. A goat bleated. And the smells. Burning wood. Animal feces. Cooked meat. Where had all of the equivalent smells been when he was against the concrete wall, getting ready to be sent back in time?

The only commonality between the basement and the chaos around him now was that in both situations he hadn't moved from where he stood. In the basement, he had credited his firm stance to his devotion to the mission. His life was of small importance if it meant the world could be saved from the State. That was why he had stood in place even as Sterling's and Trenton's faces exploded. And it was why he would have remained standing there and let the man in black tackle him if he hadn't disappeared first. It had been proof that he was dedicated to the mission. But now, standing in the exact same paralyzed fashion, in a village that had nothing at all to do with saving the world, he knew his actions back in the basement had to be called into question.

It wasn't because he was saving the world that he hadn't moved from his spot within the glowing oval tubes. He had been frozen in place because he was overwhelmed, and when he was overwhelmed, fear had overtaken him. Deep down, he still knew the mission was more important than his life or anyone else's life, but that idea hadn't been the glue under his feet, holding him in place as his fellow time travelers were either disappearing or being gunned down. It was terror. Terror had crippled him then and it controlled him now.

It was only when Chetnik came over and put a hand on Springfield's shoulder that he snapped out of his stupor. At the same time, his fingers fell away from the wood in his palm. All but two of the warriors disappeared in the direction of the village that was under attack.

The two who had been told to remain behind and guard the huts looked like they wanted to take their anger out on Springfield. One of them stared at the time traveler while sharpening the blade of his spear. The other muttered what Springfield assumed were the worst words someone could be called in their language.

Springfield went to the farthest corner of the village and withdrew a protein bar from his canvas bag. The polite thing to do would have been to offer one to Chetnik as well, but he had a limited supply and the sticky food, unlike anything the old man had eaten before, would probably pull out the last of his teeth.

When he finished the snack, he tossed the wrapper in the nearest campfire, remaining there to ensure the flames destroyed any evidence that he had ever been there. It was then, as the wrapper's embers turned to ash, that a woman called out. The warriors had disappeared toward the southeast, but the woman was pointing to the northeast.

On the horizon, a lone figure was approaching. Not a

group of people, not the warriors returning after a false alarm, but a single person dressed from head to toe in black armor. Even someone like Springfield, without any tactical experience, could guess that the man in black had planned it this way all along. He had known that a fire at the other villages would be reason for reinforcements to be sent. Circling wide, he could remain hidden in the brush, without being seen, until most of the warriors were gone.

Upon seeing him, the village's women disappeared into huts. Chetnik stayed out in the open, but shuffled further back so he wouldn't be in the warriors' way.

The man in black held one of the long spears that Springfield had seen so much of since arriving in the village. As the assassin approached, sunlight glared off the spear's blade, giving it the appearance of possessing special powers. With his normal allotment of weapons, the mercenary could have remained on the hills and picked off each villager one by one with his assault blaster. With only a spear, he would need to be more intimate with the people he was going to kill.

The weapon had no doubt been gathered from an unsuspecting warrior in one of the other villages. Without the first villagers knowing a threat was nearby, it would have been easy for the man in black to wait until it was dark, then sneak into the village, killing its warriors in silence, using their knives and spears against them. Only then would the assassin set fire to the huts. As reinforcements approached, he could simply sneak away and know to expect fewer men at the next set of huts.

This suspicion was reinforced by the smile that flashed across the man in black's face when he saw that only two warriors were walking toward him. The assassin actually laughed and clapped his hands as if two opponents was the punch line to a joke.

Twenty feet away from the pair of guards, the man in black stopped and let them come to him. They did exactly as he wanted. As they approached, the man in black scanned the village for his true target. When he spotted Springfield at the far edge of the huts, he laughed even harder.

The first warrior lunged with his spear while the second moved to circle behind the enemy. The man in black shuffled backward too, refusing to let either of the warriors out of his sight. The next thrust of the warrior's spear came down hard in an arc, the blade impacting with a crack against the assassin's forearm. For the briefest moment, the warrior paused, happy with the damage his strike must have delivered. Pride is not a recent invention. The warrior had defeated the demon! He had defended his village! The other warriors had left him behind and now he was the one who would earn all of the glory. And it had been so easy. But then, when he tried to withdraw his spear from the demon's arm, he realized the blade was stuck.

Springfield knew what had happened. The blade wasn't lodged in the man in black's arm, it was embedded in the advanced synthetic armor the mercenary was wearing. Maybe the blade had impacted hard enough to give the man in black a small cut on his forearm. Definitely not, as the warrior had first suspected, a serious wound.

But before Springfield could yell this information to save the warrior—as if it would have mattered since Chetnik would have had to translate everything, a lengthy process in the middle of battle—the man in black lunged with his own spear, driving it through the warrior's stomach. The assassin pushed with so much force that the spear burst through the warrior's back, driving him downward and stabbing the dirt beneath him. Pinned to the earth, his panic-stricken face pointed toward the sun as the life drained from him. The warrior, as he lay dying, tried to push himself up from the ground. Even as he struggled to breathe, his fingers scrabbled at the dirt beneath him. Finally, the defeated warrior's hands stopped moving and his body became motionless.

The man in black did not have time to celebrate his victory. The other warrior's spear came down with enough speed to make the air whistle. The blade sliced off the tip of the demon's ear before lodging itself in the armor protecting his collarbone.

Learning from what he had just seen, the second warrior did not try to yank his spear free from the demon's shoulder. Instead, he reached to his hip for his knife. The man in black gave an angry growl. The first warrior's spear was still attached to his forearm. With his own spear holding the dead warrior to the ground, he yanked out the one from his arm and used it as his new weapon.

With only one warrior left, the man in black no longer needed to backpedal. Instead, he lunged forward and, grinning, swung the spear back and forth as the warrior retreated from the longer weapon.

The man in black wound up and swung the spear as hard as he could. The warrior met the swing with his puny knife. But instead of deflecting the blow, the weapon was thrown to the side and the spear drove into the warrior's arms without slowing. One of the warrior's forearms bent grotesquely where bone broke through the skin. The other forearm was sliced open, blood spraying everywhere.

In shock, the warrior looked at the red liquid all around him and at the bone sticking out of his forearm where nothing but skin should be visible. The man in black had as much time as he wanted to take the final step forward and end the contest.

Another man, young and muscular, came out of nowhere and tackled the man in black. Once they were on the ground, Springfield could see that it wasn't a man at all but a boy who was probably not considered old enough to be an official warrior yet.

The young attacker's courage was admirable, but as soon as they were both on the ground, the man in black was able to duck under one of the young tribesman's arms and ended up on the boy's back. The assassin's arms circled the teenager's neck before the other could put his hands up. Only seconds later, the boy was unconscious. But even then, the man in black refused to let go of the choke. A minute later, the boy was not only unconscious, but dead.

He pushed the young body off himself, retrieved the nearest knife, and faced the second warrior once more. The injured man, his arms mangled, was on the ground, crying at the extent of his injuries. Springfield suspected the warrior wasn't crying because he was going to die or because he was in pain, but because he had let down the rest of the village; the man in black was now free to kill as many women and children as he wanted. The assassin stepped toward the warrior, rolled his eyes at the lack of dignity he was seeing, then drew the knife across the man's throat. The crying was replaced by gurgling and then that, too, was replaced by silence.

With both warriors dead, the man in black looked for anyone else who might be of interest. Particularly the time traveler.

He did not spot Springfield's head poking out from behind the far shacks where he had been when the fighting started. As quickly as he could, Springfield had moved to the trees at the far edge of the village. There, he would be out of sight. It didn't even enter his mind to confront the man in black; there was no resistance he could offer and he would be dead before he could do anything. The Theta Timeline would never be shifted. And after Springfield was dead, the assassin would still kill the women and children simply because he wouldn't want to stop. That was how most of the State's horrors started in other countries, with soldiers that got a taste for blood and couldn't keep from slaughtering additional people.

Springfield sneaked around the tree line, making his way back to the spot from where the warriors had departed. He looked at the various huts and at the man in black walking, calmly, to each dwelling's entrance to see who was in each one. Sometimes, there was a scream from within the huts. Other times, there was only silence.

Chetnik was still standing at the final hut. "Run for your life," Springfield wanted to scream at the old man. No such call came, though. He could only watch.

The man in black towered over the old man. Still holding the warrior's knife in one hand, the assassin said something and Chetnik said something back. Springfield couldn't hear what either man had said but he was sure the man in black only spoke English, which Chetnik did not speak, and so nothing that could be said between them would make sense anyway.

The man in black didn't wait for Chetnik to offer more gibberish. Without another word, he drove the knife into the old man's gut. Chetnik fell to the ground, covering the grass with spurts of blood. The mercenary stood there, maybe waiting for Chetnik to whimper or to plead for a quick death. But the old man did neither. He merely clasped the bloody hole in his stomach and, unable to find the strength to return to his feet, stared up at the sun and the clouds, then closed his eyes.

This disgusted the man in black, who grabbed a wooden log from the cooking fire and smashed Chetnik's face with it. With another log from the fire, he began walking from one hut to the next until they were all in flames. Women and children began screaming, darting out from their hiding places. Some of these villagers were cut down with a spear that the man in black held. Others merely had their arms or neck sliced as they ran past—whatever could be reached without the assassin having to give too much of a chase. There was no reason to hurt them other than simply liking the sight of human suffering. That look of fear was magnified on women and children, which only fueled the man in black's appetite.

As Springfield walked away, back in the direction he had come, he heard women screaming and children crying. Although he was too far away to be sure, he thought he also heard the man in black laughing.

At the top of the first hill, he looked back one last time. All of the huts were on fire. Two had already burned to the ground. Through the smoke, he saw the man in black dart three steps, grab a boy, slit his throat, then dash toward a little girl so he could do the same to her. Springfield turned and began descending the hill before he had to see anything else. The only thing he could hope for was that the killer would get so carried away that he would still be there when the group of warriors returned.

Just like that, a small village, where everyone had lived in peace, was removed from the earth, and for no better reason than they had found Springfield and nursed him back to health. He wondered how much the Theta Timeline had just shifted. How much of the world he had come from would be changed because some obscure village in some unknown part of history was gone? Maybe a neighboring tribe, which would have been kept in check if Chetnik's warriors had remained there, would now expand until it became an empire. Maybe some great figure in history was Chetnik's great-great-grandson, but now would never be born. Maybe an important discovery would now need to be made by someone else, centuries later.

Whatever the change, a shift had occurred. The world he had come from would never know of Chetnik or his people. They had been erased, permanently, from history. It wouldn't be the first time that a Thinker's actions erased a settlement, but that knowledge offered little comfort as Springfield listened to the echoes of screams in the distance.

46 - JAMESTOWN, VA

The history books will never mention anything about a time traveler being involved with Virginia's Lost Colony, but all the signs are there. In a different reality, there were no missing people. Instead, the settlers from Jamestown established the first bustling city of the New World. In that timeline, Jamestown kept expanding, the new country growing along with it, until it became the nation's capital. The White House and the Capitol Building would have been built on farmland in Roanoke instead of the marsh of Washington, D.C.

But then something happened—the Theta Timeline shifted—and the history we know of now, an entire settlement vanishing without any clue as to what happened to them, became our new reality. The Thinkers believe they know what really happened. They took a closer look at the evidence and became convinced that one of their own was responsible for the people disappearing at the end of the sixteenth century.

The Roanoke colony was established to give England a permanent settlement in the New World. The settlers arrived at Roanoke Island in 1584. Once on land, one hundred and eight men and women set about building a fort, homes, and exploring the surrounding terrain. Minor skirmishes erupted with the local natives, but the two sides quickly formed a truce. A few of the colonists went back to England with new crops they had discovered, but the vast majority remained behind. In 1587, a follow-up expedition was sent to check on the status of the Roanoke colonists.

No one was there.

In fact, not only didn't they find living settlers, they didn't even find dead bodies to explain what had happened to everyone. Only one partial skeleton was found. Everyone else, even the dead bodies, was simply gone.

One hundred and fifteen new men and women set about re-establishing Roanoke as an operational fort. Three years later, in 1590, more people and more supplies were sent to reinforce the colony.

But once again, they found it completely deserted.

This time, there wasn't even a single skeleton left behind. Other than the settler's possessions, which were still scattered about in the fort, there was no trace that people had ever been there at all. There was no sign of a battle, no indication that disease had wiped the people out. There was simply nothing.

If they had to abandon the fort for any reason, the settlers had been instructed to carve a cross into one of the fort's trees. There was no cross. It was as though the people had simply walked off into the wilderness or vanished into thin air.

Ever since the colony disappeared, people have tried to come up with explanations for how so many people could evaporate without leaving any clues as to where they went. Some people tried to make the case that the settlers had died at the hands of the natives, but there was no sign of struggle, no cross etched into a tree.

Because the word "Croatoan" was carved into a post at the fort, it was thought the settlers had moved to Hatteras Island, which was called Croatoan Island at the time. At this new location, the Roanoke settlers joined with another local tribe, which was then attacked by a different group of natives. But no sign was ever found of the colonists there either.

Over the next two centuries, some of the local natives were found to have grey or blue eyes. This was taken to mean that they must be the descendants of the missing Europeans. But if they were, why had none of them passed down stories of relatives who came from overseas? Why didn't they share any other physical traits with the settlers?

Some people tried to say the Spanish killed all the settlers so they could have the territory for themselves, but this didn't make any sense because the Spanish, upon finding the remains of what had been the Roanoke Fort, chose not to settle there.

None of the theories held up to scrutiny. But along the way, more details came out. A team of researchers found the remains of a canvas bag. A scrap of brown paper, no bigger than a postage stamp, was found by the remains of a camp. Along with it was a partially petrified bean. The Thinkers began to piece the puzzle together.

In addition to the corn and potatoes that the first settlers took back with them to England in 1587, they also took a type of brown bean that the local natives didn't grow because it wasn't indigenous to the area at the time. It's rumored that the first batch of time travelers, the group starting with Adamsborough and ending with Charlottsville, were supplied with such seeds. This was in case they needed to make friends with local tribes or had to live on their own in the wild. At the time, none of the Thinkers realized that the brown bean, now extremely common, might not have been known in whatever time the men would be sent to. Not even a Thinker can think of everything.

What the Thinkers hypothesize is that one of the time travelers was sent too far back in time to be of any good in preventing the State. After knowing he wouldn't be useful to the Thinkers, he joined one of the local tribes. How shocked he must have been that day when the first sails appeared off the shore, the colonists deboarding their vessels and thanking

God for finally guiding them to solid ground. The time traveler's mind immediately started racing. Instead of giving up the mission, he improvised and made his own plan for how to alter the Theta Timeline.

A settlement would be established there. Those people would be joined three years later by another set of colonists. The new world would continue to expand and the Roanoke colony would become its centerpiece. The time traveler knew all of this was going to happen.

But, he thought, what if he could make the British never want to colonize this new land? Or, if that was too ambitious, what if he could postpone the establishment of their colonies until the natives made peace with each other, until they became unified in their distrust of the White Man and joined together as one group. Maybe, he thought, if the British could be held off for a while longer, the New World would still eventually be established, but the natives would be better prepared and wouldn't have their land stolen. By the time the settlers did come over, they would have no choice but to accept the local population as their equals. In this altered Theta Timeline, the natives and the British would form a country together. By the time the War of Independence started, if it still took place in this shifted reality, it wouldn't be a war of disenfranchised British versus red coats, it would be the settlers who wanted to be away from British rule, combined with the existing government of Indians.

Anyway, that's probably what the time traveler thought he could accomplish.

As the settlers went about building their colony in Roanoke, the Thinker watched, along with a group of natives, from the cover of trees.

"I know they don't look like much of a threat," he would tell the Indians. "But trust me, they are."

The colonists went from having a camp, to a fort, to being a real settlement. Other ships came and went and took news back to England that verified there was an established base full of healthy men and women.

Once the first boats sailed back to Europe with updates from the New World, the time traveler befriended the colonists. They were no doubt shocked to see a white man, but even more shocked to find him living with the natives.

Seeing that the settlers were having a difficult time growing healthy vegetables in the foreign soil, he told them they should visit the tribe's land so they could see how crops should be grown in warm, dry weather.

Once the colonists were away from the fort—their guard down after so many pleasant meetings with the natives and this mysterious white man—the slaughter commenced. The Native Americans wouldn't have liked what the time traveler asked them to do, just as the time traveler wouldn't have liked telling them how necessary it was. He convinced them, though, that it was critical unless they wanted these people to come and take all their land. It would make the Thinker sick to know he was killing a hundred innocent men and women, but he did it with the knowledge that killing one hundred people would one day save billions of others.

After the slaughter was over with, the time traveler made sure the natives buried all the bodies to keep them from ever being found. Then he went back to the now-empty fort and made sure no one would ever want to return to it. From his bag, he deposited the remains of one skeleton. Only one. A way of saying, *Don't come back, this land is haunted.*

But if that wasn't enough, he also wrote *Croatoan* on the fort's wall, his tribe's word for the equivalent of "hell." New settlers would arrive and ask the locals what the word meant. When they were told, they would get back on their boat and sail away. If they went north and spoke to the tribes there, they would be told that this land had been claimed by the devil. The British would never want to return.

The Theta Timeline would shift from a reality in which Roanoke had never been abandoned and had eventually become the center of the New World, to a history where the white man never stole an entire continent of land.

The only problem was that it didn't keep the British away. Not for long. This was why the killings had to be repeated a few years later. This time, the time traveler didn't bother with leaving a skeleton behind. The bones hadn't been creepy enough. This time, he left no remains at all.

Maybe he died shortly thereafter, or maybe he realized nothing would keep this land from being colonized by the British. In the end, the mass murder resulted in one fairly minor change to the Theta Timeline. The State still rose. The mushroom clouds still left much of the world under a veil of dust.

Looking back at the smoke rising in the air from where Chetnik's village used to be, Springfield couldn't help but wonder if the Thinkers would one day try to piece together what just happened at this village as well.

47 - AFTER THE FIRE

Springfield might have missed the neighboring villages the first time he passed through the stretch of fields and trees, but they were easy to spot with smoke rising from them. He stayed as far away from them as possible. The warriors wouldn't be kind if they saw him, not after all the death and misery he had brought. After having failed to find and kill the man in black, they would take vengeance out on him, regardless of whether or not Chetnik had taken a liking to him.

He guessed the warriors would have arrived at the already destroyed village, only to spot smoke rising from the place they had just left. They would come sprinting back. If they saw Springfield along the way, he would be treated like the demon they had suspected him of being, and understandably so. Springfield had been the one that the man in black was looking for on his rampage. He had also sat and talked to Chetnik when he knew the assassin would be looking for him. And he had stood by and watched as the villagers were being slaughtered.

Even if he pretended to be severely injured when the warriors saw him, motioning for them to ignore his wounds and save their fellow villagers as quickly as they could, he had a hunch one of them would linger just long enough to drive his spear through the evil tree spirit's throat. It was better to avoid them all together.

He rubbed at the smooth piece of wood in his palm. If he had been one of Chetnik's people and had seen a man near their homes, a branch growing out of his hand, mumbling nonsense, he would have taken the visitor's arrival as a wicked omen too. The only reason he was still alive was because poor Chetnik had believed that compassion outweighed superstition, and now his blood was all over the ground.

Although Springfield was sure the warriors were no longer there, he did not approach what remained of the second set of huts. There would be dead bodies, young and old, male and female. They would be scattered about just as they had been in Chetnik's village.

After what he guessed was another three miles, he came upon the third set of huts. These homes, like the other two sets, were completely destroyed. Made of grass and twigs and mud, the burned-out remains were nothing more than smoldering ruins.

Since this was the first village in the man in black's warpath, there would no longer be anyone looking for survivors. This time he did approach. There were bodies everywhere. The surviving warriors would eventually give their loved ones proper burials, but as Springfield passed through what remained of the village, he saw corpses strewn across the ground in the same spots where they had taken their last breaths. Some were charred from fire. Others were drenched in blood where an arm or leg was missing. Bugs and vultures were everywhere. With his own eyes, he saw what the State's men were capable of doing.

He saw a baby, still in its mother's arms, with only a few cords of muscle keeping its head connected to its body. The child's mother, also dead, had been stabbed in the stomach and chest. A trail of blood wrapped around the side of the hut, ending where she lay with the baby. She would have known she was dying, that her infant was already dead. She would have used her last bit of strength to drag herself to a quiet spot where she could hold her baby in her arms one last time, in peace, as death came over her.

He saw part of a body under the remains of one of the ruined huts. Probably, the woman had seen the man in black standing right outside her home and decided to brave the smoke and fire rather than face the spear and knife.

At the center of the tiny village, where meals were prepared, a group of vultures swarmed over a heap of bodies, ripping flesh away from the stack of arms and legs. He looked for any supplies he might be able to use on the rest of his journey. There were no tarps or blankets, though, nothing to keep the rain off him. There was food, but all of it was also covered in bugs. A small knife was lying on the ground. This was the one thing he deposited into his bag before turning and leaving the village forever.

He never saw anyone from the tribe again. The warriors, wherever they went after confronting the man in black or giving up their search for him, might have tried to rebuild their village. Or, knowing they had been conquered by demons, they might have wandered off to make a new home elsewhere, roaming the earth for a place free of such evil. It was also possible that they were finished off by another tribe who took advantage of their weakened condition. However it happened, the tribe, the name and precise location of which he would never know, was gone forever.

48 - THE RESPONSE

The State had to offer a response to the explosion at the apartment building. The checkpoints and AeroCams had been touted as safety measures that would prevent future attacks. Now, one had occurred, and the measures that people had grumbled about but finally accepted had failed. Every night on the news, the country was shown footage of people evacuating the building. As soon as the clips were over, the leaders cried that something drastic had to be done.

The people waited to see what the response would be. Two different ideas were passed around. One leader proposed making it illegal to call people by anything other than their real name. The great evil: nicknames! Another leader suggested creating a new agency that would monitor and approve every financial transaction made by the State's citizens. The Ruler was very happy with these proposals. The new set of laws, the State's sense of humor never waning, was titled The Liberty And Justice For All Act. The LAJFA Act would finally make everyone safe.

When a reporter asked for examples of what would now be illegal, the Ruler said, "Well, pet names for loved ones—that will be against the law. Hey, I like free speech as much as everyone else, but nicknames aren't really speech,

212

they're just tools used by radicals to hurt everyone."

"And how many people would need to be hired to work for the new agency that's going to review and approve all financial transactions?" the reporter asked.

"A lot."

A protester stood up and yelled, "Can't anyone see how crazy this is? We used to be led by great men who would have known these laws were outrageous."

Just before the State's guards grabbed the man, the Ruler raised a hand for them to pause. Then he looked the young idealist in the eyes and said, "We live in different times."

And with that, the Ruler gave a nod and the Security Service agents dragged the protestor away. It was the last time anyone saw or heard the heckler.

The reporter cleared her throat before asking her next question: "And the new agency will have to approve it every time someone wants to charge something to their credit card or withdraw money from an ATM?"

"That's correct. Listen, I know it sounds like a hassle. But the numbers don't lie. If we had these laws earlier, none of the recent attacks would have occurred. It makes sense for the people because it ensures their safety."

The first person arrested under The Liberty And Justice For All Act was an eighty-year old man. When asked what he did to get arrested, the man replied, "I called my wife Schnookums. Next thing I knew, I was being taken away."

The officers who cuffed him and drove him to jail couldn't be blamed; they were only following orders. And by calling his wife anything other than the name she had been given at birth, he was, under the terms of the new law, engaging in criminal behavior.

A grandmother who said she would only stop calling her two grandchildren by their pet names—Little Stinker and Little Dinker—if she was dead, was found the next morning, the victim of an apparent suicide.

A man who showed up to the bank to withdraw

money was told he would have to wait while the teller called the Department of Monetary Review so they could approve the transaction.

"I don't need permission to withdraw my own money," the man said, slamming his fist on the counter.

"I know, sir. Please, it will only take a minute."

"I know you're doing your job, but give me my god damn money."

That was when the bank's security guard subdued the man. When the police arrived, they were told what happened and the man was sent to prison for trying to break the LAJFA Act.

Kids were still taught that they were free, and they still believed it because it was repeated to them every day. At night, as they watched the evening news with their parents, those same children saw protestors arrested and beaten by police for no other reason than they disagreed with the new laws. Even as they watched a girl get shot in the face with a canister of tear gas, the children knew they were living in the freest country in the entire world.

The Ruler went on television in hopes that cooler heads would prevail. "Humans can adjust to anything," he said. "Give people a little time and they'll settle into following the new laws. A month from now, they won't even remember what life was like before nicknames were outlawed."

So many laws were added that most people no longer had an idea of what was still legal and what was illegal. People no longer spoke in public because they weren't sure what they were allowed to say. For the State, it was perfect. With so many laws, any time they wanted to get someone, they could think of ten crimes the person was probably guilty of. The sheer volume of codes and regulations made it impossible to be law-abiding. With thousands and thousands of laws, you could be guilty a hundred times over without even leaving your house. Everyone could be guilty of something.

The real beauty of having so many laws was that eventually some laws contradicted others. You were guilty if you did something, and you were guilty if you didn't. But the State never noticed unless you gave it a reason to.

49 - RETRACING STEPS

Following a stream, Springfield walked the entire rest of the day. Now aware of how the local villages blended in with the surrounding hills, he kept a better watch for other people. Even so, there were no signs of civilization.

Before sleeping, he built a small bed of leaves and grass under a tree and lay there. Even though he had inspected the ground for anthills, each time something tickled his fingers or ears, he brushed it away as though it was an entire swarm of insects. After the incident with the ants, it would be a long time before he would be able to have an itch without his heart racing.

In the morning, he began walking again. By the end of the next day, he reached the spot where he had first appeared and where the man in black had fallen out of the sky. There were no lingering signs of his arrival, no singed earth or dead grass, no faint glow remaining in the sky. If time travel worked the way he had seen on television—an open portal allowing him the chance to return home whenever he wanted—he would have considered leaving this place, where he had already caused so much pain and suffering, and rejoining the people he loved. They would be miserable, and the world would never be free of the State, but he would be back home, and that had to count for something. If there was a way to get back home, however, and he took it, he would never be able to face his parents or Jessica ever again, not after giving up on saving them from the prison of their lives.

Eventually, the stream he was following met up with another brook, and the two joined to become an even larger current. An hour later, another stream combined with the one he had been following to form a river. Knowing there was a good chance that a village or town might be situated near such a water source, the current became his guide.

For two days, he followed the river without any sign of the man in black or anyone else. Even so, he couldn't help but feel the footprints he was leaving in the mud were providing an easy trail to follow. No matter where Springfield went, the assassin, if he was still out there, would be able to find him.

This was probably the man in black's version of heaven. Away from modern technology, he had no fear of someone recording his actions and filing a complaint against him. He could slaughter as many people as he wanted without being put on paid leave. The entire landscape was his to use as a safari, until he got the one kill he really wanted.

It didn't matter how much of a lead Springfield had on the man in black. The footprints would give the mercenary all the information he needed to keep moving in the right direction. Springfield thought about jogging in different directions, then back-tracking and veering off in a slightly different course. But that would only confuse the man in black for a couple minutes before he was able to pick up the correct trail again. He thought about carrying leaves with him and dropping some on top of his footprints, but that would only slow him down more than it would the killer, and the wind could easily blow the leaves away to make the entire endeavor a wasted effort. Really, he had no idea how you were supposed to lose someone who was hunting you. *The Most Dangerous Game* was a fascinating story, but it had no practical application when being hunted by someone from the State.

As the river increased in strength, he came to a place where trees had been washed down stream until they formed a natural dam. Water rushed under and over the collection of logs, but a path of branches and trunks connected his side of the river to the far side. If his parents knew what he was thinking, they would send him to his room without dinner. If Jessica knew, she would withhold sex for a month.

He walked a hundred feet past the dam, ate one of the protein bars, tore off the edge of its wrapper, and dropped it on the ground for the man in black to find. Then, walking backwards, he retraced each step so there was still only the one set of prints, all heading in one direction. It took him so long to copy each footprint that he kept alternating between thinking the scheme was silly, and feeling like it was taking too much time. The man in black would inevitably catch up with him, see the Thinker walking backwards like a complete idiot, and begin laughing so hard he would need to get his breath back before killing him.

But finally Springfield got back to the place where trees were stuck in the river. Now that he was back at the dam, even he didn't think it seemed like a very good idea to try and walk from one side to the other. His parents' voices, along with Jessica's, agreed with him.

A vision kept playing in his mind: him being halfway across the logs before his weight caused one of them to dislodge. All the trees, with him still on top, would begin moving down stream again. Within two seconds, he would lose his footing and be carried away by the current. The wet tree trunks wouldn't give him anything to hold on to. The towback would grab him and make sure he drowned before he could get back to shore.

But what other option was there? If he kept walking in one direction without trying to lose the man in black, the trained killer would eventually get him. It was inevitable. Something drastic like this was his only chance.

His right foot stepped away from the muddy banks and reached out toward the collection of logs. He thought about all the other time travelers who had been sent back in time, only to never be heard from again, and pictured himself becoming just another one of them. Forty other men had been sent back in time before him. Yes, more than half of those men had died before they could start their mission, but the rest had survived long enough to begin a new life. And yet none of them had done anything to prevent the State. Many of them, in fact, hadn't even done anything to give the Thinkers a clue as to where and when they had appeared in history. If Springfield did die right here, would the scientists chalk up his disappearance as yet another ocean drowning or another elevation death? Maybe they would assume they had sent him too far back in time to be of any use. Maybe, he thought, that's exactly what they had done.

Was this the point, one foot still on solid ground, where Springfield was supposed to realize that what he was doing was foolish, and decide better of it? Were his doubts reasonable, or was fear trying to make him turn away from uncertainty?

No. This was his chance. If he wanted a way to escape the man in black and begin a serious effort toward the mission he had been sent on, he needed to do this. It wasn't as if he had to jump out of a plane without a parachute or walk in front of an oncoming train. All he had to do was put one foot in front of the other, carefully, and keep his balance.

And with that, the foot that was still on solid ground stepped forward and he was entirely on the fallen tree trunk, water rushing underneath him.

"Son of a bitch," he said, both feet immediately soaked by water.

One of his feet inched out further than the other and he began making his way across the river.

50 - LEAVE AND DIE OR STAY AND BE A SLAVE

It was likely that the man in black had tracked targets through the wilderness before. He and men just like him, an army for hire, had gotten their start in the deserts and mountains of far-off countries. There, it didn't matter who they gunned down; everyone was a potential threat. It was a mindset they had brought home with them.

When the Thinkers first decided it was easier to get away from the cities and from the State's rule rather than continue putting up with it, there was a pattern of families selling their expensive suburban homes and moving out to abandoned farms or cabins in the woods. These were people who had grown disillusioned with the State and thought, innocently enough, that if they quietly left society they could once again be free. But the State was even more threatened by people who went silently in the night than they were by people who spoke up in public. Someone who went on television and cried about injustice could be labeled a crank or be charged with any number of embarrassing crimes that would ruin their reputation. The State actually liked limited amounts of this form of dissent because it gave them a chance to make an example out of someone, and in the process, discourage anyone else from doing the same thing in the future.

What they didn't like were the families who gave up their normal nine-to-five jobs and the hours spent in rush-hour traffic and the noise of city life in favor of places where the AeroCams weren't constantly circling or where the State's checkpoints weren't set up to control where they could go and where they couldn't go. Moving away and making a new life for themselves reminded everyone else that there were alternatives to putting up with constant surveillance and pat-downs.

That was why people like the man in black were sent in to eliminate them.

People can only be forced into tolerating the intolerable if they think they don't have a choice. But when they see their neighbors leading happier lives after they have left, well, it was proof that a better life was possible. The leaders couldn't allow people to see that. They needed everyone to think the State was necessary for their safety or else they lost all of their power.

That was why, one by one, the families who left the cities in favor of the wilderness, were greeted in the night by assassins just like the man in black. Originally, AeroCams had been sent in to destroy the homes, or a team of men dropped out of a helicopter and gunned everyone down. But the State had been burned by these types of killings in the past. Anonymous videos posted to the internet showed an AeroCam in the sky right before a log cabin exploded. The official story, that the explosion was the result of a faulty gas line, was debunked. Another video showed a group of men rappelling down from a helicopter before gunfire broke out. Until the video was leaked, those deaths had been declared part of a cult's suicide ritual. The videos would disappear, along with the people who posted them, but people wouldn't forget what they had seen.

It was only when video proof showed how far reality was from the official story that the State was forced to change its strategy. Now, they said, the Thinkers were to blame for all of the deaths. When people believed this even less than they had the previous stories, the State said the videos were nothing more than training demonstrations that had been confused for real-life events. The story could keep changing as much as the State needed.

After having learned their lesson the hard way, the State began dropping off a man or a team of men far away from the target. From there, they would hike, under the cover of darkness, to the kill zone. They would be expected to get in and get out without being detected, and the deaths would have to look like suicides or explosions from natural gas leaks. Other than that, they were free to do whatever they wanted.

People came to realize that they could either live in the city or die in the country. They could wait at checkpoints, ask for permission to withdraw their own money, all while under surveillance, or they could attempt to avoid that by living in the wilderness for as long as they survived. This was the choice the State gave its people.

51 - SO CLOSE, YET SO FAR AWAY

The river's full power could only be felt once Springfield was standing with both feet atop the first fallen tree. Looking at the river from the safety of dry land, he had been able to convince himself it was nothing more than a large stream. Now that he was directly over top it, the rapids were loud and violent.

Nor did the giant tree trunk seem quite so wide once it was slippery underneath his feet. Just step forward, then again, and again—that's all he had to do—and he would be free of the man in black. Just as he talked himself into believing he could do it, the rapids splashed over the log, soaking not only his feet, but his shins and his knees. Any confidence he tried to muster was washed away.

He inched forward, knowing each step toward the middle would be another step away from the comfort of solid ground. If just one of the intertwined trees shifted, the entire structure would give way and begin drifting downstream again. And he with it.

Another step.

"Just keep putting one foot in front of the other," he told himself. "Just stay balanced."

Another step.

The rapids splashed his feet again and he immediately bent over and held onto the trunk with his hands. When he was sure he wouldn't fall in, he stood up straight and once more began inching toward the far bank. After a few more treacherous steps, he looked away from the placement of his feet just long enough to check his progress. That was when his heart sank. He was less than twenty feet from the shore, not even a quarter of the way across to the other side.

Although his feet were still holding firm, his courage was slipping away. Each time water splashed higher up on his legs, part of his determination was carried off. He was spending more time bent over, holding the tree, than he was moving forward. If his willpower was already flailing to stay above water, it would need a life vest once Springfield had to transition from one trunk to another. Just thinking about it was enough to make him freeze in place where he stood.

But each time he stopped, immobilized by doubt and fear, the rapids seemed to grow in intensity. Instead of periodically sloshing his feet, bursts of water pushed at his knees and hips, testing his balance on the timber.

Still hunched over, he shuffled toward the opposite bank. He only made it another few steps before water splashed over the tree and—sure he was going to be washed away—he squatted and grabbed hold of it again. He thought about lowering himself to his belly and crawling forward, but the trunk was too wide for him to get his arms and legs all the way around. If the water washed him off to the side, nothing would keep him from being carried away.

He continued shuffling forward. By the time he reached the spot where he needed to leave the first tree and step over to the next, every part of him was soaked. The second log was wider and taller than the first, so he was able to make his way over it more quickly. He was doing fine until he looked up and saw he was fifty feet away from land in both directions. His heart, already pounding, began thumping in a way that made him gag. If he had eaten more than a single protein bar, his lunch would have come up right there.

Everything became a blur. He gripped the tree for safety.

Blinking hard, his eyesight came back in tiny bits. First, he saw the outline of his fingers, white and tense, digging into the bark. Then he saw individual splashes of water rushing over his knuckles as he tried to keep his weight centered on the log. Once his breathing slowed, his head cleared and he started moving again.

He tried to envision the man in black coming to the same series of fallen trees stretching across the river. The assassin would probably welcome the challenge, would probably dart onto the first section of the dam without a single thought to his own safety. After skipping to the end of the first log, he would hop to the second. This thought was what finally convinced Springfield to begin shuffling forward again.

Now that he was more than halfway across, he kept his eyes pinned to the place where he could finally return to solid ground. His goal was getting closer and closer. Another rush of water crashed over the tree and sprayed him in the face.

"Son of a bitch."

The third log was the smallest. When he stepped onto it, it shifted ever so slightly under his weight. He stood there, one foot on the sturdy trunk in the middle of the dam, and one on the slender gateway to the far side. If the final tree couldn't support his weight, he would have to turn around and shuffle all the way back. If he insisted on going forward anyway and it dislodged, the entire dam would come apart with him still on top of it. If he didn't drown first, he would be pulverized between colliding trees. His dead body would drift away and become lost to history.

Only twenty more feet before he was on solid ground again. Looking up at the bank, then back down at the tree, no wider than his shoulders, he thought about whether or not he could race to the other side before the dam fell apart. Even if he couldn't get all the way across before he went into the water, he might be close enough to grab a branch or exposed root and pull himself to safety before getting swept away.

With that thought in part of his mind and the idea of the man in black catching up to him in the other part, Springfield stood up, took a deep breath, and began to run. He made it four strides before his left foot slipped out from underneath him. But in those four strides he had crossed three-quarters of the tree. By the time his body hit the water, he was only a foot away from the shore and easily pulled himself out of the river. Gasping for breath but on dry land again, he rolled onto his back and looked up at the sky.

So happy was he with his ingenuity in going somewhere that the assassin wouldn't be able to find him that he actually laughed. For the first time, he had the feeling that the mission could be a success. Even if he had been sent too far back in time, he would find a way to make a difference. Things could work out.

His shoes, his clothes, and the bag he was carrying were all soaked through, but it was all stuff that could dry while he rested and collected his thoughts. The sun was beginning to go down for the evening anyway, so he only walked another hundred feet before finding cover and settling down for the night. He didn't bother to make a fire to stay warm and to dry his clothes. Doing so would only signal the mercenary.

For dinner, he ate another protein bar and washed it down with filtered river water. After collecting grass and leaves for a bed, he laid down with a contented groan. He was still congratulating himself on this first minor victory when thoughts of Chetnik's now-extinct tribe came rushing back and sobered him up again. At least the bed of grass and leaves he was laying on continued one tiny part of the tribe's culture. Maybe Lewis and Clark would one day need to find a place to sleep on their way to discover uncharted lands and would do exactly what Springfield was doing now. And with that thought helping him remain positive, he went to sleep.

52 - A LITTLE BIT AT A TIME

Hidden within the Liberty And Justice For All Act was a provision restricting people to cities. No one could leave, not even for a vacation. The leaders acted as shocked as the public. Someone, they agreed, must have anonymously sneaked the provision into the bill at the last minute. None of the leaders claimed to be able to find out which one of them had put it into the Act, but none of them complained about its inclusion either.

The public only found out about it when a man went on television and said he had been told by the State's men that he wasn't allowed to take his camper into the nearby national park.

"They said I had to turn around," he told the reporter, his belongings still in his truck, his kids hanging out the windows in an attempt to get airtime of their own.

"Did they say why?" the reporter asked, holding a microphone to the man's face.

"They said no one is allowed there any more. I had a camping permit and everything. Didn't matter. Said if I didn't turn around right away, they'd have me arrested."

"For what?"

"They didn't say. If I'd asked, they would have

arrested me for breaking the part of the Freedom Act that says you can't question the State."

"So you turned around and came back?"

"What else could I do?"

When the man was found dead the next day, his family was told he committed suicide.

To quell the inevitable protests that would form once people realized they were stuck within their urban prisons, the State told everyone that the new law had already prevented at least three additional attacks. When protests occurred anyway, the State said ten attacks had been prevented. After the third day of protests, the number of prevented threats was raised to twenty-five.

The mere idea of the State telling people where they could and couldn't go would have been ludicrous fifty years earlier. The press would have screamed. People would have revolted. Now, though, people grumbled, they complained, but that was it. After all, the State was adamant that this new measure was to ensure everyone's safety. After losing so many other freedoms, one more loss didn't seem like that big of a deal. Things just had to be taken away in small increments.

The Ruler smirked into the cameras as he told people, "The AeroCams and checkpoints protect everyone in the cities. But out in the wilderness, where we don't have those things, we can't guarantee the safety of our people. And so we must protect everyone from going where they aren't safe."

No one was dumb enough to ask why, if the AeroCams guaranteed everyone's safety in the cities, they hadn't been able to prevent a nuclear bomb from going off. Not to mention the most recent explosion at the apartment building. Nor did anyone ask why the State didn't just send AeroCams into the forests the way it had everywhere else. And, most importantly, no one dared ask the Ruler if there was anything the State wouldn't do in the name of self-preservation and public safety.

53 - HELLO AGAIN

In the morning, Springfield reached into his canvas bag for another protein bar. There were only four left. He was either going to have to find other people very soon or find a way to feed himself in the wild—something he knew he wasn't capable of doing.

If other people were out there, they would be near water. With that thought in mind and, knowing he was safe on the other side of the river, he continued along the bank. The mountains, prominent from where he had been on the fields, eventually disappeared from sight. Only the river and the trees were visible now.

Birds were chirping all around him. The water, now that he didn't have to cross it, sounded peaceful in its steady current. On the other side of the river, a cardinal was standing on the same limb as a bright yellow bird. Beneath both creatures stood a man, staring right at Springfield.

The man in black.

Springfield's eyes involuntarily closed the same way they had when he was a boy and couldn't force himself to watch the scariest parts of horror movies. When he opened them, the mercenary was still there, but was now smiling at the discomfort he caused the Thinker.

His first thought was that maybe if he ducked into the tree line, the man in black might not see him. It was wishful thinking, though. It was worse than that; it was completely unrealistic, bordering on delusional, because the man in black was staring right at him. Tied to the assassin's hip was a knife, maybe the same one he had used to kill all of the women and children from the village. And poor Chetnik.

Without moving, the two men stared at each other from opposite sides of the river. Springfield saw the mercenary's eyes scan the water. The man in black's first instinct was to come right at his target and kill him where he stood. But to do so, he would have to swim across the river, and he had received enough survival training to know that rapids were always stronger than they looked. He liked killing, but he liked living even more, and so he remained where he was.

Then the State's man gripped the spear he was carrying. Springfield knew what the assassin was thinking: maybe he could throw it across the river and hit Springfield. If Springfield was only twenty feet away, this might have been an option, but not even the best athlete could be expected to hit a moving target with a spear from a hundred feet away.

The man in black had no other options, and so he simply stood there, waiting for the Thinker's next move.

Springfield knew that if he continued following the river, the man in black would simply follow from the other side. If he turned and walked in the opposite direction, he would come across the dam. Not only would the assassin follow, he would have a way to cross the river. The only other option was to walk into the forest. Although this would get Springfield away from the man in black, it was his worst option because he would be walking away from any chance of finding other people, right into the very wilderness he couldn't survive in for much longer.

There was only one thing he could do, and so he did it: he continued on in the same direction he had been walking before being spotted. As soon as he did, the man in black chuckled and, from the other side of the river, began walking again too.

54 - HOW THESE THINGS WORK

Each time Jessica left her apartment, she had the feeling that one of the State's men would walk up behind her and put a blaster hole in the back of her head. The State had done much worse to the relatives of people who had done much less than Isaac was accused of. The AeroCams would just happen to miss the shooting. The news reports would say it was random crime. It was how these things worked.

Instead, she got through her days without being disturbed. She was sure an AeroCam was programmed to follow her every movement, that a live agent was listening to her phone calls instead of the usual computer monitoring. But these were things she had come to expect anyway.

At work, everyone tried to pretend the Liberty And Justice For All Act wasn't such a bad thing, but they only did this because they weren't sure if the State was listening. If they were being eavesdropped on, any complaint of the LAJFA Act would be taken as a violation of the previous laws it had put forth in the Freedom Act, which prevented anyone from saying anything negative about the State.

Even so, the woman in the cubicle next to her whispered, "How stupid is it that I had to wait at the bank for ten minutes while the teller tried to get in touch with someone from the Department of Monetary Security? Just to see if I was allowed to withdraw twenty of my own dollars?"

Most people in the office knew Jessica's boyfriend was one of the Thinkers involved in the basement explosion. Because of this, they avoided having any contact with her. It was understandable; if the State was watching her, anyone who spoke to her could also fall under suspicion. Sadly, the few times someone did acknowledge her, instead of being grateful, she found herself wondering if they had a death wish.

When she got home that evening, she turned the television on only to hear the anchorman saying there had been a shootout between the Security Service and a radical who was directly violating the new law that forbid anyone from going into the wilderness. Men in black cars had pulled up on the man as he unpacked his bags, his two young daughters and his wife assisting. The men didn't say if they were police, only drew their weapons and yelled at the family to get on the ground. When the man tried to usher his wife and kids back into their truck, the State's men shot him dead. It was how these things worked.

The man's wife said they had been planning the trip for a year and didn't want to lose the deposit they had put down on the cabin. When asked about the shooting, an official from the State said he was sorry for the woman's loss, but the man was breaking the law and, even more importantly, the State had identified the man as a Thinker.

The next day, the woman, now a widow, proved her husband wasn't a radical by posting letters he had written in which he stated the Thinkers were just a bunch of crazy conspiracy theorists. After calling into question the official explanation for the shooting, the State had no option but to arrest the woman for violating part of the Freedom Act.

The kids, orphans of a dead man and an incarcerated woman, would grow up with their grandparents. The State had gotten rid of two innocent people who it claimed were Thinkers, but in so doing, they created two more who really would be. After watching their father get blasted away and their mother shipped to a secret prison for no reason, the children would have no choice but to see the differences between what the Leaders said and what they saw with their own eyes. And when they had children of their own, those kids would become Thinkers as well. Everything the State did to get rid of the supposed radicals only created two new radicals. It was how these things worked.

55 - UNKNOWN BARRIERS

The Thinker and the man in black continued walking on either side of the river's bank on what Springfield figured to be a northwesterly course. Any time he stopped to drink water, the assassin stopped too. Although the mercenary didn't have a canteen to filter the water he was drinking, he seemed to believe it was safe for consumption.

Maybe, Springfield thought, *he thinks he can kill me before whatever bacteria is in that water can kill him.*

When Springfield stopped and ate a protein bar, the mercenary could only watch, his eyelids narrowing slightly, his jaw setting. Although the man in black was surely capable of hunting and catching his own food, even creating a campfire to cook the meat over, he wouldn't want to let Springfield out of his sight. After finally finding the Thinker, he would rather starve than let his target disappear again.

Watching the skinny radical eat a protein bar on the other side of the water only made the assassin despise his enemy even more. Springfield had the urge to rub his stomach and lick his lips, maybe even say how delicious the food was, but on the chance the man in black did catch him, he didn't want to die any worse than he already knew he would.

It was possible that this game of hunter and hunted could only end one way, and that everything Springfield did to prolong the inevitable would just make his eventual death more gruesome. In the apartment building's basement, he could have been shot in the head. No pain. No suffering. At Chetnik's village, the man in black would have slit Springfield's throat. Time to realize he couldn't breathe. Panic, short-lived but still there, knowing he was gagging on his own blood. Now, after making the mercenary walk for two more days, going without food that entire time, the killer would try to see how long he could keep his victim alive while he tortured him. Endless pain. Suffering so bad he would beg to be allowed to die.

Springfield called across the water: "What did you think of my little trick back there, doubling back and crossing the dam? Not too shabby, huh?"

The man in black looked at him, but didn't acknowledge anything that had been said.

As they made their way along a curve in the river, Springfield thought about what he would do when night returned. The man in black would still be on the other side of the river, but knowing that the Thinker would need to sleep eventually, the mercenary might attempt to cross the water under the cover of darkness. If Springfield was asleep, he would never know the man in black was approaching. Even if Springfield moved into the forest for the night, the man in black wouldn't have a difficult time finding him. The river might carry the man in black a quarter mile down stream before he was able to swim to the other side, but he could easily walk the distance back to where Springfield would be snoring.

"You can never go back home," he called across the water. "Once you go back in time, it's not possible to return home. I hope they told you that before you did this."

The man in black looked over at Springfield again, but just as he had the first time, he offered no reply.

Springfield thought, *Maybe he's been trained to keep from*

talking to the enemy so he doesn't start to empathize with them.

After another hour of walking, they came to a place in the river where a series of large rocks poked out of the surface. Bubbles burst into the air at each boulder. He watched the man in black assessing the situation. If the mercenary was getting impatient, either because he was starving or because he simply didn't like having to wait so long to kill his target, he might risk jumping from rock to rock until he got to the other side. One missed step, though, and he would go wherever the river took him.

The two men stood facing each other, both taking turns looking to the stones in the water and then back at the other man standing on the opposite bank. If the assassin did attempt the cross, it would be the end of one of them. Either the mercenary would miss one of the rocks and get dragged under by the current, or he would beat the rapids, get to the other shore, and quickly chase down his adversary.

Considering how athletic the man in black must be—the State only hired the best killers—he might very well be able to maneuver all the way to the other side. With this in mind, Springfield began walking again before the assassin could decide if risking the stone path was a good idea or not.

If Springfield had known the man in black's ankle was injured, he would have been more tempted to let the killer try his luck at leaping from one stone to another. But, struck with fear any time he saw the assassin, he hadn't even noticed the splint that allowed the State's man to move without a limp.

"What are you going to do after you kill me?" Springfield yelled. "Why would you ever come here? There's nothing for you in this place. Are you going to murder me and then live out the rest of your life in the woods? Have you even thought about when and where you are? If you cause too much death and suffering in this time, you might change history enough that the people you love are never born. Have you thought about that? If you stopped now, you could make a home for yourself. You could know that you gave the world a chance at a better future. Doesn't that count for anything? Don't you want your family to live in a free world?"

This time, the man in black didn't even bother to look over at Springfield.

But as they walked, he became more and more bothered that the person following him refused to say a single word. If the man in black was going to cut Springfield's head off, he could at least give his reasons why it was so important to continue the mission. After all, they were in the past, where the man in black's bosses would never know if he had succeeded in killing the Thinker.

"Why are you doing this?" Springfield said again. "No one will ever know if you're successful or not. They won't even know if you died in the reappearance or lived for another fifty years. There's no reason to keep doing this. Do you even know how the Theta Timeline works? In a blink of the eye, everyone's consciousness shifts and the world they knew changes to something else, as if that's been their reality forever. They'll have no idea if history shifted or not. No matter what you do, even if the world changes, it will be as if they have always been living in a world where the State never existed. They won't even know there had been a State or a mission to kill me."

The man in black looked over at Springfield, but said nothing.

"Don't you understand, you asshole? I'm saying you don't have to do any of this. No matter what you do, you'll never be thought of as a hero or as failing your mission. Why are you doing this? Why do you keep following me?"

Without realizing it, he had become so angry he wanted to scream. Taking deep breaths did little to help. As they walked around another bend in the river, he began to wonder if the man in black knew anything at all about what had happened. Maybe he didn't even know he was in the past or in a different part of the world. If he didn't trust his senses, he might think this entire journey was some kind of hallucination created by the Thinkers.

"What have they told you about time travel?"

The man in black did not reply.

"Did they tell you it's a one-way trip? Do they even know time travel exists?"

When the man in black didn't reply, Springfield said, "Did they know that's what we were doing down in the basement? Do they understand we're sending people back in time, or did they think we were trying to do something stupid, like create a nuclear bomb? I wouldn't put it past them to be that far off from what we were actually doing."

The man in black remained silent, only looking at Springfield for a brief moment, then ahead for any signs of a way to cross the river.

"The Thinkers will always find a way to be one step ahead of you. Don't any of you wonder why the room was rigged to explode? It's because we knew you might show up. Unlike you, we always have a contingency plan. Did you know there were four other departures prior to the one you finally arrived at? That means forty other men are back in time trying to keep the State from rising. Nothing has changed just because you found one departure location. Nothing. The room is complete ash. There won't be a single trace of what was going on there. Not even the State's best forensics people will be able to find evidence that time travelers were there."

The man in black didn't seem interested in anything Springfield had to say.

"Doesn't it bother you that you would be sent into a mission without being told who you were supposed to kill or what we were doing? We're trying to save our families from living in chains! We're trying to save the planet from the State's bombs and guns. Doesn't that mean anything to you? How can you keep your head in your ass and act like you're performing your duty? Your job is to kill people who are standing up for what they believe in. Are your paychecks worth that? Why do you hate us for wanting the country we used to have?"

The man in black glanced in Springfield's direction, then went back to watching for stones and fallen branches so he could avoid them.

"Why won't you say something?" Springfield screamed.

Suddenly, he was crying. He was tired. He missed Jessica. He missed his parents. He even missed the stray cat that showed up at his door begging for food. And it was unbearably frustrating having the enemy refuse to acknowledge what he was saying. He didn't even care if the man in black could sympathize with what the Thinkers were doing, but at least he could admit the country they grew up in wasn't the same place their parents had lived in. If the mercenary couldn't at least understand that much, there was no hope that the Thinkers would ever be understood. There was no hope for a world where people could forget the great things that had been taken away from them. That was part of the reason he was crying. And it was why he had to find a way to change the Theta Timeline to one where the State was never created.

"I don't care how long you follow me, you piece of shit," he said across the river.

He wiped his eyes on his sleeve, then blew his nose on a leaf. When he did so, the man in black smiled and mouthed something at him. Springfield had no idea what it had been.

"What?" he called across the water.

The man in black said something else, saw that Springfield still couldn't hear him, then rolled his eyes and smiled again.

That was when Springfield realized the current was louder than he had suspected, the distance between them further than he had estimated. They were only a hundred feet apart, but the sound of water rushing downstream prevented them from hearing anything the other said.

The man in black probably thinks I've been begging for my life.
That would at least explain why the mercenary was

smiling, because he thought the Thinker was finally realizing it was a matter of time until he ended up dead somewhere along the river.

Everything he had said was pointless.

56 - OLD NEWS

Isaac's parents rarely watched the news anymore. Once their son was no longer around to join the discussion, there was no point to listening to updates about which country was being bombed and which new laws were being passed or, during the quiet days, the distraction of which celebrity was pregnant and which one had a sex tape. It was all a waste of time.

The anchorman offered his usual cheery news: "An eighty year-old husband and wife were killed today in a shootout when representatives of the State discovered the couple was violating the Liberty And Justice For All Act by taking residence in a secluded log cabin. An official from the State said the Security Service went there merely to arrest the couple, but the man was holding a gun when he came to the door, so they had no choice but to open fire."

The picture changed and one of the State's leaders was now shown. He offered a pained smile as he said, "While this is unfortunate, it's important to note that the couple knew they were violating the LAJFA Act and were given every chance to turn themselves over to authorities. The policy of preventing people from living outside the cities has already prevented a dozen different Thinker plots."

The anchor was once again shown on the screen: "Details of the said plots could not be released to the public because they were classified."

"The same thing, just a different day," Isaac's father said, turning the news off.

As if tempting the State to come and get her, Isaac's mother looked out the window at an AeroCam that was hovering outside their kitchen and said, "The sad thing is that half the country really believes the State foiled a dozen attacks by passing those laws."

She swiveled in her chair and looked out the living room window. A second AeroCam was hovering on the other side of the glass, looking into their home, as if it too had been listening to the evening news. Its microphone was advanced enough that it could hear through the walls and listen to what they were saying. No matter where they went or what they said, the State could hear their words and monitor their actions.

She was right about what she had said, though: half the country really would believe they were now safer just because they had been told they were. Of the other half of the population, there were the cynics, the pessimists, and the Thinkers. The cynics said that of course no supposed attacks had been spoiled by the new laws; they were just a way to divert attention from more important matters or to keep the leaders looking like they were actually doing something. The pessimists were adamant that things got worse all the time and questioned how many more ways the State could find to let the people down. The Thinkers merely saw the continuing difference between the land they had called home and the land they now lived in, and they knew things had to change. Things wouldn't get better, however, by simply grumbling about a new inconvenience. Change could only occur by refusing to be quiet and afraid.

People didn't like being told where they could and couldn't go, but most people didn't feel they could do anything about it, and so they did nothing. They didn't like having to ask for permission to spend their own money, but who were they to battle a new agency whose entire mission it was to keep people safe by monitoring all financial transactions? And so these people made snide remarks, but that was it. The next day, the State appeased the masses by releasing new information: the new laws had prevented more then fifty planned attacks.

"You remember how many they said it had prevented yesterday, right?" Isaac's mother said.

Her husband clicked off the television sooner than he had any previous night, then said, "If people are still upset next week, they'll discover the new laws have actually prevented hundreds of attacks."

But the news didn't mention protests the following night. Nor did they mention how many plots had been prevented. Because the next night, the first story began with dramatic music and footage of the State's bombs falling on yet another country. A new war had begun. The most recent laws were already old news.

57 - MORE MISUNDERSTANDING

Springfield had another protein bar later in the day. As usual, the man in black could do nothing but watch his prey put more food into his stomach.

There was no telling how far they had hiked, but he was certain that he had never walked so far in his entire life. Each time he looked at the killer across the river, the other man didn't seem to realize it was possible to have sore feet or tired legs or even an empty stomach. Meanwhile, even though Springfield had just finished eating, he was still hungry. And now he only had two protein bars left.

They couldn't go on like this forever. That much was obvious. But he didn't know what to do other than to keep walking. Eventually, he thought, he *had* to run into other people.

He couldn't help but wonder what he would do if he really had been sent back in time so far that not only was preventing the State an impossibility, but that mankind was still sparse throughout the world. If they were walking around tens of thousands of years ago, humans wouldn't yet have filled every corner of the world. If that was the case, he might as well give up now and begin hiking into the woods, away from the river and from the man in black. He would only make it as far as he could get with two protein bars left, but that was also true if he kept following the river. At least if he changed directions, he might finally be able to have peace before he died.

He could even turn to the assassin and say, "I'm out of food. I'm going into the woods now. Please just let me die quietly."

He knew, though, from what he had seen so far that he wasn't tens of thousands of years in the past, maybe only hundreds. Chetnik had mentioned other merchants traveling through the area to trade their goods. Established trade routes proved that other humans must be nearby. And from the spears and knives Springfield had seen, with their finely crafted metal blades, he knew they had to have been made no more than a thousand years in the past. The final clue had been Chetnik's knowledge of modern Russian. It all added up to make Springfield think he was probably no further back in time than the Renaissance.

There had to be other towns and cities nearby. He just had to find them, and the only way he could do that was to continue walking.

An hour later, his luck took another turn. Lights appeared in the distance. People! From far off, he couldn't tell if they were on his side of the river or the man in black's, but he knew they meant food and shelter were imminent. His pace quickened.

The man in black matched his stride. Although still too far away to see individual people, the lights quickly came into view as a series of campfires illuminating the village's perimeter. Springfield thought about dropping his bag and making a mad dash of the final hundred yards, but no matter how fast he could run, the man in black would be able to run faster. And if the village was on the other side of the river, it wouldn't matter how quickly he got there because he would have to find a way to cross it and, in doing so, fall right into the mercenary's hands.

What he hadn't thought of, but what he saw as he got

closer, was that a bridge connected the two sides of land, allowing the town's people to cross the river whenever they wanted. The man in black saw the bridge and smiled. Immediately, Springfield broke into a run. The assassin did the same.

Even as he dashed toward the lights, he thought about veering off and disappearing into the forest. At least that way he might be able to sneak through the trees and appear on the other side of the town before the man in black found him. If he ran into the woods now, under the cover of darkness, and hid until morning, he might be able to find someone who would hide him until the assassin went away again.

But even as this possibility lingered in his head, Springfield continued running toward the lights. After a bend in the river, he could see that the town was on his side of the water. The man in black was running faster now. Even though he was on the opposite side of the river, he would be quick enough to reach the town first.

As the Thinker sprinted over twigs and rocks, he looked across the river in hopes of seeing the man in black trip over a fallen branch. It happened in every action movie he had ever seen, but it didn't happen here. In fact, as he watched, he was the one who almost stumbled because he was paying more attention to the killer than he was to a hole that a rodent had burrowed right in his path.

Another fifty feet. The man in black was already at the bridge, ready to cross it. However, a guard, or maybe just a man from the town who had been waiting there for someone else, was standing in the way. Either because he didn't recognize the man running toward him, or maybe *because* the person coming toward him was wearing some kind of odd-looking black suit and racing right at him, the guard stepped in the mercenary's path and put his hand out for the man to stop. But instead of slowing, the man in black lowered his shoulder and ran straight through the unfortunate watchman. Springfield was surprised the mercenary hadn't pulled a knife and slashed the man's guts open, but maybe he had calculated his chances of killing both a guard and Springfield before too many other men from the town came out and overwhelmed him.

The villager, flat on his ass and rubbing the back of his head, yelled to the other side of the bridge for help. With the town situated in a place where the water was calm and there were no rapids, it was easy for everyone else nearby to hear his scream. While Springfield tried to determine what language the guard had been speaking, two more men came running out and faced the man in black. The assassin stopped ten feet short of them, eyeing their hands and hips to determine what weapons they carried and how much of a risk they might be.

It was only after the man in black assessed the situation that he shifted his gaze back to where Springfield was approaching the village. The two men in front of the mercenary noticed him as well and shifted their attention.

You fools, Springfield thought, *don't turn your back on that man.*

But before the mercenary could withdraw his knife and slash the two men's throats, more reinforcements came running out, each with a long knife or club. They looked at the one man, then the other, then at the guard who was dusting himself off and walking across the bridge to rejoin the others.

Half the men directed their weapons toward Springfield. The other half pointed them at the killer. The time traveler kept expecting the assassin to slash his way through the entire group, but he remained in place, hands by his side, no visible trace of violent intentions. Springfield would have helped himself if he could have mimicked his adversary's calm approach, because when he ran toward one of the men, all the while pointing at the man in black, he only agitated the guards, causing two of the men to point their weapons right at his face. Seeing their reaction, he came to a stop and didn't say anything else.

Finally, a man, not as old as Chetnik, but older than Springfield or the assassin or any of the other men assembled by the bridge, came out to see what was happening. The man was all cheeks and jaw. Every other part of his face seemed only to be there because it was necessary.

"*Npnbet,*" Springfield said to the man, greeting him in Russian.

The man frowned at this.

The Thinker then said hello in Chinese. But the men, including the older man and the man in black, all looked at him as if he were losing his mind.

"*Bonjour? Parlez-vous français?*" Springfield said.

Nothing.

Finally, he greeted the man in Arabic and this caused the giant cheeks and jaw to break into a smile.

"You understand my words?" the older man said in heavily accented Arabic of his own.

Springfield smiled. But just as quickly, he grew serious again, saying in their shared language, "This man is a murderer," while pointing to the man in black.

He expected the assassin to lunge at him then, even though he wouldn't understand what Springfield was saying, simply because it was obvious the Thinker was accusing him of something and it couldn't possibly be good. But the man in black only stood where he was, without moving a single muscle. A pleasant smile remained on the mercenary's face as if he didn't care what was being said. For now at least, he was content to stand in place and let Springfield do all the talking.

"This man is a murderer," Springfield said again, speaking slowly this time in case the other man's Arabic wasn't very good. "He has killed many people."

The leader of the group motioned for the younger men to step aside so he could approach Springfield.

Within arm's reach, the time traveler held his palm out so the piece of wood could be seen by the campfire's light.

"He did this to my hand."

"This?" the man said. "He did this?"

The man's giant cheeks expanded even further when he was confused.

"Yes. He tried to crucify me. Do you understand that word?"

The giant cheeks and jaw nodded.

Springfield said, "He is very disturbed. Very sick. He did this to me, but I've seen him do much worse. At the last village we were at, I watched him kill women and children."

"Stop," the man commanded, no longer smiling. "First, what is your name?"

"Springfield."

This one word finally made the man in black shift his weight, as if hearing one of the Thinker's code words was too much for him to tolerate. Or maybe it was the confusion of hearing the name of a place that obviously had nothing to do with where they currently were. The assassin might think the time traveler was telling these people they were in Springfield when they all surely knew they weren't. The assassin, confused, started cracking his knuckles as his eyes darted from one guard to the next.

"Springfield, I am Sabir," the man said in Arabic.

"It's an honor to meet you, Sabir."

"Why are you with this man?"

"I'm not with him. He has been following me. He wants to kill me."

"Why?"

"He is evil."

Sabir seemed to consider this, then asked, "Where do you come from?"

"From very far away," Springfield said, motioning off on the horizon.

"How did you come here?"

"I got separated from my friends. I've been wandering the land looking for food and water ever since."

"And this man was separated as well?"

"No. He was sent by an evil lord to kill me."

Sabir considered all of this as if it were something he heard every day. He did not waste time translating any of Springfield's words to the men gathered around or to the onlookers who had collected near the edge of the village to see what all the noise was about.

"We cannot house you both here," Sabir said finally.

"I understand, but I can't go back out there with this man free," he said, once again pointing to the mercenary.

"What do you expect us to do? He has done nothing to us."

"Can you put him in jail for a few days, until I am far away?"

"Jail?"

"A place to keep evil men locked away."

"We are simple people. We do not have these jails you speak of."

"What do you do when someone breaks the law?"

"Break the law?"

"The rules of the town," Springfield said. "What do you do when someone breaks the rules you have given everyone?"

"We only have three rules," Sabir said, holding up the same number of fingers. "Do not hurt others. Do not take what is not yours. Do not kill an animal unless you eat it and use its skin."

"What do you do if someone disobeys these rules?"

"No one does."

"I know, but what if they do?"

"We tell them not to. People do not want to bring shame to their families, so they obey."

"That doesn't work for people like him," Springfield said, once again pointing at the man in black. "If you tell him not to do something, he'll come back when you're asleep and cut your throat. What do you do with people like him?"

"We do not have people like him. One time, we had a young man who could not follow the rules, no matter what we did. The boy could not help it. He was born different."

"Yes," Springfield said, "like this murderer here."

"We sent him away."

"Didn't he come back?"

"No. Exile is very shameful. Even sick boy knows the burden of shame. Once he leaves, we never see him again."

"This man will not leave simply because you tell him to."

"Won't he leave if you leave?"

"Yes, but he'll kill me if you make that happen."

Sabir seemed to consider this.

The time traveler added, "Please, tell the man that I will be sent to jail. Tell him I will die there."

"I just told you, we have no jail."

"I know. But he doesn't know that. If you convince him I will never be free again, he might go away. It's my only hope."

Sabir considered this for a while, then asked, "What would you be arrested for?"

Springfield held his hand up so the piece of wood could be seen again. "Tell him I'm accused of being an evil spirit. Tell him you will lock me up until you kill me."

"If this man understands your language, can't he understand what you say now?"

"He doesn't speak this language that you and I speak."

"What language does he say?" Sabir asked.

"The language of a land far from here."

Sabir frowned. "If he does not understand Arabic, and I do not know his language, how will I tell him we are sending you to jail?"

Springfield thought about this. He could tell the man in black himself, but the mercenary would never believe anything spoken by a Thinker.

"Have two of your men take me by the arms and walk me away. I'll act like I'm protesting. After I'm gone, motion with your finger across your neck to let him know you will chop my head off."

"Will that work?"

"It's my only hope if this man is out here."

Sabir took in a long breath, then exhaled. The onlookers near the campfire had departed for the comfort of their cabins. Finally, the thick-jawed man spoke in his own language to the seven men gathered there, probably explaining everything that had just been said and why he would be asking two of them to escort Springfield away as if he were a prisoner.

And then, without any questioning of what Sabir had just told them, two of the men walked toward Springfield, forced his hands behind his back—with more force than he thought necessary—and began walking him away.

Springfield called out in English, "What are you doing? I didn't do anything. I'm not an evil spirit. I'm not the one you should be sending to jail."

As they walked him away, he looked over at the man in black. The mercenary was still standing in the same spot he had been the entire time. Sabir was in front of the assassin, gesturing with his finger across his neck and then pointing at their prisoner, but the man in black wasn't watching anything the town's leader said or did. Springfield noticed, as the two villagers escorted him away, that the killer's eyes never wavered from tracking exactly where the Thinker was being taken.

58 - A FOURTH SOCIAL CLASS

Jessica's weekly status meeting should have started five minutes ago. No one had seen her boss, though. Without him, the others could do nothing but sit around the conference room, each person trying to act as if they would gladly be there even if it weren't a mandatory meeting on their calendars.

"Maybe he took the day off and didn't tell anyone," somebody said.

"Maybe it's just taking longer to get through the inspection lines today," the woman who sat across from Jessica said.

Ten minutes later, their boss still hadn't shown up.

"What do we do?" Jessica asked.

"Should we just go back to work?"

"Without a boss?"

But they would either go back to work or wait in the conference room for the rest of the day. As a group, they stood from their cushy chairs and filtered out of the conference room, back to their desks.

Her boss didn't arrive that day. Or any other day. No one ever saw or heard from him again. They never found out what he had been accused of doing or what happened to him exactly. He was just gone, like all the others that the State had taken for one reason or another. It was very possible that the man who used to write Jessica's performance reviews would spend the rest of his life in some secret prison without anyone, not even his family or a lawyer, knowing what he had been accused of doing.

It was taught in school that there were three social classes: the lower, middle, and upper. In the State, a fourth class existed: the prison class. Most people in the prison class joined it at an early age. Being in a gang made someone part of the prison class. Selling drugs was another path to joining the group. But, as with the other classes, social mobility could take someone from the upper or middle class and drop them into the prison class. Speaking out against the State could put someone who owned a fancy car or a nice house into the prison class. Exposing the State's lies was a way to ensure that even the wealthiest members of society could join the ranks of the prison class. Once there, most of these people remained behind bars for the rest of their lives. For the lucky few who managed to get out, it was a matter of time until they returned.

There was a time when the prison system was meant to reform people. The guilty served their sentence and were then released back into society to live out the rest of their lives. Now, prisons are used as a way to ensure the silence of dissidents.

This fourth class of people is never referenced during political speeches, but its very existence is one of the ways the State keeps the other classes in line. The middle class thinks to itself, At *least I have my house and my job and my family—I can be arrested at any time, but as long as I keep my head down and stay silent, I can keep the life I have.* The lower class thinks, *I'm poor, I struggle to feed my family, and I work all day for almost nothing, but at least I can come home from a long day of work and watch television with my kids.*

The State has a larger percentage of its population in jail than any other country in all of history. And more people are added to the ranks every day. With thousands of laws, there is always something that people can be arrested for. With a quarter of the population incarcerated, and another quarter employed by the State to be checkpoint guards, AeroCam technicians, and surveillance analysts, the State has effectively dealt with half the population.

The leaders learned early on that secret prisons were the perfect destination for the people who couldn't be controlled through the State's money and benefits. Not even many of the people who work for the State agree with what the Ruler and the leaders do, but given the choice between collecting a paycheck or being put in jail, the choice is easy. As far as they are concerned, the State can pass any law it wants, can bomb any country it wants, as long as the money keeps coming in.

Who benefits from more people being in jail than any other country? Not the people who could be rehabilitated but are never given the opportunity. Not the people who don't belong there in the first place. Certainly not the spouses who have to raise children in single-parent households. Not the children who grow up with one only one parent. The only people who benefit from the prison class are the State, for being able to get rid of anyone who questions it, and the corporations who run the jails.

Long ago, it was realized that war was a great way for the rich to get richer. But not even the State can be at war every single day of every year. For the quiet weeks, those times when the State isn't destroying some far-off land, the millions of people in jail provide the leaders' friends with a consistent revenue stream. The profit margin isn't as good as it is with war—there will never be another venture in the world that can make the banks and corporations richer than organized warfare—but when bombs aren't exploding, they can still collect billions of dollars off the lives of the prison class. The State wins. Their friends win. Only the prison class loses.

Back at her desk, waiting for the rest of the day to

pass so she can go home, Jessica has the sinking feeling that her boss has just joined the ranks of that fourth class. The feeling is confirmed a week later when a pair of men stop by his office, box up all of his possessions, and leave his workplace looking like her manager had never been there. It was the same feeling she had the day her brother was dragged away from their home. It was the same sensation she had when two of her best friends from college were taken in for questioning, never to be seen again. Maybe her boss was lucky and was already dead. At least it would be a relatively quick death.

Wherever Isaac was, she hoped he was doing something so this would be the last time she ever had this feeling.

59 - THIS IS ALL YOUR FAULT

The two guards left Springfield inside an empty cabin. There were no pictures hanging on the walls, no lights or anything else to remind him of his former world. Only the bed, elevated off the floor by a wooden frame, provided a hint of the future he would know. There was only one window, not of glass, but a simple square hole, through which fresh air kept the room livable. A shutter offered privacy from others.

He didn't sit on the bed. If it belonged to Sabir, and if Springfield was merely meant to remain there until the man in black left, it would be rude to make himself too comfortable. Instead, alone, he sat on the floor and waited. After a minute, the door opened and Sabir entered, a candle in hand. He held the flame to the wall, where another candle flared into life. The entire room became illuminated as though a light switch had been flipped; it was amazing what one little candle could do.

Neither of them said anything. Sabir, also avoiding the bed, lowered himself to the floor.

Sitting across from Springfield, the town's leader said, "He is gone."

"Are you sure?"

"My men walked him to the other side of the bridge. The evil one waited there briefly, then vanished into the woods."

"Is anyone watching the bridge to make sure he doesn't come back?"

For the first time, Sabir furrowed his brow. The man's cheeks, when he became irritated, turned from gobs of putty to mounds of grey stone.

"What I mean," Springfield said, "is that I know people like him. He will not be happy until he kills me."

"You do not need to worry," Sabir said. "I have a man watching the bridge." Then he leaned back and let out a long breath because another day was finally coming to an end. "Tell me, you must have done something to make this man so angry. Evil or not, people do not go seeking to kill others without some reason."

Springfield considered this. Obviously, he couldn't provide the actual reason the man in black wanted to kill him. Sabir would think his guest was crazy if he started talking about tyrannies and time travel. But he also owed the man an honest answer after the kindness he had received.

"Where I come from, we once had a town like this," he said, holding his palms out to gesture at the homes around them. "People wanted nothing more than to grow old and be happy. Life was simple. But then, the leaders liked the power they had over everyone else. The more they liked the power, the more they were afraid they might lose it. Over time, growing old and being happy were replaced by war and prisons. Eventually, the original town could no longer be found."

Without moving his mighty cheeks or jaw, Sabir listened to everything Springfield said. The time traveler couldn't tell if the town's leader was simply taking in everything he was hearing, or if he thought he was being told a fairy tale.

"And?" Sabir said, when his guest stopped speaking.

"And I am one of the people who wants to return

that town to what it once was."

"Ah," Sabir said, nodding. "Very difficult to return something once it is gone."

"That's very true."

"Tell me, even if you can change it back, what makes you think it won't just change again once you are gone? You will die some day and then it will once again revert back to the thing you are fighting against."

"There is that risk. But you have to hope people understand how important it is once it's returned to them and they remember what they lost. If your child goes missing, and then you find them, you never want to let them out of your sight again. If the people can regain what they had, they will cling to it and never let it go."

"They did not think it was important enough to keep the first time?"

"They did, once. But they forgot."

Sabir considered this, then nodded.

Springfield said, "You must never let your village veer from what it currently is. One little change causes another. The differences add up. Before you know it, it's no longer the place you knew."

"You have jails?" Sabir said.

Springfield nodded. "More than you can imagine."

"Why?"

"To control people. One out of every four people is in jail."

Sabir's eyes grew wide and he whistled.

"You have three laws here. We have more than all the clouds in the sky."

"Do you really think you can change things?"

"Maybe the evil man will kill me one day. But before that happens, I need to try to save my town."

"How will you save it?" Sabir asked, as if he might learn some great insight about how to keep his own town safe.

"I'm not sure."

The village leader opened his mouth to say something else, but just then, a woman screamed. Sabir jumped to his feet and ran to the door.

Looking out at the rest of the village, he said, "A cabin is on fire."

"It's the evil man," Springfield warned.

Without saying anything else, Sabir darted into the night. With the campfires extinguished for the evening, the town was dark except for the candlelight coming from within a few of the homes and from the cabin that was on fire. But then, on the opposite side of the village, another burst of light appeared. Another cabin was engulfed in flames. Then another. More people began screaming.

Springfield closed the door, blew out the candle, and backed himself into the corner. There was nothing he could do except huddle on the floor while everyone screamed for their lives. In the dark, he could hear people running past the door, some toward the fire, and some away from it. One person ran past in silence. The next shouted as they went by, as if words could save them from the evil that had entered their village.

He heard what sounded like a hiss, then a man choking and gurgling before going quiet. There were more yells. A woman's scream of urgency was interrupted by a grunt and a thud. Her bellowing immediately changed to panic as she realized she was going to die right there on the ground. Yelling and agony were everywhere. It sounded like the entire town was going mad.

Peaking out from the wooden shutter, he saw so many cabins on fire that the entire town was lit, as if the sun must already be coming back up.

The cabin door opened. Two things struck fear into Springfield. The first was how the screaming of children and women and the groaning of wounded and dying men intensified once the door was open. It sounded as if the flames were right in front of him. The scared children were loud enough to be crying in his arms. The second thing was how the figure in the doorway simply stood there, staring at him. With the fire behind the man, Springfield couldn't see who it was, only that the man stood there, watching.

It's the man in black, he thought. *There's nowhere I can go.*

But when the man stepped forward, closing the door behind him, Springfield saw it wasn't the man in black at all. Sabir took two steps forward, then stumbled. When Springfield rushed forward to help him, Sabir growled in frustration and pushed the time traveler away.

"This is all because of you," Sabir said, struggling to breathe, his chubby cheeks swelling to cover part of his eyes. "This is all your fault."

"I'm sorry, I didn't mean for this to happen."

"What you intend to happen is not important. What you actually do is what matters. When you die, no one will talk about what you meant to do, they will only say what you actually did."

"I know. I'm sorry."

Sabir smacked Springfield's hand away. "Do not apologize. Do something about it."

"What do you want me to do?"

The question drove Sabir into a fit of rage. Maybe because he was dying and he thought it would be for nothing. Maybe because all of the people he knew were also dying while an imbecile asked stupid questions. Sabir lunged forward and grabbed Springfield by the throat. His hands were sticky with blood.

"What do you do?" the town's leader asked, still holding Springfield by the neck with one hand while the other offered weak smacks across his face. "We had a simple life here, and now it is gone because of this man you brought to us. So you keep going until this man and people like him do not exist anymore."

Sabir's hands relaxed a moment before he crumpled to the floor. When Springfield knelt on the ground next to him, he saw a dark puddle forming next to the man's gut.

"I'm sorry. I'm—"

"Do not stand over me," Sabir said. "It is bad luck where I am going. I am not afraid to die. You will die like this one day as well."

"I'm sorry. I'm—"

"No more talking. Go next door. There is food and a blanket. Take these and anything else you need, then go past the town, along the river." He coughed. "In two days, the river divides. Go to the right. In another day, you will find a very large town. Maybe they can help you."

"Thank you," Springfield said, but Sabir was pushing him away.

The town's leader would die where he lay. Nothing would change that. The Thinker got to his feet and walked to the door. As soon as he stepped outside the cabin, screaming and flames were all around him. He paused there to make sure the man in black wasn't waiting for him around the corner. When he didn't spot anyone, he ran to the next cabin. He saw the stack of blankets Sabir had mentioned. Behind them, a child, no older than three years, was huddled in the fetal position, trying not to make a noise.

"I'm sorry," he told the toddler, knowing there was no chance the kid would understand anything he said. "I'm so sorry."

He took a blanket off the top, making sure the child was still covered by the rest, then grabbed a packet of what looked like rice and beans. Outside again, a man ran past him, almost knocking him over, before disappearing around the corner. Almost immediately, the sound of two clubs hitting each other echoed in the air. The man grunted and thudded on the ground.

The man in black was only feet away.

Springfield backed into the tall grass and the cover of trees. Hidden in the dark, he waited there so the mercenary wouldn't hear him stepping on leaves and twigs as he made his escape. He heard a cabin door open, more screaming, more flames. A figure appeared in the light of the doorway. Fire engulfed yet another home. The home next to it, already burning, collapsed.

When he was sure the man in black wasn't near him, Springfield began walking in the dark. Just as Sabir had directed, he followed the river. He did not stop to rest when he got tired. There was no chance he would be able to sleep, and stopping would only give the assassin time to pick up his trail again.

As he walked, he heard Sabir's words echoing in his head: *This is all your fault. You must keep going until this man and people like him do not exist anymore.*

He continued throughout the night.

60 - TAKE AWAY A LOT, GIVE BACK A LITTLE

After a month of forbidding its citizens from leaving the cities, the State relented. People still weren't allowed to take up permanent residence at beaches, parks, or forests, but, if they were willing to pay a tax, they could once again visit those places for short periods of time. After being cooped up in the crowded streets and packed freeways, everyone was happy to pay a fee if it meant they could see the ocean and get away from the smog and honking car horns.

Of course, it would take a lot of people to work at the new checkpoints that everyone would need to pass through to visit such destinations. Just like that, the State found a way to employ millions more people who had once complained about the leaders. Instead of saying how absurd it was to have to pay a tax just to visit a place that used to be free—both monetarily and personally—these new checkpoint guards remained quiet and happily collected their paychecks.

Lines of cars stretched for miles to be inspected by the State's expanded workforce. One of the guards would ask everyone to get out of the vehicle so he could pat them down and check their identification. Another worker would search inside the car, including, if he felt like it, going through everyone's luggage, while a third person walked around the car's perimeter with a device that was supposed to detect anything illegal. After the all-clear was given, assuming the State hadn't found anything it disliked, the family was free to go. The next car would pull up and the process would begin all over again. The lines wrapped all the way around the exit ramp, blocking traffic back on the highway. Some cars ran out of gas while they waited. Other people, realizing they would never get to the beach in time to enjoy the waves before having to turn around and go through the same inspection on their way back into the city, simply turned around and went home.

Guards stole money out of cars. Some threatened to detain people for no reason, unless they were given a couple dollars on the side. Women were groped. Every once in a while, an old woman was shot to death for refusing to let one of the State's workers reach up her skirt. When people complained, the State reminded them how many plots had been prevented because of the new inspection stations.

The Ruler went on television and said, "These shootings, as unfortunate as they are, have only occurred because the State is nice enough to let people once again go on vacation. If people are so outraged that they don't want the inspectors to go through their belongings or put their hands all over them, the State can always go back to disallowing all trips outside the cities."

After that, the people kept their complaints to themselves.

61 - WALKING AND THINKING

Springfield was still walking when the sun came up. Pausing only long enough to withdraw the second-to-last protein bar from his bag, he continued forward as he ate. When he needed something to drink, he bent over in mid-stride, scooped his water pouch through the river, and continued walking as it dripped through the filter. Finally, when his legs couldn't move anymore, he collapsed on the ground. It had been two days since he last slept.

When he did sleep, he dreamed of Jessica. They weren't fighting the State or making love. They were merely sitting on the sofa, holding hands and laughing at the television show she had wanted to finish watching with him before he left. When one episode was over, a new one began, Jessica said something, and Isaac laughed and kissed her.

Then he woke up.

Memories of how happy he had been with her, even in the world of the State, made him groan. Pain shot through every part of his legs when he forced himself to his feet and started walking again.

A series of thoughts cycled through his mind as he followed the river. He thought about the time traveler from the Roanoke Colony and what it must have felt like to give up his life, only to travel back too far in time to be of any use. For nothing more than a hope that it would impact life four hundred years later, the man had killed over two hundred people. Was the need to change the future so great that Springfield would be able to do the same thing?

He thought about how, instead of feeling lucky that he had survived the roll of the dice by appearing on land instead of in the ocean or falling out of the sky, the entire journey had been a waste. He was one of only roughly fifteen men, out of fifty, who might have survived their reappearance. Instead of appreciating that, however, he found himself wishing he could be back with Jessica and never think about time travel again. He would gladly watch the rest of the television show she had wanted to watch. After his next dinner with his parents, he would ask his dad if he wanted to finish the half-complete model they had put away so many years earlier.

Yes, he would be living in a world where nothing the State said was true, where people could vanish and never be heard from again, where a new war seemed to start each day. It was a world where his best friend from high school was either dead or spending the rest of his life in prison for a crime he hadn't committed. It was a world where his college roommate, knowing the State's men were outside his home, ready to take him away, had committed suicide rather than face being tortured. And for what crime? He had started a blog that tracked which of the State's leaders received the most money from the companies that got lucrative contracts during each war.

He was in a world where none of those things existed, and yet he found himself longing to return if it meant he could see Jessica and his parents again. Ashamed, he let out a long sigh and let his head drop to his chest. His legs began to move forward so slowly that they were barely moving at all, and he thought about stopping, laying down on the ground and not waking up. Either the man in black would find him and kill him, or he would wither away to become a set of sun-bleached bones on a barren path.

This is all your fault. You must keep going until this man and people like him do not exist anymore.

Sabir's words made him move on. Thinking of Jessica in the State's prisons, he quickened his pace. Images of all the people he had ever known who were now dead or in secret jail cells pushed him forward. For each person he knew of, there were thousands of others he didn't know. Jessica's brother wasn't the only person escorted away by the State's men and never seen again; all around the country there were brothers and sisters, fathers and mothers, who were also victims.

As he walked around a bend in the river, he thought about people having to accept what they were told by their leaders, even if it didn't make any sense, because doing anything else meant risking their livelihood. He thought about generations of kids who were taught to believe that war, no matter the reason, was patriotic. Yes, it was when fighting evil. But when war wasn't necessary, when it was war by choice and for profit rather than war of necessity, there was nothing patriotic about the State's bombs.

The thoughts distracted him from the smattering of bug bites dotting his arms and neck, but not even memories of the State could keep him from thinking about his aching legs. Each time he noticed he was slowing down, he darted forward again. Just as quickly, though, his feet would become heavy and stick to the earth. So stiff were his knees from walking for two days straight that he almost fell when his legs refused to step over a fallen branch.

It was obvious that he was pushing himself too hard. He wasn't some outdoor adventurer who had spent his life climbing mountains, hiking through the countryside, or preparing meals at a campfire. The longest he had ever jogged was in high school, when his gym teacher instructed everyone to run two miles if they wanted a good grade. He had completed the task in eighteen minutes. It had been a very average time back then. Now, he was lucky if he could hike a single mile in twice that time.

He couldn't start a fire even if he wanted to, and anyway, starting a fire would be suicide as long as the man in black was out there. Instead, he reached into the pouch of food that Sabir had left for him and nibbled on it. The uncooked rice and beans actually made him thankful for the bland protein bars that the scientists had given him.

He wished he could go back and have one more brainstorming session with his fellow time travelers. He would have raised his hand and asked if anyone in their group realized they were scholars, with absolutely no outdoor experience, and then said, "Maybe we could have a tarp, some waterproof socks, and mosquito repellent added to our canvas bags."

While it was possible that someone from Sabir's village had struck down the mercenary during the previous night's attack, Springfield seriously doubted it. In the dark, it would have been too easy for the killer to blend in with the havoc and slice people down one at a time. The mass confusion of screams and flames would have been the perfect atmosphere for him to murder until he was content, and then slip away in the night. It was wishful thinking to hope the man in black would be vulnerable without his assault blaster. It was almost as if he was an even better murderer when he killed with his hands and a blade, where he could see the life drain from each victim's eyes. Springfield had the suspicion that the assassin had never been happier. Some people dream of a beach villa in the Caribbean; the man in black probably dreamed of the indiscriminate killing of entire villages.

Birds chirped all around Springfield as he walked. Squirrels darted onto and off the path. A red fox watched him before disappearing into the brush. If he were on this trail with Jessica, these sights would reaffirm his belief in the beauty of the world. But with tired legs, a stomach wrapped into knots, and the weight of knowing both Chetnik's and Sabir's villages no longer existed because of him, the carefree animals only made him mad.

Eventually, the path opened to present a giant lake that stretched into the distance as far as he could see. Panic made his heart thump. Not because he thought he had run out of land and had nowhere else to go. Not because he was afraid of water. But because Sabir hadn't mentioned anything about a lake when he gave directions to the next town.

A series of doubts made Springfield's hands shake: *Did I take a wrong turn? Did I misunderstand what he said? Was Sabir just trying to get me away from his town as quickly as possible?*

But as he stood on the lake's shore, taking in his surroundings, he noticed what looked like tiny homes on the north side of the water. Once he noticed them, other homes and buildings also came into focus. His heart lurched. He couldn't help but smile. Sabir had been right all along.

Springfield's feet felt like they were going to fall off and he was so hungry he might throw up, but none of that mattered now. Without another thought, he made his way along the lake's edge, toward the town. It wasn't long before a woman, catching fish in a cove, saw him. He expected her to be frightened by the dirty and disheveled man coming out of the forest and go screaming back to her people. Instead, she laughed. She actually laughed!

As he approached, she put down her fishing net, smiled, and said something in a language he didn't understand.

Son of a bitch, he thought. *Why is it so difficult to find people who speak English, French, Arabic, Russian, or Chinese?*

Rather than attempting to find a mutual language, he smiled and nodded toward the town. The woman made an encouraging cooing noise and motioned him onward. As he continued past her, he looked back and saw that she had returned her attention to the fish. She was still smiling, though, as if she had placed a bet that very morning on whether or not a strange man would appear out of nowhere.

He passed a boy playing in the dirt with a collection of beetles. When the boy saw Springfield, he jumped to his feet and spoke excitedly in what might have been a combination of Arabic and some other local language. The beetles immediately became uninteresting and the boy followed three feet behind Springfield as he continued on.

A pair of farmers, inspecting the soil near a row of crops, noticed him and waved. The boy, still right behind Springfield, waved back at them on his guest's behalf. He had never seen a group of people so happy to have a visitor. Part of him wondered if this might be a town of cannibals who had just stumbled upon their next meal—proof that his mind had been warped by watching too many senseless movies.

When he got to the town proper, more people came out of their homes to greet him. A girl giggled, tugged on the time traveler's sleeve, then darted away. A woman brought him a tiny cup of water, which he drank and thanked her for.

For once, his heart didn't sink at the absence of power lines or running motors. Somewhere along the way, he had given up hope that he was in an age where he could be of any use to the Thinkers. Nor did he think about Chetnik's three sets of huts, all destroyed, or Sabir's town, burned to rubble and ash.

In place of all of those thoughts, as children ran in circles around him, a single idea formed: *I could get used to this.*

62 - A SHOOTING

The lines at the inspection stations kept growing as people queued up to be allowed out of the cities. At some of the longer lines, the first day of a family vacation would be spent inching forward, stopping, and then inching forward again, for miles. The routine was repeated the final day of vacations, when everyone had to return to their homes in the city. Half of a four-day vacation was spent in lines.

All it took was one frustrated driver for everything to unravel. Fed up with spending his vacation in his car with his family instead of at the beach, he growled and pulled around the marker that said STOP. The guards yelled, but rather than waiting for men in uniforms to grope his wife and kids, the driver ignored the commands and sped away. Another car immediately did the same thing. Then another.

Presented with the possibility of being at their destination that same day, rather than waiting in line for hours just to be harassed by the inspectors, the entire line of vehicles swerved to the side so they could attempt the identical maneuver.

"We can't let them get by," one of the inspectors said.

There would be hell to pay when the AeroCams alerted the State's watch center that a group of cars had gotten through the checkpoint without being searched. The guards and everyone else working that day would surely lose their wonderful new jobs where they got to boss people around all day.

"Well, stop them," another guard said.

None of the workers were sure what to do. During their orientation, they had been told they had full authority to detain anyone they wanted, for any reason they wanted. But a week-long training session, mainly covering the proper way to pat someone down, hadn't prepared them for a revolt. They *had* been given assault blasters, though, just like the army carried—didn't that mean they deserved the same respect that a soldier received?

One of the guards tried to stand in front of an oncoming car, but the driver only swerved further to the side, refusing to slow down.

"If I step out any further, they'll run me over."

The other guard yelled, "Stop," and leveled his rifle at the next car that was passing by.

But this vehicle also passed by without the brake lights flickering.

"Stop," he said again at the next car.

It passed too.

They were being paid to make sure each car was inspected and each person inside the cars was patted down and questioned. They got sick leave, a retirement plan, and all the other benefits they could ask for. It was the best job any of them had ever held. Finally, they felt like they had the positions of authority they had always deserved but were never given. Without this job, they would go back to being nobodies. That could be the least of their troubles, however. If the State found out how many cars they had let slip by, they might even be accused of being associates of the Thinkers. They would be sent to a secret prison or end up dead.

"Stop," the guard said one final time.

When the next driver also ignored the command, the

guard pulled the trigger of his assault blaster. The station wagon's rear windshield burst away. The trunk exploded open. Both back tires blew out.

The car drifted slightly to the left, away from the line of other vehicles that were escaping to an early vacation. Ten feet off the road, it reached the guardrail. Sparks shot out from the driver's side door where it dragged against the wall. The driver didn't try to accelerate away. Nor did he step on the brake. No one inside the car made any noise. Both parents were slumped forward in their seats. Only bits and pieces of their child remained in the backseat. An infant's arm was on the dashboard. One of its hands ended up by the driver's feet.

The driver in the car directly behind the station wagon saw the carnage and panicked. Flooring the gas pedal, he swerved around the destroyed car and tried to get his family to safety. The guard who had been standing motionless while the first vehicle was shot up, broke out of his stupor and opened fire on this second car. This time, when the driver died, his foot didn't relax from the gas pedal. The car drove full-speed off the road into a ditch and then a tree. Of the four people who had been in the car, only one, a little girl, made any noise. Her howls were endless. She would, one day, grow up to be a Thinker, along with all the other children who witnessed the scene that day.

A third guard came running over and pointed his assault blaster at the cars still waiting to pass through the inspection station. None of the other drivers were trying to get through the checkpoint any more, but after being so close to blaster fire, the third inspector was in shock and took his lead from the other two men. He emptied his rifle into the line of parked cars in front of him.

People abandoned their vehicles and ran back in the direction they had come. The first guard had a new clip in his rifle and was looking for anyone who wanted to start a fight. By this point, though, everyone was either dead or fleeing the scene.

When it was over, nineteen people were dead. The inspection station was closed for a month while the State performed an internal investigation. At the end of the review, the official report stated that the guards had acted in self-defense and that those who had died in the two cars had been Thinkers trying to evade the checkpoint. Two of the three guards involved in the shootout were given no punishment at all and immediately returned to work. The third, the man who started the shooting, was given a year's paid leave.

People were outraged, of course. To quell the anger, the State released additional information about the people who had died in the shooting. Not only had they been Thinkers, but inside their trunks the State had supposedly found weapons capable of destroying a major city.

No one believed this, so the official story changed again. New evidence, classified of course, showed that the people in the cars had actually shot themselves so they wouldn't be captured alive and end up revealing information about Thinker plots. People didn't believe this either, but a few days later, the State's bombs started falling on another country and the shooting became old news.

63 - A CELEBRITY SCANDAL

Springfield was welcomed with open arms. The townspeople watched as a wrinkled, little woman gave him a washcloth that he used to clean his face and hands. A portly woman brought him another cup of water to drink. Someone even handed him a small plate of rice and meat. He thanked them all while he shoveled food into his mouth.

None of them understood Russian or Chinese. Two of them understood a few words of Arabic, but not enough to be useful. He was surprised to find that the language he had most in common with them was French.

When they asked him where he was from, all he said was, "A land very far from here."

None of them asked how he had come to wander into their town. He assumed it would be part of later conversations. As he spoke to the townspeople, children ran by and tagged him on the shoulder. He smiled, assuming they were making him a part of their game, but didn't have the strength to play along.

Trying to determine what country he was in, he asked if the town was part of a larger community. Not even the people who spoke French understood what he was trying to get at. One of the men, upon hearing Springfield's question, said their town was part of Braclawskie, but Springfield, for all of his knowledge of geography and history, had no idea who or what Braclawskie was.

It would have told him a lot if they at least knew who Napoleon was, but none of them reacted when he mentioned the name. Not a good sign for his future prospects.

He was in the middle of a second bowl of food when a man came running up, speaking in the language Springfield didn't understand. Whatever the man had to say, it made everyone groan with horror. The nearby children not only stopped playing, they all went indoors.

"You came from the town southeast of here?" a man said to Springfield in French.

Springfield nodded.

"This gentleman says the entire town is destroyed."

Another man walked up and yanked Springfield's bag from his shoulder. Too busy thinking of what he should say and what he should keep to himself, Springfield didn't try to stop the man. With the bag untied, the man withdrew Springfield's short knife, holding it in the air for everyone to see. Only a few people didn't gasp.

The person who had come running up with news of Sabir's village said something else, which caused the man holding Springfield's knife to drop it back in the bag and say, "This man reports that everyone in the town was killed with a blade."

"I can explain all of this," Springfield said, but that was all he got to say before two men, one on either side of him, were hauling him into the city.

As they walked, Springfield offered comments like, "This is a misunderstanding," and "I didn't do it," but the men dragging him either didn't care to hear what he had to say or didn't understand French.

They took him to a small two-story building near the center of town. Except for a few tiny windows, the entire structure was made of grey blocks of stone. Another man was already waiting at the building's entrance when Springfield's two escorts deposited him on a wooden chair. The man had thick, black eyebrows with matching dark eyes that made his entire face look like it was cast in shadows.

"My name is Wladyslaw," the man said in French.

"My name is Springfield."

"Springfield, tell me, were you at Sabir's town two nights ago?"

"Yes, but—"

The man motioned for silence. "And tell me this, was the town unaffected? Was Sabir healthy when you left?"

"There was another man, he—"

Wladyslaw motioned for silence again. The two men who brought Springfield to the room were still standing on either side of him. It was then, maybe because of the way he was being questioned, or the way the two men remained there, or the fact that the building's windows were tiny—much too small for a man to climb through—that he realized he was in the town's jail. A burst of fear caused his spine to tingle, making his ass and throat clench tight. He had never expected something like this when the glowing oval tubes sent him back in time. He would have rather appeared in the middle of the Pacific Ocean and drowned or been eaten by sharks than walk all this way just to spend the rest of his life in a dungeon.

"Listen," he said. "I can explain everything."

The interrogator held up a hand, then said, "Silence. The constable will be back tomorrow morning. You will have a chance to defend yourself then. You will spend the night here."

There wasn't much the time traveler could say to this. Wladyslaw was already turning to leave. The other two men took Springfield down a hall to a room that would be his cell. He had expected something so small that he couldn't lay flat on his back with his legs straight out, but the room they put him in was large enough for a crowd of people.

"Get a lot of protestors here?" he said with a smile, trying to make friends with the men who had become his wardens.

Neither of the men smiled. Probably, they had no idea what a protestor was because it was a fairly recent invention in the history of man.

He was in the room for two hours when a woman brought him a bowl of soup.

"*Merci*," he said, but all of the good cheer he was initially welcomed with was gone now. The woman did not acknowledge him or even look in his direction before disappearing back down the hallway.

Still, it wasn't so bad. At least he would have a chance to explain things in the morning. He was sure a reasonable man would hear his side of the story and know that what he was saying was plausible. In the meanwhile, he was eating warm food, much better than the protein bars he had quickly gotten sick of, and he was on dry ground. It would be the best night of sleep he would get since disappearing from the apartment building's basement. No, things weren't bad at all. In fact, this could even be considered a good night.

He was dumb enough to think this until the two guards reappeared later that afternoon. They weren't alone. Between them, another man was being escorted into the jail cell. The prisoner was going to be spending the night in the same small room as Springfield.

Springfield found himself scooting backwards, away from the cell door, even though his back was already against the stonewall. It wasn't that he thought a good night's sleep was ruined. It wasn't that he was afraid of being stabbed in the night by some gang member trying to make a name for himself. It was who the guards were escorting that upset him. When the prisoner saw Springfield, he not only smiled, he burst out laughing.

It was the man in black.

64 - BUSINESS AS USUAL

A week later, the State's bombs had stopped falling. Yet another country was turned to rubble. A private army of contractors would remain behind for another decade, collecting billions of dollars for their services.

It wasn't until the violence was over that the State bothered to justify the most recent attack. First, they said the country's government had been providing support to the Thinkers. But when a group of Thinkers released documents online that proved they had no relationship with the doomed country, the State said they had dropped the bombs because the foreign government was engaging in genocide on its own people. When evidence didn't support this claim either, the Ruler went on television and said the war was to liberate the people from their corrupt politicians. No one could be sure if this was intended as black humor or was just ironic.

At home, the State had reopened all of the inspection stations that people needed to pass through to leave the cities and visit the parks and beaches. Now, though, twice as many guards manned each checkpoint. There was no money to pay for the additional guards, and the State was already in a debt it would never be able to get itself out of, but it was the only solution the leaders knew.

No one questioned if the inspection stations were actually effective because the State had already offered countless reassurances that the security checks had prevented hundreds of attacks. And anyway, once the inspection stations were there, nothing could make them go away. As soon as the State found another way to control people, it would never give up that power, not even if the threat they had supposedly been created to address no longer existed. People would just have to get used to having their genitals groped and their luggage inspected if they wanted to go to the beach. Just as they would have to get used to asking for permission to withdraw money from the bank to pay for the vacation.

Whenever the next disaster did happen—it was inevitable that one would, because nothing could ever guarantee everyone's safety for the rest of time—the State would create more laws and find additional ways to give themselves power. It was business as usual.

65 - UM, EXCUSE ME

"*Um, excusez moi,*" Springfield said as the guards opened the door to the jail cell, ushering the man in black inside the same room as him.

The two guards looked at Springfield with a frown. If neither of them understood French, he wouldn't live long enough to tell the constable his story in the morning. The two guards looked at each other, then back at their first prisoner.

"*Oui?*" the guard on the right said finally.

Springfield stepped closer to the door, his peripheral vision on the man in black just in case the mercenary grabbed him while the guards were still there. He noticed, though, that the killer was smiling, was more than happy to wait until the two of them were alone together.

The room had seemed large when Springfield was first ushered into it. Now, it seemed like a coffin. Once the cell door closed, he would be trapped. It wasn't as though the time traveler could put up any kind of fight against a trained killer.

Although the man in black could hear everything Springfield would say, he wouldn't be able to understand anything that was spoken in French.

"If you leave me in this cell with this man," he said,

"I'll be dead in the morning."

The guards shrugged and pulled the door closed anyway.

Springfield gripped the iron bars. "The constable will be here in the morning to hear my story. When I'm finished, he's going to set me free. If I'm not able to meet with him, he'll be very upset with you."

"It will not be long," one of the guards said in broken French as he fumbled for the key to lock the cell door. "Only few hour."

"Even one minute is too much," Springfield said. "As soon as you leave, this man will kill me."

"We will be down hallway. We come if trouble."

"You don't understand. This man is a trained killer. I'll be dead by the time you get back in the jail cell."

Still holding the key in the lock, the guard considered what Springfield said. The second guard, who had been standing there silently the entire time, said something to the one who was speaking with Springfield. The first guard translated everything that had just been said. The second guard kept frowning, not interested in the story their prisoner had to tell.

"Please," Springfield said, "just move me to another cell until the constable arrives."

"We have only one room," the first guard replied.

"I tell you, I will be dead if you leave me here with him," Springfield said, gesturing with his eyes to the man sitting on the ground behind him.

The two guards spoke some more, then the first guard turned back to Springfield and said, "We may have something."

But instead of helping Springfield, the guard turned and walked away, out of sight.

"Please don't go!" he called.

Only the guard who didn't understand anything Springfield said was still there. The time traveler turned and looked at the man in black. The mercenary was sitting with his back to the far wall, smirking at how panicked the Thinker was. He knew it was a matter of time until the guards left the two of them alone. Until then, he was happy to watch the show.

A clanging could be heard. The first guard reappeared, a thick chain draped across one shoulder. When he got back to the cell, the second guard reopened the door. The man in black didn't move.

"Don't get too close to him," Springfield warned the guards. "He's more dangerous than he's acting."

The guard who understood French gave a sigh, as if irritated with the inmate's suggestion, but at the same time he whispered something to his friend, who withdrew a knife from his pocket and held it toward the man in black. The mercenary would not make a good poker player; his grin disappeared, replaced by a look of hatred.

With a loud clang, the guard let the chain fall on the ground in front of the assassin, then motioned for the prisoner to pick it up.

At the end of the metal links was an iron cuff. The guard with the knife motioned for the man in black to secure it around his ankle. The mercenary didn't acknowledge the request. Instead, he glanced first at Springfield, then at the knife and at the two guards. Even as the one guard moved his blade closer to the assassin's face, the man in black seemed to calculate if it was better to kill the men now, or wait until the morning. The guard with the knife saw how his prisoner was assessing his chances and quickly pressed the knife's edge to his cheek, causing a prick of blood to trickle down the assassin's face.

You'll pay for that, the mercenary's expression said.

But he complied and put the shackle around his ankle, then let the guard lock it closed. The other man looped the opposite end of the chain through a metal ring that was bolted to the wall.

"*Dormez bien*," the French-speaking guard said to Springfield on his way out of the cell.

"Yes, I will sleep well," Springfield said. "Thank you."

And with that, he was alone with the man in black in the dirt cell. The two men sat on the opposite sides of the room. There they remained, motionless. Other than the sound of their breathing, there was perfect silence. No noise of an air conditioner. No sound of an audience's laughter coming from a television. There weren't even any cars or motorcycles outside.

"Do you know where and when you are?" Springfield said, returning to English.

"Shut up."

"What I mean is, do you—"

"Shut up, Thinker. I'm going to sleep."

And with that, the man in black laid out straight, turned on his side so his back was to Springfield, and let out a long breath. After that, he was silent and still. If he wasn't asleep, he was good at pretending he was.

Springfield was left to think of what he would tell the constable the next day. How could he make someone believe that the man in black alone was responsible for so much killing? And beyond that, what would he do with the rest of his life? Would it be spent in this cell, with a man sworn to kill him?

These were the things he thought about until his eyes eventually closed and he too was asleep.

He awoke in the middle of the night to find the man in black standing over him. The mercenary's arms were outstretched, reaching for any part of Springfield that he could grab hold of. With a gasp, the time traveler tried to scurry backwards. He was already against the wall, however, and managed only to hit his head against the stone. There was no place he could go to get away from the killer, but also, luckily, no more slack on the chain to allow the assassin closer.

Any sense of resignation that the man in black pretended to have was gone. He was growling, arms outstretched, but the shackle kept him from crossing the final third of the room. Undeterred, the mercenary leapt forward like a rabid dog jumping against its collar, not caring that it choked itself each time it tried for blood. With his free foot, the killer kicked at Springfield. Failing to wrap his fingers around his intended target only made him despise the Thinker even more.

In the darkness of night, the man in black appeared like a demon. Not the glowing red, fiery eyes variety. No horns or long fangs. He was the cloaked version. The kind sent by the Grim Reaper itself. The type that appears whether someone believes in God or they don't. The kind that leaves a bloody mess behind as proof that pain and suffering are real things.

Once the mercenary was sure he couldn't stretch any further, he went back to the corner and lay down again. Springfield remained against the far corner of the room, his knees to his chest. Neither of them had spoken during the entire episode.

For a long time, Springfield sat there, motionless, expecting the man in black to jump up and try again. But the assassin didn't waste the energy. He was a murderer and a savage, but he wasn't without a sense of tactics and common sense.

With a man who wanted him dead only a few feet away, Springfield didn't think there was any chance he would be able to go back to sleep again. But an hour later his eyes grew heavy and no matter how many times he tried to blink himself into remaining awake, his eyelids stayed shut longer and longer. With resignation, he finally gave in to sleep.

It was still dark outside when he next awoke. It took his eyes a moment to adjust to the darkness. The man in black was still on the ground at the opposite corner of the cell. Instead of sleeping, though, the killer was trying to use a section of the metal chain to whittle away the stone where the bolt was keeping him tied to the wall.

In the dark, Springfield couldn't see if the mercenary was making any progress. There was nothing he could do except hope that he didn't hear the chain drop against the ground, followed by the rush of footsteps coming toward him. The assassin worked quietly, without giving up or taking breaks, running the chain links back and forth around the bolt.

Morning couldn't come soon enough.

66 - THE NEW NORM

"How was your vacation?" Jessica asked the woman in the cubicle next to her.

"It was okay. We were in the inspection lines longer than we were at the beach. One of the guards touched Jill under her dress. They went through all my clothes. But it was nice to get away for a couple days, I guess."

Jessica lowered her voice and leaned closer to the woman before saying, "You do remember that two months ago, you could go to the beach whenever you wanted, right?"

The other woman frowned, as if the checkpoints had been a part of her vacations back when she was little. People had no alternative if they wanted to leave the city, and so they quickly grew accustomed to the invasion as if it had always been a normal aspect of their time away from home.

"It's not so bad, though," the woman said. "The extra two days off, while we were waiting in line, gave me more time to spend with my kids. I was mad about the guard touching my little girl like that, but he said the Thinkers have started planting weapons on little kids as a way to sneak them out of the city, and he had to make sure Jill wasn't carrying a nuclear bomb."

"And you believed him?"

"You make it sound like he just wanted an excuse to touch my daughter."

Jessica turned back to her computer. What else was there to say to someone who would let their own children fall victim to the State's men so easily?

"Well," she said over her shoulder, "At least it makes you feel safer. I suppose that counts for something."

She thought to add, *If I had kids, I wouldn't let them be touched like that,* but then she realized she wouldn't have a choice in the matter. If she complained, the guard would have her arrested and she would never see her children again. The only other alternative was never going through the inspection stations in the first place, becoming a prisoner in one's own home, the way Isaac's parents were in theirs. Ashamed, she turned to apologize to the woman, but her co-worker was already gone.

Hopefully not to report me as a possible Thinker, she thought.

But again, what could she do if she was or wasn't reported other than to stay quiet, keep her head down, and hope no one ever had a reason to take notice of her? For the first time, she was glad Isaac was gone. They had only recently begun to talk about having children. Now that he had vanished, she didn't have to worry about whether or not she would have a son or daughter to raise. And without children, she didn't have to worry about how to protect them from the State.

67 - THE MOST IMPORTANT MORNING OF A TIME TRAVELER'S LIFE

Springfield was already awake when the two guards arrived in the morning. Behind them, the constable took inventory of the new prisoners. Springfield was sitting against the opposite corner of the room from the man in black, his knees to his chest and his head down. The mercenary was lying on his back with his legs out straight, looking up at the ceiling.

The constable was a middle-aged man with thinning, grey hair. Even when he didn't talk, his mouth hung open an inch, putting his gigantic teeth on display. Although wider than the two guards in front of him, he was also shorter, making him look like a walking sea lion.

A grin spread slowly across the man's face. Either the sight of two prisoners in a cell made him happy, or else everything made him happy. He spoke to the two guards in their native language, pointing first at Springfield and then at the man in black. Springfield offered a polite smile. Not interested in making a good first impression, the man in black stared at the three men on the other side of the cell door as if they were already dead and just didn't realize it yet. Even this made the constable whistle and grin in a childlike way.

The constable said something else to the two guards. The one who understood French mumbled an answer and left.

Unlocking the door, the constable turned to Springfield and said, "*Bonjour.*"

"*Bonjour,*" Springfield said, smiling.

The little round man motioned for the remaining guard to help Springfield to his feet and then led him out of the cell by the shoulder.

"Where are we going?" Springfield asked in French as they were walking down the hall, leaving the man in black shackled where he had been all night.

"To chat," the constable said. "Over breakfast. You must be starving."

After walking up a flight of stairs, they came to a room with two big windows looking out over the town. Following a night in the dank prison cell, he appreciated the sun and the sounds of people and animals. He saw a man with a mule hauling a cart of hay or wheat. A group of women carried baskets of dirty clothes. A circle of children huddled together as they played some sort of game. The clangs of a blacksmith, hard at work, hammer against anvil, rang out. A rooster made sure everyone was awake.

The guard motioned for Springfield to sit in one of the chairs while the constable sat in another.

As the second guard left, Springfield said, "Aren't you afraid I might be a killer?"

The sea lion laughed. "You are like me." When it was obvious Springfield didn't know what this meant, the still-smiling constable added, "You don't look like you could kill much of anything."

"Thanks, I guess."

"My name is Mikolaj."

"I'm Springfield."

"Tell me, Springfield, what brings you to our part of the world?"

But the time traveler thought there were more

important things to discuss. "You have to believe me that I had nothing to do with what happened to Sabir and his people. The man downstairs did all of that. He wants to do the same to me. I'm—"

Mikolaj raised his hand for silence, his big teeth still on display. When Springfield was quiet, the constable said, "What part of the world are you from?"

"Past France."

"Past France?" Mikolaj said, and Springfield nodded.

It was doubtful the constable had ever been to the country, let alone travelled past it. Probably, like the others Springfield had met, he knew the language from doing business with French traders.

"And the man downstairs is trying to kill you?"

"Yes."

"Why?"

"Because I believe something different than he believes. It threatens him. He doesn't understand how to settle differences other than by killing."

"Ah, you are a man of ideas. Ideas can be very dangerous."

"That's true," Springfield said, thinking back to all the people he had known during his life who had either been arrested for their beliefs, disappeared for their words, or killed for their actions.

"Tell me, what idea does the man downstairs want to kill you over?"

"Freedom," Springfield said. "A man should have basic rights. Leaders should govern with respect for their people, not rule with fear and deception."

Mikolaj stopped smiling. When he spoke, he said, almost in a whisper, "These are very dangerous ideas indeed."

"The most dangerous. Because they are worth dying for."

The constable frowned. Springfield wondered if the man across from him lived in a town where the people had no such rights, or perhaps didn't even know they could.

293

"If they are worth dying for," Mikolaj said, "why do you not confront the man downstairs instead of running from him?"

"I'm not a killer. People like me don't fight with weapons. We use reasoning to show others that there is a better way to live."

"And your words bother this man so much that he would hunt you across the lands until you are dead?"

Before Springfield could answer, one of the guards came back into the room, a plate of food in either hand. He delivered one to the constable and the other to Springfield.

"Ah, breakfast," Mikolaj said, suddenly jovial again.

On Springfield's plate were two eggs, a biscuit, a few slices of what looked like apple, and meat of some kind. The smell was intoxicating.

"*Merci*," Springfield said before shoveling the food into his mouth. While he wasn't proud of himself for his lack of manners, he was even more embarrassed that he was weeping as he ate. "It's been a long time since I had real food," he explained.

"Slow down. Enjoy."

But the food was gone before he could savor it. He didn't even care that there was no milk or water to go along with the breakfast.

"Did the man downstairs really destroy an entire town by himself?" Mikolaj said as he put a piece of fruit into his mouth.

"Not just Sabir's town, but three smaller villages also."

The constable's eyes widened.

"Why would he do that?"

"Because he was following me and I went to those places. He will murder anyone he comes across until he kills me."

"If he is going to keep murdering until he has you, shouldn't we hand you over to him right away so the killing stops?"

"You can't do that!"

"Why not?"

"Because then," Springfield said, struggling for something more meaningful to the constable than the only words he could think of, "because then you would be saying that it's okay for a ruler to treat his people however he wants. It would be okay to live in fear. You would be no better than him."

"Why do you assume that's not how I feel?"

"I—" Springfield began, but he didn't quite know how to continue. Based on the limited use of metal in town, he assumed he was living before the nineteenth century, somewhere between France and India. But without knowing more than this, he really had no idea what someone like Mikolaj would believe. Maybe the town did abide by the commands of a ruler who required complete obedience. But the way the children played outside told him different. The way the women sang while they carried baskets of clothes to the river. Even the way the constable smiled. All of these things made Springfield believe he couldn't be in a land where people had to do as they were told or else they would be executed.

He looked at the constable and said, "Everyone I've seen here seems too happy to be living without respect for each other."

Mikolaj regarded this statement as he nibbled on a piece of meat. After swallowing, he said, "I have seen many people smiling the day before they are sent to their death. Even under the worst conditions, people find things to be happy about."

"Maybe that's true, but it's also human nature to treat people the way you want to be treated."

"What do you think I should do with you?" the constable said. "Don't you think it would be easiest if I just had both of you executed? That way it would be like nothing ever happened. The town could go back to how it was before you arrived."

"You would give me breakfast, just to have me killed?"

"Why not?"

Maybe it was the way Mikolaj said these things, with a half smile, but Springfield got the impression the constable was more interested in the debate than in actually deciding outcomes.

"Because men deserve better than that. Living things deserve to have a chance to make their own lives, not to be thrown away on the whims of those who only care about power."

"Maybe so," the constable said. "Maybe so."

The guard came back in and retrieved the two empty plates. He said something to Mikolaj and the constable nodded. Then the guard was gone again.

"Tell me, what should I do with the man downstairs?"

"I don't know."

"You don't know? Shouldn't he be killed?"

"I don't know. I've seen him kill more people than I thought anybody would be capable of killing, and I know he'll keep on doing it as long as he has a chance to murder me."

"Then why not kill him?"

"If I say he should be killed, am I any different than him?"

"My friend," Mikolaj said, smiling again, "You would make an absolutely awful constable."

68 - THE NEXT MOVE

"Our top story tonight," the anchorman said as the evening news started, "Flooding and storms continue to batter the Midwest."

"Thank God," Isaac's mother said.

Isaac's father understood exactly why she would say such a thing. It wasn't that she was happy that people were losing their homes to torrential downpours; she was relieved that another day had passed without hearing of a fresh attack or another shooting. There had always been people willing to inflict violence on others, and there always would be. What she dreaded was the State's response to whatever happened. What other part of people's lives could they control?

Each time a bomb went off or a computer was hacked or a plane crashed, the State passed more laws. They couldn't, as the old saying went, let any tragedy go to waste. And because the new restrictions rarely served to prevent of a similar tragedy from occurring in the future, there would always be more chances for another disaster. Everyone was left to guess which aspect of daily life would change next.

Yes, there would always be violence and people able to make violence. The Thinkers knew this, and so they accepted it. But the State refused to acknowledge it. Not only that, they also insisted that the public refuse to believe it. Because if the public knew that additional laws wouldn't prevent every single future attack, they wouldn't tolerate the conditions they were subjected to. A man who is trying to provide for his family only puts up with being searched and frisked each day because he has to get to the job that pays for his family's food and shelter. If he could support his loved ones without wasting part of each day standing in line just to be harassed and answering the same stupid questions every time, he would quickly grow impatient with not only that specific intrusion, but with the entire State.

That's why the State needs the next attack. If one doesn't happen quickly enough, they make their own or start another war. Through it all, the people are told the State is protecting them, and so they believe it. Meanwhile, more laws are passed. Another restriction is established. More guidelines need to be adhered to. But no matter how many laws are passed, no matter how much control the State has over its population, it can never keep people safe forever. And so life will only keep getting worse.

Isaac's father said, "Maybe tomorrow's headline will be another recall of spinach."

"I'm keeping my fingers crossed."

69 - A NEW HOME?

After breakfast, Mikolaj gave Springfield a tour of the town. Occasionally, the constable had to scold children for being pests as they ran in circles around their guest. Even the adults stared at him as he passed.

"What will you do with the other prisoner?" Springfield asked.

"We do not have the resources nor the desire to keep him in that cell for the rest of his life. But we also don't kill people. No matter what they do. I can't say I always agree with that; there are some crimes deserving of the guillotine. But it has always been that way in this town, and so I follow the tradition."

"What will you do then?"

"Our traders sometimes travel to faraway posts. The few times we have had a prisoner who cannot be set free in the immediate area, we take him out in the wilderness and let him go. It has only happened twice in all the years I have been doing this."

"If you try that with the man in the cell, he will simply kill the people transporting him, take their wagon, and ride it back into town."

"We'll have him tied up. The wagon will be long gone

by the time he frees himself."

"Even so, aren't you concerned that he may come right back?"

"It is over five hundred kilometers. He will never find his way."

"You underestimate this man's resolve. He'll never stop as long as he thinks I'm alive."

Mikolaj sighed. "If the unlikely occurs and the man does show up again, my guards will have no choice but to kill him."

The constable motioned for Springfield to enter one of the wooden buildings lining the main thoroughfare in town. Inside, the time traveler saw a collection of rugs and tapestries. Some looked Middle Eastern. Others, Asian. A set of plates and dishes was arranged at the end of a long table.

Mikolaj picked up a curved metal shaft and handed it to Springfield. It was an intricately carved dueling pistol.

"If the man insists on coming back to the town, we have these." The constable smiled at the object in Springfield's hand. "They are becoming very popular. Do they have them where you are from?"

"A version, yes," Springfield said.

The weapon in his hand was a beautiful piece of craftsmanship, inlaid with real gold and silver, but all Springfield could think of was his parents and Jessica. In his hand was an item that would win people their independence, then, hundreds of years later, become the symbol of the State's rule.

How many times had journalists ended up dead—always of what was declared to be a suicide even though it obviously wasn't—after covering a story critical of the State? How many writers had ended up in a dumpster or in the desert, a single shot to the back of their head, after their book exposed the State's treachery? Somewhere along the way, the item in Springfield's hand no longer symbolized individual freedom, but rather the lack of it.

He handed the pistol back to the constable, then said,

"When do you plan on taking him out into the wilderness and releasing him?"

"Our next trip to Samara is next month."

So that was it, Springfield thought. He had a month to decide what he was going to do.

Next, Mikolaj took his guest to an empty home at the edge of town. There was nothing on the structure to let Springfield know if it was reserved for guests who were traveling through the area, or if it belonged to someone who had recently died. Whatever purpose it had served, the constable intended it to become something else.

"This will be your new home," the sea lion said.

Springfield had no idea what he should say other than "I have no money. I have no way of paying for this."

Mikolaj laughed. "You can work in town. There are always things to do."

And that was what Springfield found himself doing. Each morning, he woke up and asked people if there was anything he could do for them. His first two weeks there, he showed two of the local farmers how to build a better irrigation system for their crops. Although not a farmer himself, he did have the benefit of knowing various advances that would be developed during the next centuries. He made sure not to reveal anything that would change the course of history. There was no telling how the Theta Timeline might be affected if two obscure farmers in Eurasia were given credit for sweeping innovations in crop growth. But he didn't think it would hurt anything if he helped them get additional water to more of their land. For his work, the farmers provided him with three meals a day.

In the field with them one day, he said, "I've been traveling for so long, I can't remember what year it is."

Thinking he was making a joke, the farmers only laughed.

As one of the farmer's wives presented him with breakfast, he said, "I've lost track of how many years I've been away from home. What year is it anyway?"

But the farmer's wife didn't understand French.

The next week, he taught French to all the school children. He had no idea how to speak their language and almost none of them knew French, so he had no idea how much or how little they were actually benefitting from what he was teaching. The parents seemed happy, though, because they too offered him as much food as he wanted.

During his very first lesson, he stood in front of a chalkboard and said, "Who can say the date in French?"

A boy raised his hand.

"Yes?"

The boy cleared his throat. "*Un, sept, six, un.*"

"*Très bon!*" Springfield said. Very good indeed.

One, seven, six, one. That was how he was finally able to determine the year he had been sent back to. He continued the lesson, all the while thinking about what it meant to be living in 1761.

Life didn't change just because he had finally discovered the year. Roosters woke him each morning. Cows sauntered past during the day, always offering their casual moos. At night, he listened to the wolves far off in the mountains. Through all of it, there were no AeroCams above him, no guards telling him to empty his pockets or trying to determine if he should be detained. There was no war, no suffering. It was a nice life.

Everyone around him seemed happy just to go about their business and to live their lives. Thoughts began to creep into his head that he never would have thought possible. He reminded himself that no one from his own time would know if he changed the Theta Timeline or not. It wasn't as though they would wake up one day with the realization that the world they knew was altered. If the Theta Timeline did shift, their awareness would shift as well, and everyone would see the new world as if it were the place they had known all along, because in some reality, it had been. He thought about how his parents and Jessica would never look outside, notice a sky free of AeroCams, and know he had altered history for them. Their consciousness would simply transfer into another reality as if that reality had always been their life.

And then he thought that if those realities existed anyway, why should he try to change the Theta Timeline at all? Just because their collective consciousness was set on one reality didn't preclude the other, happier timelines from existing. And likewise, just because he might shift the Theta Timeline to give everyone a State-free consciousness didn't mean that other timelines, even worse than the one they knew, wouldn't still exist. No matter what he would do, there would still be timelines in which everyone was free and timelines in which everyone was ruled by the State. In the end, did it really make any difference what he did or didn't do?

Hell, no one he cared about even knew he had been sent into history. If enough time went by, they would all probably come to regard him as the radical that the State had labeled him and be glad he was gone. Maybe Jessica and his parents, the very people he was trying to make a better world for, had already begun thinking of him as someone they had never truly known. The constant reports on television, each saying how much of a danger he had been, would eventually cause them to view him as the State wanted him to be viewed.

None of it mattered anyway, because he was too far back in time to make a difference. There were things he could try to do to change the Theta Timeline, but they were all long shots, like the Roanoke Settlement.

"Damn it," he groaned from the comfort of his new bed and shut his eyes.

With only darkness in front of him, his mind was quieted. When he reopened them, he realized the internal voice was the same one that always managed to convince people that quitting was okay. A similar voice had told him it didn't make a difference if he stopped building the model aircraft carrier with his father or if he stopped watching the final few episodes of the television show that Jessica had enjoyed. The only difference was that this voice also had fear and fatigue behind it.

He hadn't left his parents and Jessica just so he could live in some forgotten town and teach children a foreign language. He had risked his life for this mission. There was only one thing that could make it okay for him to leave his old life, to never kiss Jessica again, never hug his parents again: freedom for the people he loved and for everyone else too. Not the version of freedom that the State talked about, but the real thing. Not being told they were free, but knowing they truly were.

And yet, in a quiet town, surrounded by people who adored him, away from the troubles of his old life, he began to understand the power that time travel could have over someone. There was an allure that came with appearing in a new time and place. That much he knew for sure. He thought of the pyramids and the pharaohs who had commanded them to be built. Only then did he realize how dangerously close he had come to repeating the lapse made by another of his fellow time travelers.

No matter how much of a long shot changing the Theta Timeline might be, he owed it to his parents and Jessica and everyone else who lived under the State's rule to try.

As if to confirm these thoughts, he said aloud, "I can't stay here."

Alone in his tiny house, no one was there to agree or disagree with his comment.

70 - THE PYRAMIDS

In addition to the hieroglyphics that line the inner walls of the pyramids, there are also a series of illustrations etched into the stone. Both the words and the pictures offer stories about the pharaohs, the people they ruled, and their gods. Most of the hieroglyphics recount what daily life was like for the Egyptians. Some narrate what could be ancient fables.

One illustration in particular, however, has interested archeologists for centuries. The drawing is of a man-like being floating in the sky, glowing with sunlight, as he presides over the entire Egyptian civilization. The god, identified by historians as Ra, the Sun God, even hovers over the pharaoh. Only a god as powerful as Ra could be depicted above a pharaoh without mass executions being carried out.

The pyramids, located just outside Cairo, are on the 29 N latitude, the same parallel that runs through Mexico, Texas, Florida, Africa, India, and China. In fact, if someone were to jump from the 29 N latitude, they would have a 47.1% chance of landing on solid ground.

Not bad odds for a time traveler.

It was from that exact latitude that a group of ten men departed on one of the Thinker's expeditions. What archeologists didn't realize was that the illustration doesn't show Ra floating in the air at all. Rather, it shows a man falling out of the clouds.

Knowing this, it isn't difficult to reconstruct what must have happened. Sometime, during the hundreds of years it took to construct the pyramids, a burst of light appeared and a man fell from the sky. If he only fell ten or twenty feet before hitting the ground, he would have been able to gather his senses, brush the sand off his clothes, and look around at what was happening. By the time he understood his surroundings, thousands of people, mostly slaves whose job it was to construct the great structures, would already be on their knees in his honor. Their actions would have been reasonable. How else would they explain a burst of light and the appearance of a man from the sky other than to believe it was heavenly? Likewise, it was understandable that the time traveler kept up the appearance of being Ra. If he admitted he was just a normal man, even a man from another time, the pharaoh would likely have him executed for being the recipient of his people's adoration. But if he were a god, even the pharaoh would have to fear him.

The time traveler would have no choice but to live out the rest of his life pretending to be their most powerful deity. Anything else would lead to his execution. If there was a drought and the people begged for rain, he would be forced to say he was upset with something the pharaoh or his people had done. Admitting he was powerless to bring the rain would make him worthless, and thus, expendable.

But to balance out these demands, he would try to do as many good things for the people living under the pharaoh as was possible. He would let the pharaoh know that gods do not like cruelty and abuse, that each time a slave is beaten or whipped, the gods become restless. When this happens too much, they send locusts or a flood or a drought. The pharaoh would have no choice but to be kinder and gentler. After all, the person telling him to be more compassionate was Ra, the father of gods. It wouldn't happen overnight. But slowly, the

Egyptian people would be treated with more respect. Tired workers would be given rest instead of a beating.

The time traveler's actions wouldn't prevent the State, but they would at least make a better life for hundreds of thousands of Egyptians. Sent back too far in time, it was the best the Thinker could do. Not only was it a good deed, though, it was intoxicating. A man went from being an enemy of the State, to being treated like a god. Anything he wanted would be delivered with the snap of his fingers. Having his every whim serviced could quickly turn him into someone like the very people he had hoped to stop. It was a daily battle to do as much good as possible without becoming corrupted by the power he held over everyone.

Another problem was that the time traveler would grow old over the years. And as he aged, his mortality would reveal itself. Maybe he would close himself in a private chamber for the rest of his life. That way, at least, the pharaoh would never find out his guest was a mere mortal and have him killed. Or maybe, when the first sign of sickness or disease showed itself, the time traveler would command the pharaoh to give him a camel and simply ride off into the desert.

There is no telling how the time traveler's life ended—the hieroglyphics don't reveal that part of the story. What they do reveal, however, is that a man who was accidently sent back too far in time could be seduced by the love of the people around him. They reveal that a man who had sacrificed his past life to do one thing might falter when surrounded by affection in a new life.

The same thing was beginning to happen to Springfield. It was why he knew he could no longer stay in Mikolaj's town.

71 - A LONG TALK

"It has been four weeks," Mikolaj said during one of his walks with Springfield. "Do you remember what that means?"

Under different circumstances, in another point in time, this could be the discussion where the landlord evicts his tenant, or where the man who has been given a second chance must prove that he has made the most of the generosity he has been offered. But Springfield knew what the constable was getting at.

"The man in jail will be taken away," he said.

Mikolaj nodded.

"You still have the same plan: take him far away and release him in the wilderness?"

Mikolaj nodded again.

"Do you mind if I go and talk to him before then?"

This made the constable turn his attention from the cows and the sheep and focus it back on Springfield.

"He leaves tomorrow morning. Make any peace with him that you can before then."

Springfield hadn't been back to see the assassin since the morning of his release. On his way to the prison, he watched as a man led his cow through the street. He saw a group of four goats standing next to a house, not tethered to anything, just milling around as if they were perfectly happy to be where they stood. A little boy ran down the road as fast as he could, followed a moment later by his friend. These were the things that had made it possible for him to forget that a trained killer was being kept in a cell right down the street from where he slept. Chetnik's three villages and Sabir's town were gone because the man in black had followed Springfield's trail. He was thankful that this town was spared from the same fate.

He was sure the assassin spent the entire month wishing he had killed him when he had the chance. Probably, that made the man in black despise the Thinker even more.

At the jail, he saw the same guards who had originally escorted him into the cell. Each time he had seen them since that first occasion, they all enjoyed a good laugh together. Now, instead of treating him as a prisoner, they welcomed him as a guest.

They did not follow him down the hall to the cell, where the man in black was still being held. With each step down the hallway, Springfield's stomach tightened further. By the time he was halfway to the cell, his throat felt like it was full of rocks.

Looking inside the stone room, he was amazed he had ever spent the night there. It was smaller, dirtier, and darker than he remembered. He could hear the scurrying of a rodent but couldn't see it. The assassin was no longer shackled. Although the man in black didn't stand up, he did smile when he saw who had come to visit him.

"They're taking you away tomorrow," Springfield said.

The assassin didn't say anything, only looked at the time traveler's face, as if trying to remember every minute detail. The way the mercenary looked at him made Springfield finger the piece of wood in his palm, the same way he played with it any other time he got nervous. His body hadn't yet rejected the foreign object and possibly never would. Nor had the skin grown around it. The wooden disc remained there in plain view like an ornament. The town's children were fond of running up and touching it, then squealing in horror and running away laughing.

"You don't have to be worried," Springfield said. "They aren't going to hurt you."

The man in black laughed. And although Springfield could tell the man had been determined not to say anything, he couldn't help himself. "Trust me, I'm not worried."

"They aren't going to execute you. In fact, they aren't going to hurt you at all."

"Do you think I care what you have to say?"

"You're lucky," Springfield said, ignoring the killer's façade. "There are many places in history that would chop your head off for a lot less than what you've done. Hell, they aren't even going to chop off your hands."

The man in black didn't have anything to say to this. Maybe he figured that when the time came, if they did try to drag him to the chopping block, he would kill them with their own weapons or die trying.

"Do you know where or when you are?"

"I don't care," the man in black growled. "It doesn't matter."

"What *does* matter?"

"Killing you."

"Do you understand how time travel works? Do you realize that no one from our time will ever know if you killed me or not?"

"If that's true, why are you set on doing whatever it is you want to do?"

"Because it's important to me that I keep the tyranny from ever forming."

The man in black burst out laughing again, but not his usual, evil version. This was a genuine belly laugh, as though he had just seen a donkey kick a man in the nuts.

"Tyranny? Can you hear yourself? Don't you hear how crazy you sound? We have elections. We elect our leaders. How can there be a tyranny? You do realize you're the crazy one, right? I might go a little overboard during my missions, but you are absolutely, one hundred percent, bat-shit crazy."

The man in black continued laughing.

72 - LET THEM ELECT THEIR TYRANTS

"Are you going to vote, tomorrow?" the woman in the cubicle next to Jessica said.

Her response could have been, "What's the point?" or "It doesn't matter," but those were things that could be construed as violating the Freedom Act. Instead, she said, "I think I'll sit this one out."

"If you don't vote," her co-worker said, "you can't complain about who wins."

Jessica turned back to her computer without acknowledging this last comment.

Each election offered the promise of change. If the people were unhappy, they had the power to vote for the other party and things would surely get better. It was one of the guiding principles that children in the State were taught from an early age.

Looking at her monitor, Jessica wondered how her co-worker would have responded if she said the only thing that would change was the formal name of their ruler. Would her co-worker laugh and say, "How can there possibly be a tyranny when we have elections?" Or would she turn serious and say, "You better not be so cynical if you know what's good for you."

The election system did allow some people to feel optimistic for the future. After all, that was the point of the elections. They were surrounded by war, corruption, and prisons crowded with people who didn't deserve to be there, and they saw a chance to vote for someone who would make everything better. What they didn't notice, though, and what only the Thinkers seemed to understand, was that the entire system was rigged; even though the people were given two options, nothing ever changed. It was a simple magician's sleight of hand carried out on a national scale.

Party A's Ruler created yet another agency to monitor yet another aspect of everyone's lives. People complained. So Party B's Ruler came into power. Instead of disbanding the agency that no one liked, he merely created a sub-council to monitor its actions. But then Ruler B also passed a law that made it okay for people to disappear without a trial or without being charged with a crime. That made people uncomfortable. Party A's Ruler wouldn't have let that happen. But after A was elected, the laws that B passed were continued. Not only that, a new bill was signed that allowed AeroCams to have x-ray technology so they could see directly into everyone's homes. The people were told this would only occur if the State had reason to believe someone might be a Thinker, but everyone had the potential to be a Thinker, and so everyone was monitored.

Both options, A and B, believed wars should be fought any time the State had the opportunity to wage them. Both options thought the only way to prevent possible threats was by controlling and monitoring every aspect of people's lives.

At least in a casino, depending on the game, people have a slightly less than fifty percent chance of winning. In the long run, the house always wins, but a gambler can get lucky every once in a while. In the State's elections, both options play for the house. If someone outside of Party A or B tries to run for office, it becomes the house's mission to make sure everyone knows that only A and B are viable candidates. After being told this a hundred times, people believe it. After being told anything a hundred times, people will believe anything. The other options don't receive election coverage unless it's to disparage them. The system is rigged so that only A and B have a chance. And the beautiful thing for the State is that it doesn't matter which one of them wins because things keep getting worse for everyone else.

In his memoirs, one Ruler even said: "You can flip a coin as many times as you want. Sometimes it will land on heads and sometimes it will land on tails. But you are always flipping the same coin."

The comment was supposed to show how he had never lost his sense of humor. But to the Thinkers, to the people who understood the principles their country was founded on and knew the type of leaders they were supposed to have, the remark spoke to how blatantly corrupt the system had become.

73 - A LONG TALK (CONTINUED)

"You are absolutely, one hundred percent, bat-shit crazy," the assassin said, laughing.

It would have been a waste of Springfield's time to explain why the elections were a sham. If the killer was willing to silence anyone the State told him to, no questions asked, he would be too far gone to understand. An illusion didn't have to be performed by a magician for a small crowd, it could be played out by an entire group of people for an audience of millions.

Instead, Springfield said, "Tell me, did you kill because you liked the money it offered, or did you really believe all those people deserved to die?"

The man in black rolled his eyes. "I guess this is where you try and get me to think like you. Right, Thinker?"

"I just want to understand how you can do what you do."

The mercenary picked a mosquito off his arm, crushed it between two fingers, then smeared the pinpoint of blood across his palm.

"You're this mosquito," the killer said. "That's all. We lived in the greatest country before the Thinkers were around, and it will still be the greatest country after you and your buddies are gone."

"If it was so great, why was it always destroying other countries?"

"It always had a good reason. Either a crazy dictator or someone who posed a threat."

"Why was it always killing its own citizens?"

The man in black could have denied that there were executions, but he didn't. He shrugged and said, "The only people who died were the ones that didn't deserve to live. When you speak out against the State, even if you're pointing out something they shouldn't be doing, you make people question their leaders. That's not right."

"What if people should be questioning their leaders?"

"They shouldn't."

"A great man once said that there's nothing more patriotic than to do just that."

"Lies."

"What?"

"That's just more of your propaganda. No one actually said that, you just create fancy quotes to serve your purposes."

"Okay. If the State is so great, why do they have to monitor everything we do?"

"You can't be safe unless the State knows everything that everyone is doing."

"If that makes us safe, why are there still attacks?"

The man in black didn't laugh this time. Instead, he took a long breath, then gave the time traveler his middle finger.

The Thinker said, "Wouldn't you rather live in a world where you don't have to pass through a checkpoint just to get where you want to go? Without having cameras in the sky recording everything you do?"

"If they weren't there, there would be crime everywhere. Without the checkpoints, there would be attacks everywhere."

"We seemed to get by just fine before the checkpoints

and the cameras."

"That's just more propaganda. You know the checkpoints prevented hundreds of attacks. That's the only reason they started the searches in the first place. Same with the cameras."

Springfield stood up. There was no use trying to convince this man of anything he didn't want to believe. Without an understanding of the freedom he had lost, the mercenary could never want it back. The State's man would always think of Springfield and people like him as traitors.

"They're going to take you about five hundred kilometers away, then drop you off in the wilderness to fend for yourself."

The man in black barked with laughter. "Do you think that's too far for me? I can easily find my way back to this town."

"I won't be here when you do come back. I'm leaving as well. I'll be hundreds of miles away by the time you return."

The man in black shrugged. "Doesn't matter. I have the rest of my life to find you."

"That's how you'd spend the rest of your life— chasing after me instead of trying to be happy?"

Already knowing what the assassin's answer would be, Springfield stood up and walked away without waiting for the inevitable response.

In the morning, the guards took their tied and bound prisoner, still dressed in all black, to the back of a wagon. Springfield wasn't there to witness it. He was telling children how to say "good afternoon" in French. Better to teach the next generation than to try to change people who were already set in their ways. As far as he was concerned, he never needed to see the assassin, or anyone like him, ever again.

The future was what mattered.

74 - WALKING ON PINS

"We should try leaving the television off for a week," Isaac's mother said. "We wouldn't have to hear whatever the leaders have to say, and we wouldn't have to watch more bombs fall on another country."

"I'd love to, honey," her husband said. "But how else will we know about all the new laws the State passes? We don't want to miss something and then suddenly become criminals for buying too much toothpaste or whatever other asinine rule they come up with next."

They never spoke about whether or not they thought their son might still be alive, and if so, where he might be. Every once in a while, Isaac's father would pause at the attic steps, remember the half-completed aircraft carrier, and then let out a sigh. Those were the worst days, the times when he would refuse to let sunlight in the house if it meant having to see the AeroCams hovering outside their window.

Each day, they noticed another change to the country and to the people around them. Some were minor: the cost of bread increasing, or more reality shows on television. Some were more significant: televisions with factory-installed cameras so the State could watch the watcher, and more scripted news than ever before. And some would change the

State forever, such as people reporting their neighbors to the State before they could be reported themselves, and a new law that forbid the State's citizens from traveling to other countries for any reason (other than to fight the State's wars, of course).

Instead of being given a Pulitzer, a reporter who exposed the State's real motivation for their previous war was found in her apartment. No one had to be told that the official cause of death was, of course, apparently suicide. And yet no one questioned the report because they knew what would happen if they did.

A man who saw his neighbor beating his wife turned the volume up on his television instead of calling the police because once they showed up, they might arrest the caller just as easily as they would the abuser. Ironically, the cops still kicked in his door and emptied their blasters into him after someone else reported the domestic violence and the police showed up at the wrong address. The body of the woman who had been beaten to death wasn't found until a month later.

People put their heads down. There was no longer a sense of community, only self-preservation. What was legal one day was illegal the next. More people filled the already overcrowded jails. A new war started. More laws were passed. Another election was held. This time, things would get better. But it never did.

By themselves, each new law, each new invasion of privacy, didn't change day-to-day life so much. The whole— cameras everywhere, checkpoints at every corner, men and women being dragged away and never being seen again—was greater than the sum of its parts.

Jessica stopped expecting to see Isaac's face on the news. She didn't believe he was in a secret prison somewhere. Nor did she believe he had been in the basement when it exploded. Maybe it was just her optimism sneaking through, giving her something positive to think about, but she liked to imagine he was still out there. He would never make her his famous Lobster Mac and Cheese again. He would never be able to put his arm around her and tell her everything was going to be all right. But maybe he was out there. Somewhere.

Even so, she knew it was time to start moving on with her life. That didn't necessarily mean packing up all of his photographs and moving them to the back of her closet. It simply meant she needed to think of other possibilities for her future.

She didn't intend to have children, but it had nothing to do with her first love no longer being in her life. How could she bring children into a world where checkpoints and surveillance were part of a normal routine? Could she teach them to ignore the AeroCams recording everything they did, to simply act as if they weren't there? Was it irresponsible to teach children not to challenge something when it didn't make sense, or was it a simple matter of teaching them not to give the State a reason to look in their direction?

If she did have children, she would want them to be able to speak out against the wrongs they saw, not disappear for questioning them. Maybe she would change her mind. If she did, she would make it her duty to teach her kids to appreciate history. And she would teach them to think for themselves. After that, it would be up to them to determine their own paths.

75 - THE THINGS THAT MEAN THE MOST

The man in black had been taken away a week earlier, but Springfield continued to volunteer at the school and in the fields. If the wagon wasn't already near the place where the killer would be released back into the wild, it would be soon. There was a chance the assassin would return to the town one day. More likely, he would accidently veer off course somewhere and never find this place again, or he would succumb to the elements and die in the middle of the wilderness.

It was also possible, however unlikely, that the State's man would find himself hundreds of kilometers away from where he needed to be, realize nothing he did mattered anymore, and become disillusioned with his quest. If that happened, maybe the man in black would finally make a new life for himself and fade into history.

Springfield was determined to stay busy because when he stopped moving thoughts of his parents and of Jessica crept into his head. The worst part was not being able to know if the State had come for them merely because they were associated with a Thinker.

Still, Springfield spent his days cultivating crops and teaching children to speak French. He had become separated from everything and everyone he had loved and, instead of fighting to change the Theta Timeline, he was being greeted by children who could say, "*Bonjour, monsieur,*" to him in the mornings. How could he make a new life for himself when the world of the State still existed? Just because he had convinced himself that he had been sent back too far to be of any use?

That was what tormented him each night. What would Jessica and his parents think if they saw him now? They wouldn't have expected him to sacrifice his life to change the Theta Timeline, but now that he had accepted the mission, they would be disappointed to see him cast it aside as easily as a model or a television show.

Upon seeing the constable outside his jail, he asked, "Would you like to go for a walk?"

Mikolaj was always happy to have an excuse to talk rather than work. They discussed the coming winter as they passed by the blacksmith's shop and then by one of the carpenter's sheds.

After leaving the middle of the town, Springfield said, "I need to go."

Mikolaj walked in silence for a while longer, his round sea lion belly bouncing with each step. A brown cat hid behind a bush, a dead mouse dangling from its mouth. Above it, a pair of yellow birds chirped back and forth to each other.

"Where will you go?" the constable asked finally.

"France."

"You have made a home for yourself here. The people like you. The children like you. The fields have never had such healthy crops."

"In a few years, there will be a man in France who I need to speak with."

"He is not there yet?"

"No."

"But he will be?"

"Yes."

"How do you know?"

"I just do."

"Do you know how far away France is?"

"No."

"No one from this town has ever been that far."

"I need to try."

"You will never make it."

"All I can do is try."

"You would risk your life for the uncertainty of meeting this man?"

Springfield nodded.

"Why?"

"Because he helps mold the course of my country, and I need to explain to him the importance of never letting it change from what he envisions."

"You sound like you have lost your mind."

"I know. But if you could have seen the world I have seen, you would know that there are more important things than my life or anyone else's life, and this is one of them. Because when a man has a chance to stand up for what he believes in, he had better stand up or else he'll never stand up for anything."

"Are you doing this for love?"

"In a way, yes, but it's not only that. The people I love will never know if I do this or if I don't. But that doesn't mean I shouldn't try. I will never see my parents again. I will never see the woman I love again, but it will be worth it if I attempt this one thing. I know I will almost certainly fail, but I must make the attempt. Everything I have gone through so far is only worth it if I keep going."

They kept walking until finally they were on top of a hill overlooking the entire town.

"When will you go?" Mikolaj asked.

"Tomorrow."

The constable did not try to convince Springfield to stay. Not for another week, another month, and certainly not for the rest of his life. He merely nodded and watched as the goats gathered around a pond to drink.

"The man in black may come back for me."

"My men will be ready."

"If you have no choice, kill him. But if he only wants to know where I have gone, I want you to be honest with him. Tell him where I am going. Tell him democracy doesn't have to deteriorate into tyranny. It doesn't have to."

Mikolaj shook his head, the corner of his mouth curling into a frown. "What is the point? Why not tell him you went to St. Petersburg or Constantinople?"

"I want him to know how things can change if you fight for what you believe in. I want him to know one man can make a difference if he follows through with what he believes rather than what he is told to believe."

The two men watched a group of children playing underneath a distant tree. Someday, they would grow up and fight their own battles. Some would die at the hands of other men, and some would die of old age. Some would have children of their own, and others would never have the chance. But all of them, right then, as they played around the tree, laughed and yelled. An entire world of possibility was ahead of each of them.

As Springfield and Mikolaj watched, one of the boys pushed a girl to the ground, only to be thrown down himself by a different boy, who then offered a hand to the girl. Once the girl was back on her feet, and once the boy who had pushed her was also standing again, the kids acted as if nothing had ever happened; all the children immediately went back to playing their game with screams of laughter echoing through the town.

"They are very resilient." Mikolaj said.

"Yes, they are. And if they are lucky, they will stay that way."

And with that, the two men began back down the hill.

QUESTIONS AND ANSWERS ABOUT
THE THETA TIMELINE

I get a lot of questions about this book. More so, probably, than any other book I've written. Below are some of the most common I've received, as well as my responses.

Question - *Why does the ending stop so abruptly? Is it supposed to be a cliffhanger for The Theta Prophecy?*

Answer – The Theta Prophecy is a completely different story with different characters and a different plot. It just happens to take place in the same world of the State as this book. My intention with the ending of this book was to provide a resolution of character. Springfield will go on with his journey and he might be successful (or not), but to me that's not the interesting part because you can infer from the stories of the other time travellers' adventures whether he is likely to be successful. The point of the ending is to show that the main character has changed. Specifically, he has gone from being someone who leaves toy models unfinished and who doesn't follow through on many things in life, to becoming someone who is willing to continue fighting and journeying, no matter how dismal his chances, because he has found something worth fighting for. That's the resolution I was trying to convey with the ending.

Question – *It seems the Thinkers, quite accidently, cause more harm than good in many of their misadventures. Were you trying to make a political point here that the Thinkers aren't as "good" as they think they are?*

Answer – Not at all, but that's a fascinating idea and one that had never crossed my mind. My main point in all of the different side stories related to time travel was twofold. The first was to show how delicate time and history are, and the second was to show that everything that can go wrong will go wrong. And to be honest, one or two were put in there simply because I love the unsolved mystery of some parts of history and wanted to give another possibility, in my world of time travel, of what might have happened.

Question – *In some ways, the world depicted in The Theta Timeline seems eerily similar to today's world. In other ways, it is the worst case scenario of the future. What blend were you going for?*

Answer – When I wrote the book, it was entirely focused on present day developments and the troubling stories filling the news. As scary as the world in this book is, I personally don't think it's anywhere close to a worst case scenario. Keep in mind that if there are an infinite number of realities out there, there are also an infinite number of realities in which nuclear war has already wiped out civilization and an infinite number in which the State is worse than we can imagine. In contrast to that, the fact that we still live in a world where people can stand up for what they believe in and cry out against any form of injustice they come across is a great world to live in.

Question – *Where did this idea of time travel come from? It's not like any other I've found in fiction.*

Answer – The way time travel works in this book is a result of reading many other books and watching many movies and TV shows where characters can somehow travel back in time to a specific place without any explanation for what anchors them to that spot of the world. (After all, the world is constantly rotating, so how do they miraculously end up in the same exact spot?) That was what spurred the idea of highly unreliable time travel. The closest I have found to a similar concept of how time travel might work was in Robert Heinlein's *The Door Into Summer*. It's not the same theory as *The Theta Timeline*, but it's closer than most.

Question - *How did you settle on the term The State?*

Answer - In an earlier version of the book, the authoritarian government was called The Tyranny. Part of what I wanted to convey was that the government had gotten so used to its own sense of invulnerability that it had the gull to refer to itself as a Tyranny and the masses of people still wouldn't do anything. However, as I wrote more stories set in the world of The Theta Timeline, the Tyranny began to feel forced and unrealistic. The State provides a more subtle yet definitive term while also being comparable in tone to the dystopian classics I love. After all, Orwell didn't have to call the evil organization in '1984' by some ominous name. He simply referred to it as The Party.

ACKNOWLEGDMENTS

As always, I am indebted to many people for their support: Jodie McFadden, for her constant encouragement and optimism; Matt Butterweck, for his comments on the story; and everyone at Authors On The Air, GoodReads, and in the BJJ and MMA communities who read my other novels and recommended them to their friends. Without their support, I would be nowhere. Of course, I am also thankful for my parents and brother, each of whom constantly encourages my dreams and aspirations.

Want to receive updates on my future books and get some great freebies? Sign up for my newsletter at: http://chrisdietzel.com/mailing_list/

ABOUT THE AUTHOR

Chris graduated from Western Maryland College (McDaniel College). His dream is to write the same kind of stories that have inspired him over the years.

His others novels have become Amazon Best Sellers, been featured on Authors on the Air, and were voted as some of GoodReads top 10 "Most Interesting Books" the year they were published.

www.ingramcontent.com/pod-product-compliance
Lightning Source LLC
Chambersburg PA
CBHW030413180626
46812CB00005B/1990